HAVOC

DEBRA

USA Today Bestselling Author

ANASTASIA

Editing by Paige Smith

Dustcover: Depositphoto image: mimagephotos

Laminatephoto **mimagephotos**

Laminate Design: by Hang Le

Dedication

T, J, and D

As always, everything I do is for you.

In memory of the original Anastasia

1

I looked from one mob boss to the other. They were sitting in my friend's house, but I was clearly in charge.

Bat Feybi's son was on my left. Mitch Kaleotos was on the right. They were unhappy. I didn't give a damn.

"Those are the terms. You both report to me. Understood?"

They cursed under their breath, but they agreed. I stood and they did the same. I folded my arms over my chest instead of reaching out for a handshake. We were not equals. I was better than they were. I was harder, smarter, and meaner—if I needed to be.

Kaleotos responded using my street name, "Yeah, Havoc."

I lifted my eyebrows and they shuffled toward the front door.

Nix came into the room. Both Feybi and Kaleotos startled at his presence. Nix didn't have on his ever-present hoodie, so they could see his full skull face tat. He widened his eyes and hissed at them.

I had to bite the insides of my cheeks to keep from smiling. My man. He was my brother in the only way it really counted —in our souls.

Feybi bristled.

I followed the two men into the foyer. They seemed like they wanted to say something more. I settled my command of the atmosphere in my chest. My inner essence was calm, cool, and collected.

They wouldn't fuck with me, simply because I wasn't scared of them. A mountain of a man with a reputation that had burned up the town.

Both Feybi and Kaleotos reached for the doorknob. Kaleotos was faster and yanked open the huge door.

On the other side, with three backpacks, a suitcase, red heart-shaped sunglasses tangled in the hair at the top of her head, and a miniskirt that made everything below her waist illegally good-looking was Nix's baby sister, Ember. Her long brown hair was streaked with all different colors and her fingers were littered with glittery rings.

I saw the whole scene play out in my head like I was a psychic. Ember was going to tease me, and I'd tease her back. Nix would immediately lose his scary demeanor and worry about his sister being too close to these murderers that we were escorting out. And Ember would get made as family. In this lifestyle, connections were best kept murky if possible.

Giving people information on who was most important to you might have consequences.

I rolled my eyes briefly. Because the most obvious answer was surely going to get me punched in the dick.

I swooped forward and grabbed Ember around the waist. I hefted her against my chest like I'd just come home from war and she'd already birthed three of my kids.

"Baby." I kissed her hard on the mouth. On her nineteen-year-old mouth.

I could almost hear Nix's anger engulfing him like a wildfire.

If I were anyone else, I would have been dead four times already. As I walked Ember back into the house, she clung to me like she shouldn't know how to do.

I pushed on Nix's puffed up chest and peered around Ember's forehead to see that his eyes were wild as I predicted.

I was barely kissing Ember now that my back was turned to Feybi and Kaleotos, but Ember was all into it.

Shit. Double shit. All the shits.

I was able to slam the door with my foot, thankfully before Kaleotos or Feybi could make out the farce for what it was.

I pulled Ember off of me. Her hot pink lipstick was smeared around her mouth, and I was betting mine as well.

"Step away from Animal, Ember. He and I are about to beat the fuck out of each other." Nix rolled his head on his neck. Snapping, cracking noises accompanied the movement.

Another gorgeous woman stepped between Nix and me, her face half-etched in a faded version of his skull tat. His girlfriend, Becca, put her hands on both of our chests, and she looked at Ember and me and then turned to Nix.

"Hothead. Animal would never touch your sister." I couldn't see her face anymore, but it was clear from her tiny sweat shorts and tank that Becca had been relaxing upstairs.

"He *kissed* her. Kissed her!" Nix was fuming. I considered Ember. She looked frazzled. And embarrassed. And slightly infatuated.

Crap.

Becca shook her head, her ponytail bouncing all around. "No. Hear them out." Becca grabbed onto Nix's arm. It was tatted like a skeleton's bones as well.

Nix looked at me with venom, but I wasn't dead yet, so I knew he still loved me.

Then he glared at Ember. Instead of words, he just pointed from her to me and back again. The question was undoubtedly *what the fuck*?

Ember grabbed her own hands and kicked her sandaled foot against the tile behind her before answering, "I'm in love. That was the best kiss of my life."

I felt my jaw drop. "Ember Ann Fenix Mercy Churchkey!"

She started to laugh before dropping the act. "Please, Nix. Obviously, I interrupted some of your business, and Animal was making sure I kept my big mouth shut."

"You cannot be like that. He would kill me." I pointed with my pinkie at Nix. He was a murderer. An assassin.

Ember laughed. "He'd never touch you in a million years. He's addicted to all the sweetness and baby talk you lay on him all the time."

I dared a glance back at Nix. He had visibly relaxed. "Ember, don't play with fire like that. Shit. What the hell are you here for?"

Ember wiped her pink lipstick off of her face and then got up on her tiptoes and wiped my mouth as well.

I looked into her giant, gorgeous blue eyes and knew she was super duper trouble in general.

"I'm moving in. I'm leaving college and Aunt Dor to live here."

"Um." Ten minutes ago I was so eloquent, I'd convinced two mob bosses they were my bitches. I had nothing now. A teenaged girl made me tongue-tied.

Nix looked like his head was going to pop off again except for a whole different reason now.

2

I've stood next to this man through a lot of shit. Not ever have we been at such a loss for words and direction as we watched Ember make herself at home in the guest room.

Her phone was propped up on her dresser. There were two girls on the video chat, as if they lived their lives like that. Everyone was involved in different things. One was curling her hair, the other was typing on a computer, and Ember was unpacking her suitcase.

There was music piping through. I wasn't sure which girl had it playing, but it was filthy.

Nix touched my shoulder and tilted his head toward the hallway. He wanted to talk.

I ducked closer to him as he leaned against the hallway wall. "She can't stay here."

Despite his ink, he looked pale. Becca had left for her shift at the tattoo parlor. It was just Nix, Ember, and I.

"Obviously."

We were in a volatile situation. Nix had a past with the Feybis. He'd killed the patriarch after working in the family for a year. They feared him for his skill, but some sins were not easily overlooked. Lighting a mob boss on fire in his favorite chair was one of those touchy subjects.

The Kaleotos had been in charge of half of Midville and were in a war with the Feybis for longer than anyone remembered.

When Nix left to work with the Feybis, I knew I needed to prepare for when he finally returned. I had assembled an army of broken souls over my lifetime, and bunches of them worked for me.

My family was small, but it now required that I run the entire entity that encompassed the criminal element in Midville. I slowly turned Kaleotos into my puppet. I went to their foot soldiers and offered better. Offered a future. Because there was no getting out of Feybi's with your life. With me, on my crew, loyalty earned a way out. I treated people like people instead of pawns. I used Nix's purple Hummer to gather them. Soon, gossip was what it was and I was getting approached by needy people, instead of the other way around.

By the time I got Nix back, I had a nice group of Kaleotos' best men.

And I had a formula that worked.

Nix was allowed to wallow in his happiness for a little while, but I used his knowledge of the Feybi organization to my benefit. I moved swiftly during the upheaval in power caused by Feybi Sr.'s demise.

After the meeting I had today, I was going to focus on eliminating the most vicious of the loan sharks. Then the independent drug dealers. I had Nix with me now, so we were running at full capacity.

I was magnetic. It was just something I had about me. My gift. Bad people trusted me. Good ones, too. I was ready to defend Nix from whoever came sniffing for his blood and retribution.

I was an unknown factor. Mysterious to the warring families. Where they had goals of crime and money and power, I just wanted my people to live— in comfort as well.

Nix wasn't my first "family" member, but he was one of the dearest to me. And he was currently close to hyperventilating.

"Did your aunt do anything to cause this? I mean, like what the hell?" The music cut out from Ember's room. She stepped into the hallway.

"She lied to me."

Nix rolled his head in her direction. I peeked past her and saw that her phone had a dark screen.

"Your friends are gone?" I watched as she shifted her eyes and hips in the same direction. "Because if they were still there, they could hear stuff that could put them in danger."

Ember snapped her gum and went to her phone. I watched as she unmuted herself and then ended the video chat session with a middle finger.

She stuffed her phone into her bra and came back into the hallway.

Nix put his hands through his thick hair. I knew that his scalp was tatted up to complete what he thought was a necessary permanent disguise as a skeleton.

"She lied to me," Ember repeated.

"Aunt Dor?" I offered because Nix was too busy sliding his hand over his face to ask.

Ember narrowed her eyes at her brother. "She said that you're dangerous. No one speaks about you that way to me."

I loved Ember. She was always special because she was Nix's sister. He'd done a great deal to make sure she was safe. More than she would probably ever know.

He never expected any kind of reciprocation from the women he watched. Nix rubbed his fingers on his chest. I knew he had the names of four females tatted there. His mother. Becca. Christina, the special little girl he'd rescued. And Ember.

He was feeling the love.

We were all goners now.

"You're my brother, and I'm proud of you. You'd never hurt a soul!" She had fire in her eyes and the sureness only someone who was still a teenager could project.

She was wrong. He'd never hurt her. Or me. Or Becca. Or Christina. But I'm sure we'd both lost count of the amount of assholes we'd ended. Hurt them so much they stopped breathing.

I saw the conflict in his expression. It was just because I knew him as well as I did. He had a great poker face.

"Just unpack for now. But don't get too comfortable. This is no place for a kid." Nix clearly wanted to talk this one out with me.

Ember leaned in and gave him a kiss on his cheek. "Thanks, bro. I'm not a kid. Aunt Dor can pound salt." She twirled and her long brown hair with streaks slapped me in the chest and Nix in the face.

Nix turned and headed toward my room. I knew we'd have to hash this out.

Because we knew something about Ember that she didn't.

We knew who Ember's father might be.

3

Animal

Fourteen Years Earlier

The trick to getting food out of the trash at school was mumbling about how you tossed out your homework if anyone walked by. I was supposed to have a hot lunch provided by the school. My foster "parents" were out of town. Honestly, I liked it better that way. I was biding my time.

They were assholes. They got a check for supporting me, and they shot that into their arms. I saw it all. And I didn't have to 'fess up to my social worker. Because she was so swamped with work, actually dealing with the kids on her list was a rare treat for her.

I could avoid the "parents".

I felt someone bump my elbow. Probably ready to bust me for dumpster diving. I had a million excuses on the tip of my tongue and the chip on my shoulder sharpened to a point, but her brown eyes brought me back.

She passed me a chocolate chip muffin tightly wrapped in plastic. I took it and pushed it into the pocket of the jacket I rarely took off.

"You boosted this?"

My girl T was trouble. Thick black eyeliner and a sneer kept her safe from everyone but me. But she'd let me in and I'd never hurt her.

She lifted her chin at me, letting me know I'd guessed correctly. "Shit, girl, you're gonna get your ass caught."

She almost smiled. The black fingernail polish added to the mystery and she touched the upside down star pendant she wore on a chain around her neck. She was giving me her excuse, not saying anything. T was spoken about in hushed whispers. She was a witch maybe. A Satan worshipper *definitely*.

None of it was true. T was homeless. She used the other kids' imaginations to enforce the distance she craved.

She bragged that she was invisible, and maybe she was right. She was a good thief.

She knew my deal, and I knew hers. We tried to watch each other's back. It was hard, though. We were tied to separate rafts in the middle of a monsoon. We were trying to survive.

"They getting closer to getting you locked down?" I stepped near her beat-up Converses.

Her eyes glazed over and her lips made an O.

She was a runner. Some people couldn't take locked doors. T wanted an open door or a cracked window. When she was locked in, she started dying—so she said anyway.

I'd offered to mention her to my caseworker in the past. I wouldn't make that mistake again. The answer had been a firm no. She had a mother. One she didn't want to discuss. Undeniably, something about it wasn't working.

After hanging her head so her thick hair could swing over half of her face, she poked at the pocket holding the muffin with her index finger.

She wanted me to eat now. My stomach grumbled. I'd had the cheese sandwich I was given at the cafeteria. The foster parents were arrears in payment to the school so that was all I could get on the menu. I got the poor man's meal.

Shit, I was just thirteen, but even I knew that signaling out kids who couldn't pay for lunch with the goddamn cheese sandwich was cruel bullshit. Cheese gave me wicked gas on top of it all, so I threw the cheese out and ate the bread.

I knew she wouldn't stop picking at me until she saw me swallow some food. I rolled my eyes at her and heard her snicker in response. I unwrapped the muffin in my pocket and broke off a bit. I had to be stealthy. The cafeteria manager, Ms. Dadish, didn't like me. If she saw me eating, she'd know I had food I shouldn't. Like her job was to slap a cheese sandwich onto my tray, and also make sure it was the only thing that crossed my lips for lunch.

I watched as T tried to make her slight form bigger to provide a shield. I palmed the food and put it between my lips. T watched my mouth move. It made her happy to help me. I allowed that. She was the only one that got this me. The walls-down, chip-laid-at-my-feet, ready-to-smile Animal.

I looked past the top of her head and made eye contact with the manager. I stopped chewing and watched as her eyes narrowed. I bent my head and

leaned down as if T had said something. I bopped my head up and down as if agreeing, using the time to swallow the bite half-chewed. I all but choked, but was able to get the lump down my throat.

It was time to go. T and I had to walk in different directions. Our rafts crashed into each other's in the monsoon once in a while. It was brief, but it was a connection we both valued.

She was homeless, and I was hungry. We were surrounded by shiny-faced kids that seemed like they lived in a different dimension. I had to stop before clearing the cafeteria door to let a kid step ahead of me to dump their lunch into the trash. Their whole lunch. Uneaten.

A beautiful sandwich. A goddamn pudding cup with a plastic spoon. That was all I could make out. My fingers itched to snatch it up. A homemade lunch, prepared with love, by a mom. I could feel the heat of Ms. Dadish's glare on the back of my neck. I took my eyes off the prize and straightened my posture. I'd walk out, head high. I was long past crying in this life, but I felt my nose burn. I wanted that lunch.

I went without it.

4

A common misconception is that quiet people are missing out on all that goes on around them. I could see you. I just choose not to speak. He saw me, though. Beyond the cement walls I'd put up to save me.

There was this thing about me. I love once. Just once. I didn't stop doing it, and I'd never change once I'd placed my heart with you.

I loved my mom. She's the only one I've had. Or will ever have. Anastasia wasn't well enough to be my mom. But I was strong enough to be her daughter.

Seeing her face both broke and soothed me when I took a breath. I'm not going to lie about it. It made me cry.

I had my mom's hospital bracelet from one of her trips. I helped her cut it off and then kept it. I kept it in my pocket and clenched my fist around it and felt the edges dig into my palm when I wanted to dissolve and run up to her. Just to get that hug one more time.

The scent of her. Her heartbeat. They say nothing's as soothing as a mother's heartbeat for her child. I knew it to be true because I craved it.

I had to have the willpower not to put myself in her orbit because her face would spread into a smile. And nothing else but her hugging me would matter.

The last time we had a visit, maybe two years ago now, Anastasia started a fire in the home where she lived. She almost killed herself and her caretakers by accident because she was too excited and wouldn't take her meds.

I knew I had to do this for us both. It hurt. It was the kind of pain that covered my heart like a blanket. The ache was so deep, a forced death.

We could live our whole lives like this. I could hurt for her every moment of every day. I *would* hurt for her. And she for me. The type of manic depression she had could be a merciless bastard. I liked to believe the love we had for each other lived outside of the pain. Maybe I'd know if it did in the next life.

I had one mother. I wouldn't love another. They said I was stubborn, but I was just sure. Few people put it together that I was homeless. I was good at pretending, and I was resourceful.

I could find clothes. I stopped by houses when the owners were off at work. I borrowed a showerful of water. Sometimes I snuck a few pieces of clothes, but never enough for them to realize I'd been there. I was a temporary hazard.

It was fascinating how convinced people could allow

themselves to be. I did my homework. I got good grades. I loved to read. The school I went to was so big, I could blend into the camouflage of other kids.

If you didn't call attention to yourself, you'd rarely get it. I could forge my mother's name. I was "sick" on days I needed to bring money in. Homelessness could be an art.

He knew.

Animal.

That I was homeless.

Not that I loved him.

Don't forget.

I love once. I'm good like that.

5

Animal

The fosters were home, so I took that as my cue to leave. I didn't want to get roped into their addiction or the mania it brought.

I started to walk, thinking of finding T. She'd been keeping to the park in town. Though she hated it when I found what she used as shelter—she was embarrassed. I got it. I respected it. We could allow each other to be kings in our imaginations if we didn't see reality sometimes.

Instead, Boon and Fleece met me on the corner. They're assholes, way older than me. But I was bored tonight. Boon had been bounced around the system like me back in the day.

It had broken him. Fleece had parents, but he lived on the side of town that people avoided at night. They were reckless. The lack of a goal was evident in how they spent their downtime. I shouldn't have hung with them, but I didn't want to be with the fosters, so I walked with them.

They started talking about jacking a car. And I hated it. But I knew how it was. I had to be as tough as they thought I was. Fleece was going on and on how he'd been watching videos on how to hot-wire a car. That might have been knowledge I wanted to hoard—if he was telling the goddamn truth. He probably wasn't.

We walked together to the part of town that had the fancy trash cans and every bench was dedicated to some old, dead rich person. I hopped on one and walked across it looking for old cars. The whole plan was shit. We were in the wrong part of town to ever find an old car. A lady pulled out from a parking garage real slow. She was at the light at the entrance. It was red. She started applying lipstick in the rearview mirror. I saw her start to talk, smiling as she put away the lipstick.

But Fleece was shit for impulse control. He hissed, "Go, fuckers." Fleece snuck up the side of the BMW. Stupid impulses happened quickly.

Boon pulled a gun out of the pocket of his jacket. Fleece opened the

driver's side door and yanked the woman out by her hair. She scrambled up the second she hit the pavement.

I got chills up my spine when I saw the car seat in the back just as she screamed, "Not my baby!"

I read scenes. It's what I did. The choices flew in front of me. These fuckers were taking that car. I watched as Fleece punched the mother in the face, knocking her out cold.

Boon's eyes were wild as he yelled, "Come on!" to me.

I leaped off the bench and ran to the car. I had to step over the mother's body, and I hated to leave her like that. I didn't know how her head was—if she'd hit it way too hard. But I'd seen how mothers were. At the park. In the street. In school. They'd die for their kid. I got in the back seat as the wheels started spinning.

I turned to look at the lump of lady next to the car. Unbelievably, and thankfully, she tried to sit up. At least she wasn't dead. Fleece and Boon were in the front seat. They were slamming the steering wheel and cursing up a storm. I looked to the car seat. I was right. A little baby—crap. As tiny as it was, maybe it was six months old? Who knew? It looked back at me and I watched it pout.

Oh no.

"Don't," I tried to warn the baby. The baby didn't care. The crying shocked both the assholes in front.

Boon turned in his seat. Instead of a question, he slid me his gun. "Kill it."

I took the gun, smooth as I could, and pointed it at the floor. I had to get the kid out of here.

The baby started crying harder.

I met Fleece's eyes in the rearview mirror. I watched his left eyelid twitch. "That crying. Make it fucking stop."

I slipped the safety off and checked the chamber. There were four bullets in the gun. Enough. If I had to. I sure as shit didn't want to.

Boon and Fleece had connections to gangs. What I did next could put me on a few hit lists. I was fucking thirteen years old.

I glanced at the car seat. The baby was inconsolable. Babies could sense stress, like dogs. At least the ones I had encountered could. I knew how this kind of seat worked. Two fosters ago had a set of twins, and I helped with their shit. If I pressed the red button, it would separate the seat from the base. I leaned over the seat and unlocked the handle, shifting it up so it acted like the handle on an Easter basket.

Aiming the gun at the floor became aiming the gun at the back of Fleece's head.

"Stop the fucking car."

We were barely out of town. Woods and a few rundown buildings were all that was left as the scenery before it was just wilderness.

"Don't start, Animal."

We were screaming at each other over this baby's crying. Boon started hitting the handle of the car seat. I didn't let my eye contact leave the mirror, but I was watching Boon out of my peripheral.

I reconsidered everything I was doing, and the plan became clear, like someone wearing a halo and a pair of wings whispered it into my ear. I pressed on the car seat and it snapped back into its base. I wasn't trying to get us out of the vehicle anymore.

I worked to calm my voice, though it still cracked a little. "Get out of the goddamn car before I blow your head off."

Fleece was enraged. Maybe he was on something. "You won't fucking do it. You're a goddamn kid."

I shot the gun between them, the windshield shattering. I covered the baby with the built-in canopy without looking at it.

Fleece and Boon exited the car like a gun just went off. Fast.

My hand was shaking, but I had to act like I was confident. I wasn't really looking to kill anyone tonight.

I kept the gun pointed toward the windshield as I tossed myself between the seats and took over the driver's side.

Fleece and Boon were showing their irritation by picking up rocks and branches from the side of the road to toss them at the vehicle.

I shot the gun toward their feet and they hopped back. I saw the whites of their eyes bug out with shock.

I had two bullets left. The baby was screaming.

I looked at the dashboard. I'd never driven anything before. I managed to slide the gearshift into drive, and the SUV lurched forward. I hit the gas pedal hard and over steered, hearing the back wheels spin on the gravel.

The open doors closed themselves from the force of the car speeding forward. I tried to look in the rearview mirror, but it was angled in the wrong direction. The cracks from the broken windshield were expanding. If

I ducked, I could see the baby in a little mirror the mother must have installed for this exact purpose. The baby was purple from all the crying.

I was staying on the right side of the road. I looked at the speedometer, but I couldn't register what the hell I was doing before I had to look at the road again.

A car came up behind me and flew around, passing me on the double yellow. I held my breath. Was it possible Fleece and Boon got picked up that soon?

I exhaled when the car sped around the corner up ahead. I realized I was going slower despite the fact I was pressing the pedal hard. When the car piddled to a stop, I looked at the dashboard again. The gaslight was on.

This car was out of business. The baby was slowing down with the crying. Gasping and restarting a lot.

I put the car in park. I didn't have a ton of options. We'd only gone about five miles, so walking wouldn't be too hard. It would have been a hell of a lot easier if I didn't know that two assholes were dumped out raging mad down the road.

I got out of the car. I didn't want to give up the gun, but the pants I was wearing had no safe place to store it. Carrying the gun and the baby at the same time gave me the willies. I opened the chamber and dropped the bullets into my hand.

After tossing the gun in one direction and the bullets in another into the woods that edged the road, I turned back to the car. I needed to walk the baby back to its mom.

Lights flashed in the distance. Another car.

Fuck.

Part of me wanted to run, but the other part of me knew I couldn't leave this baby alone. A car could hit the vehicle. Fleece and Boon could come up on it.

I was the child's only defense.

Straightening my shoulders, I folded my arms in front of my chest.

Projection was half of a battle. Maybe.

The car slowed down, but all I could see was headlights. I let my nostrils flair. I was tougher than anyone else. At least, that's what I hoped it looked like.

The car door opened and I could hear it, but I couldn't see it. Those could be my last moments. Which would suck—because then the baby would be on its own.

I heard my name. "Animal."

I squinted, trying to see who was talking to me. The headlights cut out and a flashlight illuminated Officer Patrick Merck.

I dropped my folded arms and felt my spine relax. Thank God. Of all damn people to run up on me like this—he was the best one.

"What the hell are you doing with a stolen car? Is that the missing baby I hear?" Merck turned his flashlight on the car.

"Yeah. I don't know how to make it stop." I shrugged my shoulders. Merck walked past me and looked in the back seat. I peered over his

shoulder as he slid the pacifier into the kid's mouth. It took a bit, but soon the baby latched onto the plastic. It was still sniffling and shaking a little on the comedown, but we finally had silence.

"Remind me never to have kids. That thing is a lunatic." I pointed at the baby.

Merck used the blanket to wipe the baby's nose. "How the hell are you involved in this?"

He unhitched the baby bucket from the base and carefully pulled the baby out of the car.

"Dumbass Fleece and Boon. I thought we were boosting an old car. Instead, they did a carjacking. When I saw there was a baby in the car, I jumped in." Merck handed the bucket to me and waved for me to follow him to the patrol car.

I looked down at the baby. It looked up at me. It was small and delicate and made me nervous.

"Then Fleece told me to shoot the baby. So I took the gun and shot the windshield. They got out, I drove off, and now I'm here with you. The car ran out of gas."

Merck used his walkie to tell someone somewhere that the baby was safe, and that the car was found, too.

He leveled a gaze at me. "I told you those two are nothing but trouble. You not into listening? I swear, havoc follows you around like a puppy sometimes."

Merck looked a little like Superman. Tall, with dark hair and blue eyes. We met each other when I was still in elementary school. Anytime I got in trouble at school or in the community and he'd shown up, I'd tell him the truth. Whether it incriminated me or not.

There was a connection between us. Something in me told me I could trust him. On more than one occasion, Merck could've put me in juvie for things I'd done. But that damn closeness. He knew I'd tell him the facts no matter what I saw. And there was value in that—or so he said.

We both heard a car in the distance. We looked at each other and didn't need to speak. I passed him the baby in the bucket and Merck put it in the back seat and shut the door. Protection.

Merck lifted his eyebrows and chin. That was my cue that we were going to roll into a scenario. I put my hands on the hood of the police car and he made the motions of kicking out my feet without actually touching me.

The car pulled through real slow. Merck told me to keep my head down. As soon as the car pulled away, Merck stepped back. "That was at least Fleece. Couldn't see the rest of them in the car."

I turned. We'd play-acted an arrest before, but I still hated it. And I knew he did, too.

It was disrespectful to what we both knew to be true. We helped one another.

"So what's the move?" I let us skip over the uneasiness.

Merck opened the back door to look at the baby.

"You come stay at my house for a few days. They think I got you locked up. Then we spread that your age kept you out of trouble. And you say nothing." Merck pulled out his laptop and started typing. "We're waiting for the ambulance. The mother is coming, too."

"What about Fleece and Boon? You're going to get them, right? I'll testify." I nodded and flexed. It would feel good to help put those assholes in jail. I kept picturing Fleece punching the mother. I hated it.

"We let them go. For now." He didn't take his eyes off the computer.

"No." I slapped my hand near Merck's electronic.

He stopped typing and turned his head. "You need to stay safe. And they need to not think you're a snitch."

I kicked at the dirt. “I’m no snitch. They wanted to *kill* a baby. Come on. There has to be something done about that.”

“There was. The baby’s safe because you saved it. I’m proud of you. But now you have to trust me.” He went back to typing.

“I’m not staying at your house.” I looked down the road and focused on where the yellow line met the dark.

There was silence. We’d been through this before. When I was just a kid and Merck was Superman in my head still, I’d asked him to adopt me. And he’d said no.

I wasn’t going to play house with him for a few days just to go back to the fosters. It’d be like getting everything I’d wanted just to give it back.

I heard Merck sigh. Mrs. Merck had been the reason back then. She’d said no, and Merck respected her decision. She didn’t want to adopt a kid when she was trying so hard to have a baby.

I’d lost a lot of potential families before then and since then. Now I set the terms. I didn’t want a goddamn family. I’d make my own. Someday.

“You can stay at a friend of mine’s house. They have an apartment.”

I shook my head and wiped my nose. I could hear the ambulance in the distance.

“I’m good, Merck. You need someone to testify—I’m there. Otherwise, I’ll catch you around. Oh, I tossed the gun that way, and the bullets that way.” I turned my back and walked away. Merck called my name twice, then let me go.

I didn’t turn around. I didn’t want him to see the tear that was rolling down my cheek.

6

Animal

I went to school after a few days. Then the next day. And the next. While the other kids my age were playing football during the fifteen-minute recess on the pavement in front of the school, I was watching for cars while sitting on the brick wall at the edge of the parking lot.

Because Boon and Fleece were looking for me. I'd heard from a few reliable sources they were pissed and wanted blood.

I kept an eye on the cars rolling past the school. T was next to me, using a rock to scratch lines into her skin.

We were quiet together usually. But she'd been exceptionally so recently. It was due to get cold soon, and she'd expressed concern. The shelter in town was pretty goddamn horrible. The people who worked there were nice enough, but the politicians in office were cracking down on the homeless. So she could only stay three days at a time. And I knew that there was a ban on feeding homeless people in the park where she had to stay.

"You relocating?" I was curious if she had a plan.

When she looked up from her wrist, I saw what might be letters etched there, but she pulled down her sleeve so I couldn't make out the words.

"Maybe."

Her voice was husky, like she was hiding somewhere inside herself and had to fight to be heard.

"What are the options?" I kept my eyes on a lowered Monte Carlo as it drove by far below the speed limit.

"Under the toll bridge. I guess." She watched the car with me. \

"Trouble?"

"Maybe."

The windows of the Monte Carlo were tinted. I was getting that buzz at the bottom of my spine that something wasn't right.

I stood. I didn't like facing anything sitting down. They might be trying something, but I wouldn't be caught unaware.

T started mumbling the plate number. Smart girl. The car pulled away.

I looked down at T. She had the plate number etched into her left arm, some scratches going so deep they drew blood.

"I got it if you need it." She held out her slightly bloody arm to me.

I looked at the mix of numbers and letters until I had it memorized. She pulled down her sleeve when I nodded.

I scanned the school ground. I felt so much older than the

kids playing ball or lumped in groups gossiping. I knew T felt the same. Her long brown hair was covering one side of her face, but her one brown eye that I could see got me.

"We'll make it, Animal. I can tell."

The bell rang and we had to go stand in line to get back into school. It was all so stupid. I half-waited for someone to shoot me in the back. I didn't feel as young as all the kids around me, even though we were the same age.

7

They were crowding me. They saw me. All the times I was invisible, I was lucky. Tonight I wasn't. The roar in my ears was taking away my ability to think. My ability to fight. I wanted my mom. I wanted something normal as they ripped my shirt off. And then I silently prayed for forgiveness for betraying her—even in my mind. It wasn't her fault. But as they started to hit me, I tried to fill my head with her smile. She could save me in my mind, at least.

8

The cold had finally come. And I knew, on this Saturday night, that T was likely staying under the bridge. It was the worst place. It certainly wasn't safe. And tonight, it was cold. I was worried about her.

Cars had been creeping on me when I was out and about. Fleece and Boon were making themselves scarce. I got it. They were waiting to figure out if I'd snitched. And I had. And I would. But Merck was setting the boundaries. I knew that I'd face-off with them both at some point. I stole their gun and the car they wanted. Plus, the first "test" of killing the baby was one that I not only had failed, but had turned on them.

I didn't like my chances in this town right now. My birthday had come and gone. Well, the date they thought was my birthday, anyway. No one knew for sure. At fourteen, I felt the same as thirteen. Tall, older than kids my age, and antsy.

What I was antsy about was not distinctly defined. I had something I needed to do, but I sucked at figuring it out.

The fosters were binging in the house 'cause of the cold, so I beat feet into the night.

I had a warm sweatshirt on and a blanket I'd nabbed from the attic. It smelled like four people had died in it, but it was warm. And I was bringing it to her.

Under the bridge was a shitty place to stand, never mind sleep. I stood in the shadows and took in the sight.

Fires in trash cans and car noise. The stench of alcohol and piss was overwhelming. I tossed the stinky blanket to my feet. This was not going to happen. T wasn't sleeping here another night. If I had to sneak her in the attic at the fosters' house, I'd do it.

I walked into the crowd, milling around with my hands jammed in my pockets. It was dark, but all the eyes could see me. Watch me. I felt the attention crawling all over me. They were looking for drugs, jewelry, anything. It was primal out here.

A crazy man started hollering and laughing. "Shit. They got the girl back there. Shit. They got the girl." Then he started laughing and pointing.

The buzzing started in my spine. There were plenty of women here, but I knew he was talking about T. I moved fast through the crowd in the direction he was pointing.

Between two rusted out cars I saw a herd of guys. I knew it was bad. Men didn't clump up like that unless they were on something like a pack of dogs.

I heard growling and snarling, then I saw one of the guys drop his pants while another swung his leg with a kick.

The resulting yelp was extremely female. I heard fabric rip. I looked at the ground for anything and found a pipe. It was heavier than it looked, which was good.

I went for the bare ass first, because he was getting to his knees and I wasn't stupid. He was trying to mount someone.

I knew it was T without seeing her. I hit him square in the center of his back. I didn't give the other guys around her a chance. I swung and hit without mercy. I didn't try to pull the blows to make them lighter. I heard bones cracking.

A fist connected with my face. My adrenaline was so pumped up, I only registered the blow because it moved my head. I let go of the pipe and used my fists. I was skinny but strong. Taller than all the men there. And it turned out, men who try to rape women are cowards. They ran. I looked down at the girl, hoping I was wrong.

Her pretty brown eye was swollen shut. Her shirt was ripped off completely and she was using her shaking arms to cover herself.

I pulled my sweatshirt off and handed it to her. She couldn't move one of her arms. I kept watch with my teeth bared as I helped her put my sweatshirt over her head. They were coming back. They'd run, but then they figured out that I was just one guy. I bent low. The arm she couldn't move dangled as I slipped one arm under her knees and the other behind her back.

I growled, and a few of the men and women from under the bridge formed a human wall between the attackers and us. Now that they'd seen me fight for her, they were willing to as well, I guessed.

It didn't matter. T was shaking in my arms and trying to talk, but she stuttered on the words.

I carried her up the hill by the bridge. I knew the toll takers would be in the booths, and I was hoping they could call for help. I had no idea how hurt T was.

How bad it had gotten.

I didn't even register her weight; I was too fixed on the lights on the bridge. My back was made out of metal.

"It's over?" T finally made a sentence.

"It's over," I told her. I approached the tollbooth then.

It wasn't until after I heard, "Freeze. This is the police," that I realized I was a topless black man carrying a sobbing white girl out from the night.

I looked down at her face. I'd promised her it was over, and I wouldn't regret helping her, even if it meant I would be shot down in this instant.

9

Animal

I expanded my lungs with air, not sure if any of it would be the last thing I did.

"Animal?" T was confused.

"I got you, T. I won't put you down. I know you're hurt." I waited as men I couldn't see decided what my fate would be.

"Hey. No. No. Hold your fire."

I recognized the voice.

Merck jumped out in front of the searchlights aimed at me.

He jogged toward me, holding his gear as it bounced.

"What the hell?" He held out his arms for T, but she shook

her head, moving her hair enough for him to see her whole face. I watched as Merck saw how young she was.

Behind me, we both heard the sound of tromping feet up the hill.

Headlights flashed by, going over the bridge.

Merck stopped offering to take T from me and made "a round them up" hand signal. When the other cops on the scene walked toward me, he redirected them to the guys who were hunting for T and me.

In no time, the cop cars were abandoned and the police went after the guys on foot before they could even get close to us.

I felt T shivering, and then I realized I was shivering, too. I walked toward the cop cars, knowing that I could get her in Merck's cruiser for at least a short time.

Before I could set her down to open the door, the office door cracked and I heard an older woman call to me.

"Bring her here. You okay, honey?" I looked at T's face and made the decision for both of us. My arms were starting to ache. T wasn't heavy, but she wasn't too light either.

In the office, there was a small couch that I put T down on. I sat next to her. The woman was in a toll taker's uniform with a swirl of gray hair like cotton candy on her head. She disappeared in a closet and pulled out a blanket and a windbreaker. She placed the blanket gently on T and handed me the windbreaker.

"Do you guys need some water? Hot cocoa?" I could see her nametag now. *Martha Meiner.*

T was using her hair as a veil again, so I agreed to some water for us both.

I leaned close to T. "Your shoulder jacked up?"

She wasn't moving it. T looked from the floor to my face to her shoulder. "Yeah. They pushed me down on it."

"Okay. We need to get help for that." I was going to ask for help from Martha Meiner.

She bustled back in. "Okay, here's some water. Been a crazy night. Had a jumper out here, and just after they talked him down, you two show up. You I recognize. You've been under the bridge a few days now, right?"

Martha handed me both of our water glasses.

T was still looking at her shoulder, but she nodded.

I must have seemed confused, because Martha provided the answer. "I like to make the mister casseroles, and I try to make a few extra for our friends underneath. Little Miss here's new, so I made sure she got a plate."

There was a light knock on the door and Merck entered.

"How's it going?" Merck looked at T. He kept his distance. T was unmistakably putting off some "leave me alone" vibes.

"They were attacking her. I don't know how far..." I stopped. I didn't know how bad it had gotten. T was still wearing her jeans, so I had hope.

"They didn't rape..." And then T trailed off. It hadn't happened, but it was about to. I wanted to give her a hug, but I knew that carrying her had been a lot of physical contact for T. She was a private person.

"It was the clear intention."

Merck made a quick hand movement that shut me up. He didn't want me to say more and it made me angry, but I listened.

"Ms. Martha, thank you so much for watching them. We got an ambulance coming for her now."

Martha frowned sympathetically. "Can I get ice for her? And his face?" T shook her head, so I did the same. Martha didn't seem offended that we turned down her offer.

She stood and asked to speak to Merck outside.

Adult talk, I was guessing.

"I don't want to go under the bridge again." T touched my hand with the fingers that were working.

"I'll fix it. Somehow I'll make it okay, T."

10

Merck met with officers and conversed with them outside the toll both office while we waited for an ambulance.

When Martha had to go back to her shift, T spoke up.

“If I go to the hospital, they’ll want to know information.”

She didn’t want to be found out. The homeless thing. The fact that she was working a loophole in the system.

The police scared her. Reporting scared her. The hospital terrified her.

Names. Address. Phone number.

It all made her more anxious than her not being able to

move her arm. Scared her more than whatever they'd done to her.

Her hair was caught on her bloodied lip. I reached up and pulled it gently and tucked it behind her ear. Her brown eyes were wide on me. She was always so in control. I'd never seen her this petrified before.

The ambulance pulled up. The lights filled the office, bouncing off the walls. T was panicking.

"There was a kid in one of my early foster homes. He wouldn't talk, not when he didn't want to anyway. They said he was..." I thought for a few seconds as I pulled the term up from the depths of my memory. "Selective mute. That was it. He could talk, but not when he was scared. You could be that."

She nodded. "I like that."

"I'll try to stay with you, okay?"

Merck opened the office door for the paramedics. They were respectful when T tried to get closer to me. "You know her?"

I looked at her face.

"I've seen her around." I was vague. When in doubt, vague bought me time in the past.

I watched Merck narrow his eyes. He'd want to know what the hell this was about. I widened mine slightly to let him know that I had my reasons.

The paramedics were very kind and gentle. When I didn't own up to knowing T, in hopes of keeping her a mystery, I was no longer able to assert my claim to be next to her.

The paramedics loaded her into the ambulance. I tugged on Merck's sleeve and pointed to his patrol car.

"What the hell, buddy?" Merck started the car and followed the ambulance. He put his lights on, too, so we could follow just as swiftly.

And then I let it pour out. I told him that T was my friend

and how she didn't want to be in the system. I told him that we had to find a place for her to stay that worked and that I needed to be in that hospital with her.

I watched as he shifted in his seat, his gear squeaking and clacking. "That's serious." He was plainly running through ways to process what I'd told him.

The lights flooded the sides of the road as I waited to see what he would say. I knew hospitals were militant about shit. I exhaled, worried that I'd made a mistake.

"I know a lawyer. A chick that works for homeless kids' rights. I can call her in the morning. I can stay near T and you can stay near me at the hospital. For now. Do I have to call your foster parents?"

Merck slid the blinker in the right direction to follow the ambulance. "Nah, they won't answer the phone." I kept my gaze forward so I wouldn't see Merck's internal struggle on his face.

We were about eight blocks from the hospital when Merck picked up his phone and called his wife.

His side was clear. Her side was, too, because I was close. She was ripping him a new one for not coming home. Accusing him of cheating.

He took the verbal lashing before apologizing a few times and hanging up.

We got to the parking lot, and he put the car in a spot set aside for police. I finally looked at his face, and he at mine. I said sorry without the words for the shit he'd taken for me.

Merck shrugged. "I'd do anything for you, kid."

That statement opened a whole can of worms. I dropped my gaze and let him escape the obvious. Everything except be my father.

I opened the door as the paramedics opened theirs. T was spooked out of her mind. She had an IV in her arm and bandages wound around a few of her cuts. Her arm was stabilized.

I eased out and stood next to her. "Here."

The paramedics ignored me, and Merck put his hand on my shoulder to officially escort me into the building.

I was able to grab T's good hand and hold it. She squeezed me back. We were a train like that all the way to the curtained cubical in the ER.

Maybe I loved him more in the moment he stood next to me at the hospital. Consistent. I saw a fire in his eyes to keep me safe and I was feeling so incredibly out of my element. Tender. Where I was normally sharp I felt like I could be breached and I hated it. The men under the bridge had taken a confidence from me that I didn't even know I valued. But Animal was there like a knight in the night. Someone else that worried about me. His name was branded on my quivering soul. I could be brave again, soon. But right this second he was a brick wall for me.

T had to get her shoulder reset. The assholes who had attacked her under the toll bridge had dislocated it. She had some deep bruises, but nothing was broken.

That night, after she had a taste of some strong painkillers, the doctor was able to manipulate the bone back into the correct position so she could move her arm.

Merck worked his magic, and I was able to stay with T that evening. T played her part as a newly developed selective mute. The lawyer got a special social worker called, and Merck spoke to her, but there was only so much he could do.

T was assigned to a new foster mom with an amazing reputation. The lawyer had pulled some strings.

I knew T was probably against it all. T had a mom. She told me about her once. It had been a late night. Sometimes when I needed to get away from the toxic environment of the fosters, I snuck out. It wasn't hard. They didn't care where I was. At night T and I would meet. She'd steal food, and I'd keep us safe. But one night she told me she still had a mom. I had been confused until she explained how it was.

We were at the old mall, just inside a busted storefront. She was leaning against one wall, me the other.

I'd asked her to tell me why they weren't together. This was a hard question, and I knew what I was asking. The deepest of secrets.

T was silent for so long, I thought she wouldn't answer, but then she explained, "If Mom sees me, she goes off her meds. They say I make her too excited. And when she's excited, she stops taking the pill she's supposed to. She gets violent. So the one person who loves her most in the world only creeps on her from time to time."

T shrugged as if that fact was spilled milk. It was so much more. I knew the word "mother" could hurt like a slap. When it was Mother's Day. When the class was making cards for the soft ladies that got hugs from their kids at the end of the day. And T had one mom.

"How do you not go to her?" It was almost unbelievable.

She pulled an old hospital bracelet from her pocket. It had the name Anastasia on it. "I just don't. I know what works and I do that. But I only have love for one mom, and that's the way I plan on keeping it."

I bowed my head like I was at a funeral. I could hear the pain in her voice, and it felt disrespectful to stare. Maybe she was crying; her words were barely there. It was dark in the empty ghost of a store.

I knew now why she needed an open window or a door left ajar. Part of that was not wanting to be locked in, but the other part was needing to escape and get a fix of her mom. Just a visual. T had to be the strongest person in the world.

The suckiest part of being in the system was the lack of ability to affect your situations. Merck took me home to the fosters' house when T's new foster mother arrived to pick her up at the hospital.

Merck apologized for how it all turned out when he dropped me off. I knew he'd tried his best, but I was pretty sure I was a jerk to him. Either way, the fosters didn't care that I had been gone when I arrived on Sunday morning.

The following day changed just about everything for me. I was busy trying to figure out where T had gone. Finding her actual location would take some work. But when I got ready for school the next morning, I had to pause to answer the doorbell. Merck was there, looking exhausted.

"Hey, get your stuff. Something's about to go down here, and I want you in my possession when it does."

Kids in the system know how to pack fast. I was no different. I was still being a punk to Merck because I was fine living with these asshole addicts if I had to.

On my way out, another cop came in to serve a warrant.

The addicts had been caught doing whatever they did to get high. I'd tossed my bags in the passenger side of the cop car and pushed them over to sit.

The fact that I wanted Merck as a dad was going to come up again, and it was going to hurt. I crossed my arms in front of my chest and refused to put on my seat belt. Before Merck could back up, the fosters were in handcuffs on the front steps.

"I had an idea." Merck turned the heater on as we watched the fosters get marched to another squad car.

"Yeah." Hope slammed up in the center of my chest, despite me trying to tell myself to be reasonable.

"There's the home in town. You know the one? Benfell Academy? They have kids that live there. You'd have your own room. Food's good. You could stay there until you're eighteen instead of bouncing around so damn much. There's consistency."

I looked at my lap. No offer from him to be my family.

"I asked my wife again last night if I could adopt you. She said no. I asked her for a divorce. I told her if she was making me choose between you and her, I would pick you."

I opened my mouth and slowly looked his way.

"What? You're surprised? You know how it is with us. I love you." Merck cleared his throat and looked through the window. "Every time I see you with another situation that turns to crap, it kills me."

He'd just suggested the home, so as nice as it was to hear the man cared about me like I did him, there was some sort of complication.

The squad car with my now ex-fosters pulled away. The cops were obviously conducting a full-scale warrant by the way they were tearing up the place.

"She had me followed and found out about the affair. Told me she'd ruin my career if I didn't stay." Merck punched the dashboard. We sat there listening to the heater. He finally gave me his reasoning. "I need this job. I can watch over you better this way and make sure everything is going in your direction. You *will* make it out of this screwed-up childhood, so help me God."

Merck gave me a look of pure fatherhood. There was both agony and selflessness in it. I was smart enough to know that he was right. Having him as my very own police officer would be a help.

I grabbed the older man by the shoulder and squeezed. "In my heart you're my father."

Merck put his head back against the headrest. "That means the world to me, buddy. Thank you."

I took my other hand and patted his arm. I put a fair amount of hope in the man, but that was all he was. A man that I connected with. Maybe we were father and son in a past life. I wasn't sure.

"I think the home's a good idea. I like the idea of meals. I'm hungry a lot."

On the drive over to Benfell Academy, I told Merck about the stupid cheese sandwiches. He cursed up a blue streak about the injustice of it all.

My balance was always twenty dollars no matter how

much I ate at school from that day on. Merck made sure I was covered.

I met Sister Mary. She was a fan of Merck's, and he assured her that I'd be a great addition to the home.

I saw the setup for what it was that night. Sort of a place of last resort. Kids that were too wild to stay with their families, if they had any. The abuse that most of them underwent before they were placed gave a whole new definition to crazy. Humans could be broken beyond repair. Even as kids. Structure was a large part of how the home worked. There were very consistent headcounts and procedures when kids went out of their heads. The people who worked there had to love their job, because getting kicked and spit on were part of the hard days there. But I knew I could make it work.

I was allowed to attend my regular school as opposed to the instruction they had on site for the other kids. It was like a whole community inside the walls.

I arrived at school and found T in a sling at recess the next damn day.

"Good to see you here. You still in district?" We'd both moved houses and schools a lot, so she knew what I meant.

She nodded with a far-off look in her eye.

"I'm surprised that you're here. Aren't you on pain meds and stuff?" I sat next to her on the brick wall.

The car with the lowered body and the same license plate that T had carved into her skin rolled by.

"They want me to stay in my routine." She was talking slowly and a little slurred.

"What happened? Where'd they place you? Give me an address." I watched as she swayed.

"I won't be there long. I'll be out tonight. She likes all the windows closed so..." She looked at my face as if seeing me for the first time. "Thank you. For what you did under the bridge."

I nodded. "You'd do the same for me."

It was true. I trusted her. She was small, but she was feisty as shit.

"The selective mute thing is genius, by the way." She smirked after the lowered car passed. Like she hadn't seen it at all. "I should've been doing this the whole damn time."

"You okay, T?" She was off. There had to be repercussions. She was attacked just the night before. She was still bruised up.

"I think if my mom was well, she'd make me chicken soup. And I bet she'd have a soft blanket that smelled like the dryer sheets that she'd wrap around me. And we'd watch *Grease* together. She'd make me feel safe. And I could sleep on my stomach, not holding onto my stuff, you know? And she'd hum a song I liked."

I'd never heard T just gush like that. The stuff she wanted was so specific. It was heartbreaking.

"She'd do all that shit, T. It'd be great."

She wiped at her eyes with the back of her hand and sniffled. I looked at her wrist. She still had her hospital band on. My girl wouldn't roll like that. She liked her personal shit personal. I pulled a blade out of my pocket. T didn't flinch when I put it near her wrist. I could've attributed it to her being on drugs, except as I slid her sweatshirt sleeve out of the way, I saw the remnants of all the other scars.

T looked from the knife to her wrist. This version of my girl was free with her words. "Sometimes I need to see the pain I feel."

I bowed my head like she had uttered a prayer. Then I flipped it so the blade could slide through the thick plastic. I slipped it into my back pocket so I could take the evidence out of the picture. I knew better than to let the jackholes in this school have the opportunity to dig it out of the trash. It said:

Talon Devora

I was so used to her being my T, seeing her government name was a surprise.

I held open my arms to her. I knew she was a private person, and I had nothing to offer—but a hug seemed right.

She looked at the center of my chest while she filtered the action through the drugs she must have been on.

I held still. T scootched over close and gently put her head over my heart. I carefully put my arms around her, trying to remember where her injuries were so I wouldn't hurt her.

She let out a moan, but she stayed.

I didn't tell her it was all going to be okay, because I sucked at lying. I wasn't old enough to protect her, I mean really. I couldn't make it so she could stay somewhere safe. I kissed the top of her head.

"Someday, T, you and I are going to have a house on top of a hill, and no one will be able to tell us what to do. We'll make so much money that we'll use it to start fires sometimes."

She murmured something I couldn't hear. Two minutes later, she was asleep on me. I held her so she wouldn't lose her balance.

Five minutes later, I had to wake her. Recess was over. It was time to go inside and pretend like math mattered.

11

The Benfell Home made a big deal about Christmas. Sister Mary was pretty frigging Catholic, so it made sense.

It pissed me off. To see the decorations taped to the cement brick walls was insulting. I knew the adults were trying—really they were. But the cardboard cheery Santa had a Sharpie dick drawn on him within five minutes.

Merck ramped up his visits, and I took ribbing about it from the other kids and some of the childcare workers.

I didn't let it affect me. He was getting more and more

agitated lately, and finally, when we were driving back from a movie, I asked him what the hell was going on.

He looked at me a few times before he let himself be truthful.

"You're young, but I feel like I need someone to know this. You're who I've got."

"Hit me with it. Takes a lot to surprise me." I wiggled my eyebrows. Merck sighed. "Remember when I told you about my wife? About the

affair? Well, things are escalating. This woman—the one I'm in love with? Well, she's married, too, but her husband abuses her. Like rough stuff."

"So, what are you going to do about it?" It was a tricky piece of information. I respected Merck, but he wasn't perfect. I didn't think all the cheating would end well. Lies catch up. Seemed that way, which is why I tried to avoid them whenever I could.

"I don't know. I mean, it's wrong, but I feel like, I mean—I could protect her. She's got a son—almost your age, maybe a few years younger. I know that bastard hits him, too. He's one of those that makes sure the clothes cover what he's done—no bruises peeking out."

I nodded because I knew what he was talking about. No one ever hit me twice because I walked right out the goddamn door if they did, but I knew it happened to others.

"Sounds like the wife should report him to, well—you. I mean, does she want to be with you?"

Merck bobbed his head from one shoulder to the other while he thought. "Yeah. I mean, I'm sure a guy that's nice to her is a big change, but I'm married."

"And you shouldn't be. You deserve to be out of that house. If you want to leave, just leave. Worse things have happened.

And if they take your badge, you can do security or something." I gave him a hard look.

"She's had a child. A girl. I think it could be mine."

I whistled. "Shit."

"No kidding. Kinsey will lose her mind. She's been trying to get pregnant for so long. But that's my kid, you know? I don't want the baby injured. Or her. Or her son."

"Now what?" I watched as the Christmas lights on the trees in town blurred from the speed of the car.

"I want to get her and her kids out. And get you in the same house. As far as I'm concerned, you're my kid, too." Merck looked at me like he was afraid of what he'd said.

"You're going to have to deal with your missus first. Get past the first hurdle, then you can act on everything else." I turned my head.

My hope had learned not to act up in moments like this. I kept it firmly leashed. Merck had shit to deal with. He had a merry picture in his head, like T had of her mom when she'd been out of her mind on painkillers.

As if thinking about her brought her fate to mine, Merck got a call on his cell.

I could only hear his side of the call, and he looked at me enough times during the exchange that I knew it had something to do with me.

He agreed to help, and because he turned the cruiser in the opposite direction of the home, I knew I was coming with him.

He answered the question I hadn't asked, "That's a call from T's foster mom. They're trying to put her in a straight jacket right now. You cool to come with?"

I sat on my one shaking hand. With every action there's an equal and opposite reaction. T had been attacked, and she hadn't responded yet. I had a feeling tonight was her reaction.

I knew I was surrounded. The nightgown was a trap. It looked soft, but after I put it on, I realized my clothes were gone.

The new fake mom had understanding eyes. "Listen, I just want you to get some rest. I've been told that you have trouble staying in one place. I get it. It's hard to believe that this place is a safe one, but it is. Which is why we do have to keep the windows and doors locked."

I'd told her I needed a window cracked open. I probably could have done that exact action and she wouldn't have known, but the other little girl in my room had asthma. I was concerned for her with the cold air. Obviously, I was used to it.

I felt like an explosion was simmering in my chest when the woman closed and locked the window. She apologized more than a few times.

But she wasn't just closing a window. She was predicting my future. As she tried to close the bedroom door, I bolted.

I couldn't do it. It was a cage. It was an expectation of acceptance that I couldn't allow. I saw my mother's face as I ran down the hallway. The foster person yelled my given name. My name that I only liked to hear from my mom.

"Talon!"

I forgot the layout and ran into the den where there was no escape. No door. The woman blocked the door that I had run through.

"Sweetheart, listen. It's late. Let's go have some hot cocoa and relax."

It was the worst thing to say. She'd never know that in order to love my mother I had to say no. I had to do without. Even without a roof over my head. Even without a meal in my belly. I would love my mother even if it hurt me.

The things I was being offered were too tempting. I felt the tears marching up to my eyes. And those would call to this woman in front of me. Compassion came off of her in waves. Understanding. Acceptance.

She was the most dangerous thing my needy heart had ever felt.

I took to the closest window and opened it. I was crawling away from this. From her. To the cold, where I belonged. I would be loyal even if it hurt. It was how I was made. And I wasn't changing.

12

I understood Merck knew how to drive like a wild man, but the ride to T's foster mother's house really highlighted that he was like a stunt guy in a movie.

Despite my concern for T, Merck and I grinned at each other when he spun the car around a turn so quickly he left rubber.

My smile was wiped away the second I saw what was going on at T's place.

Now she was standing in her nightgown with bare feet on the front lawn. Her small, pretty foster mom was holding a thick afghan and shaking her head.

The trouble with T's foster was that the woman was great. She wanted the doors locked at night for safety, not to cage T in, I was betting. I knew that the kids in her care had a good deal. They wore new clothes to school and had fresh haircuts. It was a primo gig to get. I knew Merck had pushed and pulled to get T there. He'd told me about it before the movie.

Maybe if T's foster had been a horrible person it would have been easier. But T only loved once. And if she were starting to feel disloyal to her real mom, she would tap out. Freak out. Misbehave on purpose—it seemed. Taking in the fact that she was still dealing with getting attacked under the bridge in her head—probably, and my girl would be fit to be tied.

Her hair was a mess. Her lips were blue. She was visibly so, so cold.

She wouldn't talk. All she would do was fight. There was a social worker standing in the driveway filling out paperwork like he was anywhere in the world. A straight jacket on the grass, discarded.

Merck spared me a glance. "Stay here."

"No." I got out of the car the same time he did.

As we approached, the social worker was noticeably ticking off boxes. "So, you said she wouldn't take more of her meds?"

The foster mom gave the social worker a dirty look. "Can we do this later? I'd like to just get her inside. It's freezing."

The woman cared. Which was good, because T had only been in her house a short while.

T positioned her body so her back was to empty space. She didn't want to be surrounded.

"What meds are we talking about?" Merck didn't bother to introduce himself. T knew him from my relationship with the cop.

The foster mom hugged the blanket. "Antidepressants. For the selective mutism."

I looked at T and she met my gaze. Medication. T was flashing to her mom, I was sure of it. Obviously, for her she was totally able to talk. She didn't need the drugs.

I walked over to the foster mom. "Ma'am? Can I have this?"

She looked me up and down and then looked to Merck. He nodded. I grabbed the blanket. "Thanks."

After spreading the afghan like wings looking for an angel, I walked to T. I wrapped her up. She put her cold forehead against the base of my neck. I kissed the top of her messy head.

"T, what's going on? Just come with me. Okay?"

Just like the night under the bridge, I lifted her into my arms. I nodded at the car, and Merck jogged over and opened the back door. I leaned down and put T inside.

The social worker began shaking his head, with his mouth moving from one side to the other.

T was safe with me, and I'd do anything to keep it that way.

Merck began doing what he did best, soothing complicated situations so that the people involved could get through the night.

I slid in next to T. She was zoning out. Maybe she was allergic to what they had given her? Meds were tough. The correct combination really helped some kids. I watched how right they were when it happened. But getting the dosage correct, and the type correct was trial and error. And I was looking at an error right now with big brown eyes and a stubborn streak.

"You know, your mom would want you happy, if she had it all together. That's how I hear moms are. This is a nice lady you're with."

I watched as she fumed at me.

"Are you kidding? Right now?" she whispered so the adults

wouldn't hear. And even though she was mad at me, I put my arm up so no one could see her mouth moving.

"Maybe drop the not talking thing?" I offered.

She shook her head and pinched her eyebrows together. "I have one mother."

Merck headed in our direction. I glanced at him, and he acknowledged me. A resolution had been reached, and I knew T wouldn't be happy with it just by the way he had his shoulders set.

That night the foster mom agreed to let T keep her window open if she would come inside the house. The little girl with the asthma would sleep on the floor in the master bedroom tonight. T got out of the other side of the car, so I couldn't stop her. She was leaving too quickly. I didn't get to tell her that I understood and it was just a suggestion. I'd support her.

Instead, she walked back in the front door of the foster home like she hadn't been losing it on the front lawn at all.

I knew she was sneaking out as soon as she could. She was done with a capital D. Merck and I rolled out after the social worker had finished his paperwork.

Merck scratched his jaw lightly when we were finally rolling back to the home. "I feel like that was too easy."

"It was. T's not likely to stay put." I already knew I'd sneak out as well and try to intercept her.

I heard Merck sigh. "Yeah, I'll tell the guys to look out for her. It's really cold, and I don't trust that she would be able to stay warm."

"What are the odds that we could get T into a place like I'm in? Do they have one for girls?" I was trying to think if I'd ever heard of something similar.

"They do, but it's not in the same school district. I know you guys are close, so I was shying away from that option. I mean, that foster mom is really fantastic. She'd be great with T. She is great with T." Merck swung the car around the circular driveway to sign me back in.

"Yeah, I appreciate that. I'll mention it to her, maybe. Thanks for everything." I got out of the car the same time Merck did, and we slammed our doors in unison.

He patted me on the back after I was signed in, and I thanked him for the trip. I jogged up the back steps to my unit.

I was out the window minutes after headcount. I was good at shimmying down the latticework that normally propped up ivy in the spring. I could pop locks. Maybe that's what I had to teach T about escaping. If she knew how to get out of anywhere, no door would ever really be closed for her.

I was hustling to the neighborhood where T was, and I knew it would take a while when a lowered Monte Carlo flashed by me down the road, illuminated by the light post I was walking underneath.

I knew I was screwed when it slowed down and reverse lights came on. I turned to the woods and headed for them. Another car came up behind me and skidded to a halt. The Monte Carlo had company, and so did I.

I was able to get my clothes from the laundry room after

everyone was asleep. I had a warm jacket on and my mother's hospital bracelet. Nothing else I had mattered. I knew Marybeth, the foster mom, was a light sleeper, but I'd tuckered her out with worry. I still made sure to be extra quiet.

I was done. I didn't want to leave, but too many adults around me were involved and official. My fine art of staying under the radar was blown. And this foster cared too much. She'd make sure I had a place to stay— even if it wasn't here. I could sense she played the long game. Part of my traitorous heart wanted to lean into the welcome. The caring. The dedication.

But I shook it off. I hadn't taken the next dose of the meds, so I was hoping my head would clear soon.

I had to leave Midville, and it killed me. I would have to treat this town like I was a wanted criminal here. The scars around my determination flared up. I would miss seeing my mom from a distance. I would pine for Animal's understanding.

The only option I had was to become a missing person. Fade from memory. Become a girl that used to be. It would be best if I didn't see Animal again, but my feet seemed preprogrammed to head in his direction. I pulled my hood up and took off into the night without looking back.

13

Animal

It was pointless to run now. Stupid Boon and Fleece and their dumb as bricks friends, Brooks and Smiley, were all feeling pretty frigging pumped. Because they got me alone.

I crossed my arms in front of my chest so they couldn't see my heart pounding there.

There was no Merck here. No friends to help. And I had no weapons.

Clearly, this was going to be a mess.

"Look at this. Not so fucking ballsy without the gun I

handed you." Fleece stomped his foot and hit his own fist. I cursed under my breath when I flinched.

"We could've had a sweet car, a nice payout. But instead, I'm up at night wondering if you flipped on me." Boon was bobbing his head like there was music playing. I guessed it was his lame way of agreeing with Fleece.

Brooks decided he had shit to say and added, "Where's your sugar daddy, Animal? That cop like 'em young?"

I was going down, that was for sure. But I didn't have to cower for them. "Brooks, how many hours did it take for you to string that sentence together?" I turned my face toward him. "And you two low-life assholes have to spend your time obsessing over a fourteen-year-old kid? Are you too scared of the guys your own age?"

After the insults settled, their predatory sneers turned to grimaces and frowns. I threw as many punches as I could, but when one of them hit the back of my knee, I bowed.

And once I was on the ground, there was no getting back up. I wished darkness would take me, but I was conscious for every punch, blow, and kick.

They say your life flashes before your eyes when you're dying. That's not what happened when I was getting the ever-living shit kicked out of me on a cold road at night.

My future flashed in front of me. How mad Merck would be at me for sneaking out. How hard it would be to know T was alone in this world. That I wouldn't get to be an adult, fully in charge of my own decisions.

I kept trying to at least hurt them, take out a kneecap or something, but four guys together seemed like a monster with a million arms.

I saw her Converse sneakers in a blink. Maybe I was dreaming it. They'd hit my head enough.

The sound of gunshots blurred with the blows. With each passing thunder, there were fewer arms on the monster.

I heard growling. There were loud bells in my ears, too. One of my lungs felt like something from inside me was poking it. My left hand was numb. My leg made me yell when I tried to move it.

A cold hand lay on my forehead gently. "Stay put. Don't move. They won't hurt you anymore."

I looked to my left without moving my head.

T.

She had a gun in her other hand.

"I'm going to grab a phone and see if I can call the cops."

"Merck." I wasn't sure she heard me. My word sounded more like a cough.

The girl who was out of her mind hours earlier had just saved me.

I was in and out of consciousness. I didn't hear her phone call or if she got Merck.

But the next time I came to, my head was in T's lap and she was speaking to Merck. Sirens and lights made my head hurt worse.

"...put my jacket on that and tried to apply pressure. I wanted to keep him warm..."

Out again. Pain. Shallow breaths.

In again.

"...you did great, T. You're going to have to let the paramedics do their job, though. Let him go."

A growl. A low, female growl.

Out again.

For a long time.

Maybe this was death after all.

14

I was having trouble peeling my fingers off of Animal. I knew he needed to go in the ambulance, but letting go of him was against everything I had inside.

Watching those men hurt him had flipped a switch for me. I was ready to kill everyone. Not my person. They weren't taking one of my people. I only had two.

Merck—I recognized him, and he was firm with me that Animal needed to go to the paramedics.

I released him from my grip, but I felt like I was letting him fall off a cliff. Merck passed me to another cop.

When the ambulance door closed, I started to fight. It was

hard to make a choice. My head was foggy. The meds were still wearing off, but still.

It went south quickly. It went to fighting for Animal to fighting for my life. They were only able to subdue me when they had the handcuffs on me.

They set me on the ground, and it was the first time I had to look at the damage I'd done. Three men dead. One man getting loaded into another ambulance.

I was a murderer now, and I had not one bit of regret. Each of them would have killed Animal. And as long as I had breath in my body, I wasn't letting that happen.

I could turn off the consequences in my head. Animal had to live. That's what mattered.

15

Waking up in a hospital was confusing as shit. The monitors. The smell. Knowing somehow that time had passed, but not how much. I was tethered to the bed by an IV and lots of wires and something below my waist that I didn't want to think about.

Merck was sleeping in a chair near the bed. I cleared my throat and tried to cough. Everything felt like I'd been through a meat grinder.

Merck's eyes popped open. He looked at me hard and I tried to wave at him. Only my fingers would move.

He stood and ran out of the room so fast I thought there had to be something dangerous going on.

The nurse who ran back into the room with Merck had a much better bedside manner than he had, giving me information and welcoming me back to consciousness.

"Hey, guy! Great to see you awake. Just lie still for me. I know it feels like you're a science experiment right now. I'm going to just get your vitals and we can do a pain assessment. You hurting?" She checked the machines while talking to me and timing my pulse.

"Yeah." Gruff, grumbly voice.

Merck was on the other side of me with just his fingertips on my forearm. He'd usually pat me on the shoulder or whatever, but it was on fire right now. And he must have known that.

I turned my head to him. "T?"

Merck tilted his head to the side. "She's safe. I'll tell you everything, but first—you." He pointed at the nurse and watched her intently.

She made me answer some questions and poked and prodded me. A doctor arrived, and he was fine, but I got the sense that the nurse knew more than he did about what was going on with me.

The nurse gently recommended a different course of painkillers because I'd had some sort of adverse reaction to the ones the doctor tried on me first.

Merck rolled his eyes at the nurse when the doctor turned around. She gave him a half-smile.

True to her word, the nurse told me I had a severe concussion, a cracked rib, a sprained ankle, and a dislocated shoulder. That reminded me of T again.

When all of a sudden I started to feel lighter and lighter, I knew whatever painkillers they had settled on were kicking in.

Grateful was my overwhelming sensation. When the nurse was gone, I forced myself to stay awake.

"T's okay. She had kind of a reaction to seeing you getting hurt. She killed three of the guys beating you up. Smiley lived. He's a few floors below us right now. And T's here, too. She's not hurt, though. But..." Merck scratched his chin and looked reluctant to tell me. "She's in the psych ward. She's been growling and fighting people, but she's safe."

I nodded. I knew I would be more concerned soon. But I started floating away. The pain was dulling, and I was incredibly tired. "Protect." Was all I was able to utter.

"I'm watching her. Don't worry, son. I love you. Go back to sleep. I got you. And her."

And I listened to him.

Healing was a lot about resting, so it seemed. And it also seemed like the pain got worse before it got better. It turned out I freaking hated painkillers. The Percocet gave me headaches. The Vicodin made me nauseous. I was aching. The physical therapist was a monster. How she made things better, I wasn't sure, but soon enough I could pee on my own. When I managed that, I came out of the bathroom and looked at Merck.

"I know. T. Let me go figure things out. There's rules there and stuff." He pointed at my hospital gown. "You might want to figure out what you're going to do about that."

While he was gone, I sweet-talked a pretty nurse into letting me have a wheelchair and a few blankets so I could be in the hallways and also considered decent.

Merck came back shaking his head. "You're lucky that the

nurse in charge up there has about four million parking tickets. Let's roll."

I wanted to give a fist pump, but moving anything pretty much hurt everything.

We had to motor through the hallways and the elevator to get to T's floor. I felt underdressed despite my blanket. My bathroom didn't have a mirror, and I couldn't find a reflective surface to see if my face was going to scare her.

I tried to protect it during the beatdown. Because I'm pretty.

We had to be admitted through two sets of doors to get into the psychological center.

The nurse in charge told us that T was in the rec area. I was expecting screaming. Maybe some naked people streaking around. The reality was a quiet difference.

There were only about nine other patients in the rec room. A TV was playing a dramatic daytime show. I spotted T at the table. A puzzle in front of her. But her eyes were on me.

Her gaze was shiny and seemed unfocused. It made sense. I bet here she was on the meds she didn't like again.

Merck said hello to T and pulled a chair away so I could be pushed in next to her. Then he left us and started talking to the nurse who was watching over the patients.

I looked at the puzzle. Some sort of hairy tiger was the picture, but not all of the pieces that were jammed together were supposed to be that way.

"You doing that so they don't catch on to you?" I mumbled.

Then I touched one of the ill-fitting pieces.

I watched as a smile inched onto her lips. Just a hint. And then I knew my T was in here.

She had a soft T-shirt on and baggy sweatpants. Canvas sneakers without laces.

"I can't wear a bra because they think I'll hang myself with it." T slipped her index finger under her hospital bracelet.

I glanced around. I knew her gig was selective mute. And she was talking. But I guess that was where the selective part came into play.

"You okay?" She stopped fiddling with her bracelet and ran her index finger over mine.

"I'm going to be fine. It just hurts. Thanks, though. For saving me. I was going out, I think." I had to stop to clear my throat.

"Animal Winters." She read my name from the bracelet. Her medical fog seemed to lift a bit. "I'd do it again in a minute. Twice a day every day to keep you safe."

"I know." And I did. I knew she would be true to me no matter what. It was the realest thing that had ever been spoken to me. I looked at her finger. The nail had black polish on it. Where were you headed that night?"

"To you." She shrugged.

"That's where I was headed, too."

She clamped her lips together. A glance over my shoulder let me know we were being watched.

Merck and I were going to have a conversation about what kind of trouble T was in because of the shootings. She was a juvenile, so I was hoping that would keep her safe.

My wheelchair was pulled back and T's finger slipped out from under my hospital band.

"I'll be back tomorrow. Okay?"

She didn't respond, but she lifted her gaze to mine.

Her chocolate eyes were desperate. She was locked in here, and hated it. I tried to tell her without saying it out loud that I'd get her out of here. As soon as I could carry my own weight, I was busting her out. I didn't think she understood. That fog was creeping back in.

Merck took me back to my room, and after another exhausting piss, I collapsed in my bed. The conversation I wanted to have about the legal consequences T was facing was on pause until I could remain conscious enough to actually have it.

I took the drugs because they had ways of checking to see if I swallowed them. Being closed in was the worst part. No window or open door. He was okay—and that was the reason any of this was going to be fine.

At night I vibrated with the need to leave. Tears ran down my cheeks.

But I saved him.

And I would do it all again.

And I would stay here forever.

If I had to.

To save Animal.

16

Animal

After Christmas, Merck worked magic with T's mean social worker and her devoted foster mom. Together, the three of them were able to meet and help her avoid charges for the killing of Boon, Fleece, and Brooks. It was clear defense of the beating I had been receiving. My injuries were severe enough that T's report was filed and expunged.

My visits to her floor were daily. We worked on the puzzle; sometimes looked through a magazine or watched TV. She asked me once what happened to Smiley, and I told her he'd been in the hospital and then had been released. He was going to face charges for the attack.

She was worried about her mom. She was concerned that I wasn't going to heal well. T never once expressed regret or concern for the men she'd killed. And Smiley was out of the hospital. So that's the way it was. Our new normal.

I was cleared for release before she was. Getting to see her after I was in outpatient was a hell of a lot harder.

Our last visit was tough. She looked worn down. Her pupils were dilated in a way that I didn't like. I gave Merck a hard stare and he nodded near imperceptibly. He knew we had an issue.

"I get out today." I wanted to tell her so she'd know things were changing. That maybe she wouldn't see me as often. The last two weeks had given me comfort because I knew I'd get to visit. "Now, actually." I was figuring my street clothes were a giveaway.

I waited for a reaction, and slowly, there was one. She lifted her hand and the nurse nearby came over.

"Can I get scissors?"

T's voice was hoarse. The nurse was sweet about it, trying to encourage T's use of words.

"You'll have to tell me what for. And I'll have to stay here with you. Okay?"

T reached for my hand and pushed up the sleeve of my shirt and touched the wristband there.

I knew then she was doing for me what I'd done for her back at school during recess. After hooking her index finger underneath it, she looked in my eyes.

"I want to release him."

The nurse praised her for speaking. I didn't look away as our gazes locked.

In no time T had a pair of safety scissors, like they gave kids in kindergarten. It took her a minute to saw through it, but she was determined.

When my arm was finally free, she handed the scissors back like a model patient. The nurse wanted the bracelet, assuming it was trash.

T shook her head. "I want to keep this." She put it to her heart with her hand over it.

Again, the nurse seemed to want to encourage the speech, so she allowed it. When we had a bit of privacy, I pulled her bracelet out from the pocket of my jeans. When I had gotten my personal effects back, the clothes I was wearing were trashed, but my wallet had been returned to me. And in it, Talon Devora's hospital band. It was sort of my own way of pledging to look out for her.

"I guess we're even now."

Sheer delight crossed her face, and I was never so grateful as I was for that piece of plastic.

"We are." My bracelet was obviously staying with her.

We hugged because visiting hours were ending on her floor. It was hard leaving.

Merck had taken so much personal time to care for me, he was unable to take me to the hospital and pave the way for my outpatient visits with T.

I was walking with a limp, but I was walking. My bruises were fading. Eventually, I had to go back to school. The absence of T was in every minute.

I checked up on her mom at the facility in town. It was a house, actually —with other adults who needed help with their everyday stuff. She looked like T.

Merck told me at the last visit that T was due out in less than a week and she'd have to see a psychologist regularly.

Rumors were making their way around. Not at school—

that place was so far behind me socially. They were still concerned about video games and dates. Smiley wanted to avenge his asshole friends. Word had it that he was watching for T's discharge as well.

On her release day, Merck and I made it to the hospital. Her foster mom was there, and the social worker had sent his regards.

Merck still didn't like him, but apparently, he'd done a good job as far as T was concerned with the legal stuff.

T walked past her foster mom's open arms and instead hugged me. I watched as the woman's face fell.

I hugged T back and tried to offer a smile to the woman. T wasn't going to give her a chance. I knew that, and it made me sad. But I knew how T was. She only loved once, so she said anyway.

One mom, foster or otherwise. I looked at T's face and knew my time with her was limited.

She was a flight risk the second the locked doors were opened. If I hadn't been attacked, she would have left a month ago.

She whispered into my ear, "Meet me at the mall."

I nodded with my cheek against hers so she'd know I heard her.

We were in a warm snap for January. Yesterday was up to sixty degrees.

She'd run again tonight.

With the social worker invested in her case now, and Smiley looking for her, I had nothing but concern about her sneaking out. But I'd be in our spot tonight.

Merck looked suspicious, but he didn't alert anyone, and I was grateful for that.

Saturdays were a wasteland. It's the way it was. Food was scarce. Shelter was tricky. Pretty much everything I did was about surviving while tricking people into thinking it's easy.

It wasn't.

I liked this abandoned mall on Saturdays because he'd usually show up and then we were alone.

Just T and Animal. And today would be our last for a long while.

I heard him just as he saw me in the parking lot. It was quiet. I smiled because it's us now.

"T, you good?" He closed the distance quickly despite his healing injuries. His legs were so long.

His cheekbones were probably sharper than they should be, but my eyes followed the line of them.

I drew. He knew, but that's it. I liked to sketch. When he wasn't here and I had paper, I etched that cheekbone. I'd use my index finger to smudge it a bit. I looked at the pad of my finger. It had a hint of pencil on it now.

I was sitting on the concrete highway divider that was used to block this pothole-filled asphalt from cars. He sat on the one next to me.

"How's the home?" I looked at the sky. It wasn't cold enough for me to see my breath.

"Fine. I run the joint." Animal cracked his knuckles and

kicked his feet out, crossing them at the ankle. I asked him about the cop.

Animal told me that Merck was a dead end and I knew it was a heartbreak for him somehow.

I knew heartbreak. Between the two of us, we could've made a quilt out of the "maybe somedays" and "could have beens".

"It's going to be a show tonight." He twisted so that he could lie back on the divider. Our concrete couches. I did the same.

Because the mall was abandoned and the electric long shut off, as the night crept up on us, the stars were beautiful.

The top of my head almost touched the top of his. We had to keep our balance as we reclined, but we were good at it.

We were going to play the lotto game now. It was what we did. He would tell me what the Powerball was going for, and then we would spend the fictional money.

Money we would never see.

"Fourteen million. You start."

I watched for a few minutes as the stars started revealing themselves. I knew he wouldn't rush me.

"Well, first, I get my mom her own place."

"Okay," he agreed with me. He knew how it was. Animal had a way of getting stuff out of me that no one else ever could.

"Then you and I get a mansion. I want four bedrooms for you and four for me." I put my hand in the air and pointed at the stars that made up the

Big Dipper. Those were his stars. The Little Dipper was mine.

I could see his pinkie tracing the stars that made up me. "We living together, T?"

I stopped describing the mansion. I knew I was blushing, but he couldn't see me. I recovered. "Just until we're adults. So

I can forge notes for you. And you can relocate spiders for me." I was good at signing adult names.

He started in with his deep chuckle. "I'm down. But we're getting golf carts and a chef for fourteen million."

I let my hand fall backwards, tucking it near my head.

I watched as his hand mimicked the movement of mine. His fingers grazed the palm of my hand. I held my breath.

The touch was so incredible. That was what I missed most with my mom.

Just the touch. One human to another.

I noticed his fingers twitch, but he left them there. The warmth traveled from my hand to my heart.

This kid. This guy. Looking at the stars. He was the only friend I had. I loved him. He could make even *this* special. When we had nothing between us worth selling or bragging about, he gave me the stars.

And I gave him a home to share with me in my mind. "We're going to be all right. Someday. I promise you."

The touch that had been just an accidental graze became a full-on handhold. He adjusted his hand so he could squeeze my fingers. I heard him gasp as he kept his balance. The injuries were hurting him.

"We're going to fight for it," he promised.

I squeezed his big hand in return.

Animal saved me all the time in the smallest ways. Tonight was one of them.

"If I leave—if I had to go, would you watch my mom?"

I sat up and turned so I could see her. My rib made me wince. "You going somewhere?"

She started to sit up and I offered her my hand to help. She used it and then held it. "They're going to put me back in that place. Do you know how many doors there were between me and the outside?"

"Maybe start talking, T?" I hated where this conversation was headed.

And she'd started talking a bit when she was in, to me anyway.

"Can't. I can't let them in. It's not going to work that way. I want to go to school. But now they'll know that I'm not locked in to an address if I run. And Marybeth will hunt for me around town until she finds me."

Marybeth. The foster mom. I actually could see what T was saying. Marybeth would be the kind of person to search every damn place for T.

And the court-appointed psychologist visits would be another way adults would track her.

"Can you answer my question? About my mom?" T turned and sat cross-legged on the divider.

I rubbed my forehead. "If you weren't here? I'd be super miserable, but I'd watch after your mom until I died."

"I'll be back. You know. From time to time you'll see me." She rubbed her thumb on my palm.

I felt like I should try harder to convince her to stay. The homeless thing sucked so much.

"Can you think about it? Wait a few days?"

"Nah. You and I know that they won't let me do this. With you. Be alone when I need it. The door open at least a crack. I mean, we're not stupid. I'm in the eighth grade. I've got at least two more years where I have to be in school. This town won't let me be." She shook her head as the different things I wanted to say to her died on my tongue.

"You going to be okay?" She was worried about me now. "Please, T. You know I get what I need. I've got it all laid out."

She pulled a backpack out from behind the divider. Shit was serious. T was really leaving.

She got off and motioned for me to do the same. When we were standing in front of each other, she went up on her tiptoes and gave me a quick kiss on my lips.

"Stay safe."

"You, too." I watched her until I couldn't see or hear her anymore. I felt the pain slice through where our future should've been. I was pissed. I felt my nostrils flare, because I could hold the pain in. This wasn't my first time.

T walked out of my childhood and became a myth that I would search for for a long time. I had her hospital bracelet and she had mine. That was how I knew she was real as the years grew long. She did leave me a parting gift, though. It was just a suspicion, but Smiley's body was found floating in the river a few weeks after she left.

17

Animal

I got a new member of my family less than a year later. Merck's beautiful plans of getting me, a kid named Fenix, his mom, Elise, and the daughter in the house had crumbled.

His wife was diagnosed with an aggressive form of lung cancer, even though she didn't smoke a day in her life. His mistress went missing, and the scumbag father was cagey as shit.

Merck's visits with me dropped off, but I knew where to find him if I needed him.

His off hours were spent nursing his wife. The daughter

that he thought could be his was named Ember and living with an aunt.

The night I met Nix, I had a visit from Merck earlier in the day.

He'd told me that his wife was in remission and that Elise was still missing. He was looking for her as best he could. He'd scared off the asshole she was married to.

Merck arranged for Nix to be offered a spot at the home for children where I was staying.

"Listen, none of this is going the way I wanted it to. This kid— Elise was crazy about him. Has a sweet demeanor. Tried to protect her all the time. He's screwed up in the head. Has to be."

"I'm bringing him here. And in my alternate universe, Nix would be your brother, and my possible daughter would be your sister. So keep an eye on him if you can."

Merck had asked very little of me in all the years I knew him. He asked me to keep his secret, about Nix's now missing mother and the fact that he was likely Ember's father. The conversation we'd had was fairly despondent. Merck felt it was best for Ember to not be alerted to her possible parentage. I had to respect that. He felt she was having the best childhood with her aunt. If I were Ember I'd want to know about the possibilities, but I kept that opinion to myself.

Merck's wife, Kinsey, was not well. The cancer had ravaged her system and, despite the remission, had brought a slew of medical problems to the surface. He took his vows seriously. I didn't think it was a great idea, but here we were.

The next day I walked downstairs to a skinny, handsome kid wearing Sister Mary's nightgown while making a papier-mâché elephant head.

I made fun of him for it, just because it seemed like a good icebreaker. Then a dipshit that had been at the home about six months decided to say something, too. I reacted before I remembered I was supposed to be undercover for Merck and knocked the kid's lights out for saying anything to my man Nix.

My loyalty was a given, considering Merck had asked, but it turned out I liked Nix.

I didn't know if we'd have been friends without intervention—he was introverted. But I was glad I insisted every day that we hang out. I got to know him.

Six months in, he shared with me that his mother was murdered in front of him. I knew the loyalty I had from him equaled mine.

After we had lights out, I climbed out of the home and texted Merck. He'd been looking for Elise for years. My guess was that he wasn't

looking too hard because he suspected the truth. Maybe hope is better than despair. But now I had an answer. One I hated, but at least I knew for sure. When he pulled around in the squad car to pick me up, I realized how much he'd aged in the lights from the parking lot.

His wife's illness. The love of his life disappearing and leaving her kids —and even me. Being invested in me had drawn him out.

I got in the passenger side and we drove around for a while. His cop instincts were no joke because he didn't push me. I was guessing he already knew she was dead—or suspected it strongly. Hell, how was I supposed to know how it was between them?

He pulled the car to the edge of the river. Still we sat.

"We're friends now. Nix and I." I peeked over at Merck's stoic face.

Merck didn't respond. He just looked out over the water.

There was no easy way to say it, so I just laid it out. "Nix saw his father kill his mom. Had to help bury her in the yard."

I didn't know words could feel like knives coming out of your throat until I said those to him. I looked away while they fell on him.

Just quiet. No reaction that I could sense. I expected screaming. Anger.

Maybe resignation. But there was just nothing.

I looked over at him again, and I realized I was wrong. Tears were rolling down his cheeks. I wasn't even sure he knew they were there.

His heart was breaking deeply.

I clapped my hand on his shoulder. "I am so sorry, Dad."

And that's when he gasped, like he finally remembered how to breathe. He wrapped his hands around the steering wheel, but not before I saw them shaking. His knuckles went white.

It was the first time I'd called him Dad, and I hoped it was the right move. I had no idea how else to comfort him.

We sat like that, my hand on his shoulder for a long, long time that night. He didn't say it, but his regret was etched even deeper in his face when he dropped me off.

I didn't know he'd hoped for so long that she would still come back to him.

I thought of T that night as I lay in bed. I wondered if she would be my greatest regret. I felt like it wasn't over—whatever we had between us.

18

Animal

Nix and I clicked on so many levels. We were inseparable when we were out of school. He's a smidge younger, but I never really noticed because he had problems older than the rest of the world.

He told me about Ember, and his aunt, and how his sister didn't know he existed.

We'd ridden bikes by the house more than a few times. Welfare checks was what he called them. If he felt like it was unfair that his sister got to have a family and a life while he was in a home, he never said it.

I learned about Rebecca, the girl who possibly saved his life the night his father killed his mother. Just a little spitfire. He watched her, too. I watched his back. While he worried after the girls, I knew that the worst monster in his life was his father. I watched T's mom from a respectful distance. I wouldn't judge when she wandered out in her pajamas or with lipstick all over her face. She was safe, and more often than not —due to T's sacrifice —her mom was neat and together. Wistful looking, though.

We burst through our mid-teens and finally got to high school. I played ball, got with cheerleaders, and got crowned homecoming king. I knew how to play the superficial games. I could be whatever they needed me to be.

Nix dropped out of high school and left the home first. I tried to talk him out of it. Merck stopped by as well.

Merck went up in rank in the police force. He always made time to come to my games, planned on taking my picture for prom, too.

Which was fine. I had two dates, and I wanted it documented.

I was still looking for T.

Merck was still looking for T. At least that was what he told me.

It was two weeks before prom, and Merck and I were going down to play old versus young basketball, though he hated when I called it that.

His most recent promotion had given him access to new things. After the game, he rolled me down to the river, the place where I told him Elise was dead. I had a pit in my stomach, wondering if this would be where our fears came to roost. I was concerned that T didn't make it. That she hadn't been able to hack the world at such a young age with nothing but her knapsack.

Merck pulled a file from the back seat and flopped it open.

In it was a picture of a girl taken from a security camera. She had long dark hair covering one eye. It was T. He'd found her.

I snapped my head in his direction, and then I saw the impending bad news in his eyes. I think my heart stopped beating. I was sure that we would see each other again. This snapshot haunted me suddenly, reminding me of all the missing girls whose last picture was a grainy one from an ATM.

"She was here. In town. Came to visit her mom." He tapped the folder in my lap. "That her? Is that T? I mean, I thought so..." He trailed off.

I looked back at the picture, confused. "It's T. That's her. She's taller now. All womaned up, looks like. When was she here? Why didn't you tell me?"

I watched him swallow before he answered, "Last week. She had contact with an undercover who tipped me off. I reviewed the security footage until I found her."

And then I looked out at the same water he had when his heart was broken.

It was different for T. She'd been able to live—of that I was grateful. But she was also able to come here and be near me and not say hi. Not say anything.

"Oh." I covered my mouth with the back of my hand. I was swallowing the disappointment. That's what men do. Well, except for the few times with the man next to me.

"I'm sorry, son."

I felt what he'd done, like I had years ago. Just offered the only thing he could—his love for me.

"Hey, it'll be okay. She's okay. That's what matters." I shrugged.

Merck clapped me on my back. I felt the wetness on my cheek. I looked quickly out the window, but I didn't shrug off his hand.

We could be this for each other. Support.

Two weeks later, I went to prom with my two dates. And I only thought about T every other minute.

19

My dress was light brown. It looked nice with my eyes. Which was just luck, because at the thrift store, there were only a few choices of dresses that fit me. This one was a little too long, but it wasn't falling down. I had my Converse on underneath the long dress. I'd snuck into a beauty store and used their samples to do my makeup.

My hair was swept up into a bun, and my neck felt naked, but I wanted something different. For him. For my return.

I'd checked on my mom from a distance. She looked great. Her hair was done, and her outfit matched. I peeked at her on a day visit to the local museum.

She was good without me. My vigilance in staying away from her was paying off. And that was important.

In the years I'd come back and forth, I'd wanted to check on Animal, but I couldn't do it. I knew he'd see me. He never missed a trick, but I couldn't come back and get nabbed. I was not going back to another foster home, so I waited until my eighteenth birthday to return to town.

In my head I pictured our reunion. He would hug me. Maybe twirl me around. Because I knew he wouldn't have forgotten about me.

I had gotten a new outfit and decided to find him, but it became clear that it was prom night here in Midville.

When I tracked him down, he was dressed in a tux. And he was the most handsome man in the world. He'd gotten taller and filled out more. His features had sharpened, too. That cheekbone that I drew had even more of an edge now.

He was beautiful. I fixed my hair in the reflection of a car window. As I was getting ready to step out and wave at him, two gorgeous girls in revealing, expensive gowns flanked him.

He preened and laughed, paying attention to each girl.

I hid behind the car when I put it all together, praying that he hadn't caught sight of me.

I stayed with my back against the car until I was sure he was in the venue. It was naïve of me to assume he wouldn't have a date. To assume he would wait for me like I waited for him.

He was the home I had. Animal and my mother, and seeing him with two other girls was like watching my home burn.

I left that night. To be someone else. To be somewhere else.

This place was better off without me.

20

I had terrors from the night under the toll bridge. I excelled at blending in. Not being seen. Not being noticed. One small mistake—making eye contact with a random guy was my downfall the night they all attacked me. Maybe it was coming for me. No matter what night, the situation was dangerous, and I knew that.

I wanted choices, and I didn't think I had that. Rejecting my foster mom's attempts was probably thickheaded. Animal would've made it work to his advantage, somehow.

When he was the one to stop the attack, I saw him for who he was. When he held me in his arms in front of a bunch of cops and refused to put me down, I witnessed grace. I didn't know what it was like to be a black guy in this society, but I knew enough about how the world worked to know he'd been in danger that night. That he'd decided he'd rather be shot dead than put me down and hurt me more. His soul was crystal clear to me. His loyalty matched to mine and beyond possibly.

But I couldn't keep it up. Not this farce. Not the fight. I knew it didn't make sense to anyone but him and me. I left Animal in the parking lot, but I stopped by my mom's place to get another sneak peek at her face. That night I got lucky. I was able to see into her room through a parted curtain. She had her beautiful hair down. Usually she kept it in a bun, but when it was down, I liked how much it proved that we were matches. Mother and daughter.

I remembered taking turns brushing it back in the day. On a good day. Maybe it was a good month. Time was judged by how she was feeling.

"Talon, we could get a perm in this hair. Really amp up these curls." How old was I then? Who knew? Maybe eight? We were in the money—what I later learned was her disability check. Mom tried really hard, but money was not an impulse she had control over. I would get a cartful of toys, and then the next week we'd be hungry.

My name was Talon. Well, technically still was. I got made fun of in school for my name, even though I really liked it. Mom was reckless with her heart and my name, but it worked.

When I figured out what happened, how the ramifications of her illness affected Mom, I insisted on being called T by everyone, save for her. I wanted the person I was to stay with my mom. And by going to the first letter of my name only, I could make something that she and I shared.

A doctor had put my name preference on a chart somewhere, and when I changed schools, it stuck. It took a few years, but Talon disappeared entirely. T took her place.

The night I left Midville the first time, I had blood on my hands. I wasn't going to leave Smiley alive to hurt Animal. He was an unfinished thread in a narrative I was intent on completing. The lack of remorse I felt after killing the other three taught me something about what I could handle. Maybe I was different than everyone else. There was one quick solution. Smiley was out on bail. I spent a few minutes unbuttoning my shirt and painting red on my lips. With my hair back and a pair of glasses on, he didn't recognize me. I tempted him from the docks where he was hanging with two other guys to follow me down to the bank of the river.

When I came back from the bank alone, I knew Animal was safe. And I knew I could murder people without losing a moment of sleep. I walked out of town that night.

My time away from Midville became about making sure that I could be weapon and a watchful owl. I could see everything and be able to fight back if I was forced to engage.

I still managed to go to school. Showing up places with just my own body and a fake ID was a good way to make sure there was no trail. I got an education, and when enough questions were asked, I moved on. I spent time with courses in libraries and even snuck into college classes as soon as I could pass as an enrolled student. I just had to make sure the professors were lax in their attendance.

I took defending myself seriously as well. One of the community colleges offered a course on self-defense for free. What I learned there about simple hold breaks and punches was like having a light turned on inside my soul.

I sought out training after that. I cleaned gyms for boxing lessons, offered to do paperwork for Tae Kwon Do instructions, and proffered weapons for criminals to learn how to shoot.

When I saw Animal at the prom with his two dates, I knew I could defend both him and me.

After the prom, I became more focused. I took up long distance running. The libraries were a network of knowledge. I did my best to make sure I knew how to throw an ax. I got good at giving a massage so I could memorize pressure points. I could use that information against someone. Squeezing the right spot could take down a person twice my size.

When the police in a town I was passing through needed volunteers for their officers to work with to learn how to hold people correctly, I signed up. Learning how to get out of the holds was important.

I took time to visit Midville. I watched Mom from a distance, making sure she was being treated well. She really did best without the pressures of being a mom. It was a hard pill for me to swallow, but I did it.

I missed Animal. I made acquaintances from time to time, but with Animal it was different. I was betting Animal got bigger. And crazy handsome. And his swagger as a kid had been incredible—it probably got even better.

I made enough money working odd under the table jobs to buy a motorcycle and enough weapons that I felt safe anywhere.

When I returned to the city—that night when he cruised up on his bike with Nix—I wasn't expecting him. But I was hoping for him.

I got to know two randomly friendly hookers, and they always seemed ready to chat and make sure I was covered for the evening. I let them assume I was a hooker, too. That part of town was easy to meld into. It was my plan to hear how things were going with Animal. He'd been getting more and more into the lifestyle that Nix was living so I heard. I needed to have my ear to the pavement.

His name was easy to catch when it was tossed in a conversation. The women gossiped about him as well. I had to make sure I kept my jealousy in check. It wasn't easy, but all that distance and time helped.

Assisting him that night was a given. I'd do anything he needed. Seeing the fire in his eyes when we connected was all the encouragement I needed to stay close to him. I was patient. And I was loyal.

And then I was going to be irreplaceable.

21

Animal

My boy Nix started on his tats long before it was legal. I understood what he did, even though every new bone etched onto his skin singled him out as different. And when he took it to his face, I watched as my boyhood friend slowly buried himself.

He'd rather look like a skeleton than resemble his father. And I couldn't blame him.

It was extreme, but *he* was extreme. He'd started working for various crime bosses, getting somehow deeper and further away from reality every year. And richer. Blood money was what he called it. He used it for trappings like a house—but all he cared about was Basement Girl.

Basement Girl was my nickname for Rebecca, the little girl he'd watched all these years. She went by Becca now. Nix, through sheer stubbornness, found all different ways to stalk her. For her own good was what I understood, though I wasn't sure anyone else would see it that way.

I got my business degree. Merck helped me figure out scholarships and grants, so I was able to give two monumental middle fingers to my biological parents who hadn't thought I was worth the cost of a diaper.

I was worth far more. It turned out that I was good at theater as well. I got a minor in theater arts. It helped me magnify this personality that made me bigger than life—to those who didn't know me anyway.

While Nix's obsession grew, his sister did as well. He still had no relationship with her, believing everyone was better without him.

I started out looking for Nix's father for him. I hated to see him waiting for what he felt was an inevitable return. Nix was scared for Becca, too, as his asshole father had a penchant for vendettas.

When I was out, I looked for T as well. I wanted to make sure she was okay. I wanted to find out why she returned to town and refused to see me.

Was she still doing it?

Maybe I was as obsessive as my friend. I just didn't wear it on my skin. My family was small, just Nix, T, and Merck, but they mattered. I counted. Ember as well, because although she didn't know it, she was a sister to me.

I learned to make money like Nix. He was more high-tech and bloody; I was more personable and about cashing in favors. I went by the street name of Havoc, but it was no secret who I was. My name was semi-famous before I was even a major player in the scene. Merck used to say havoc followed me like a puppy, so it was my way of letting him name me like a father would. I was pretty sure that it was not a gesture he appreciated. He'd preferred that I took my education and ran the entire world. And I loved him for that. And although I believed he was right, I needed to protect Nix when he was vulnerable. I was the only family that would be able to watch his back. I even explained as much to Merck, and I saw an understanding there. A gratefulness.

I became a ladies' man. Maybe I always was, but it was an act I could play with little to no effort. The game was easy. I learned to ask a few pointed questions, watch for cues, and when it was time to actually throw down? I knew my way around a clitoris.

When Becca's bar had a Day of the Dead themed event, with full makeup encouraged, I pressured my boy to go in and meet her face-to-face.

I'd been to the bar she worked at with her sexy friend Henry—female, despite the decidedly male name—and I liked her. More than that, I could read Becca. She had a soft spot for the bar drunk. For the awkward guy or girl dragged out for a night with their more socially forward friends.

She picked up jackets off the floor so they wouldn't get stomped on. Just the little shit. I had a hunch she was special enough for my man.

And I was right, which I liked because it was a good habit to be in.

Nix's father decided to come to town and start creeping right as Nix took these first baby steps, so I had to help him. Nix was dealing with Bat Feybi, a shifty old bastard. We needed a hooker to pass a note to the boss and meet him in an alternate location.

After arriving on our bikes, I saw her.

She was coming out of the mist of my memories when I watched her step from behind two hookers.

T.

My T. From when I was a kid. From when I was just a pup.

Our last meeting was still something I thought about years later. She was acting like she didn't know who I was. I had my motorcycle helmet on so I doubt she could see the hurt I knew was registered in my eyes.

Of all the people to leave me, I never thought it'd be her. We'd been family. She knew more about me than even my man on the bike next to me. He was covered in ink that made him into a monster, but it didn't hide his good intentions like he thought it did.

The hookers were trying to get the job, clearly thinking it was about sex. It wasn't. T read the scene and treated Nix and me like this was fine. Like she didn't know me. Maybe she didn't. I was still tall, still very much who she should remember, but I'd filled out in a way that made me far more intimidating. Had she seen me from a distance and I'd missed her?

My soul would always know hers. Apparently, it was a one-way setup, if she could really act like she didn't know me.

I told Nix that we were picking T. She refused to talk. I wondered about that. The selective mute thing I taught her so many years ago?

Maybe.

She slid on the back of my bike. I handed her the helmet and she put it on. I tapped the Bluetooth communicator between the helmets I had on my bike. I made sure Nix was on a different channel.

"Still a selective mute, I see." I was angry. I was also shocked. Not my best opening line.

Her response was quiet, but luckily the receiver was loud enough for me to catch it. "When life requires it."

She wasn't hanging on to me. I glanced at my hip. Her hands were on her legs. That would change as we sped up.

"I've been looking for you for years." I heard the grit in my voice that time. I took a turn hard and felt her touch lightly on my middle.

Silence.

"I heard you've been back in town. You could've left me a note or something. I thought we had each other, T." It was wildly unsettling to have this meeting on my bike, but it was coming out of my mouth whether I wanted it to or not.

"So did I." The hurt in her voice made me blink a few times. As far as I knew, she stayed away from me. I had no part in it.

"When was I ever not there for you? Honestly. Tell me." I turned my head, but was not satisfied with a glimpse of her.

Silence again.

I shook my head with the lack of a reply so she knew I thought I deserved a response.

"Why'd you come back now? At least give me that?" I took one hand off of my handlebar to shake it out.

"I needed to see you." She took her hands off my middle.

I wanted to tell her I needed to see her for the years in between when she left and now.

"Were you okay? All that time?" I followed Nix down another road. "I lived."

Nix stopped and I followed suit. T got off the back of my motorcycle, like being that close to me was a problem.

She listened to the directions one more time, handed me my helmet, and disappeared down the path. I was so shocked by her sudden return into my life I finally realized that we'd sent her marching into a possible ambush.

Nix was off and driving to the next spot. We'd hired T to be a messenger girl. I hesitated. She'd been alone all this time when she could have been with me. I always planned for her and me to live together as soon as we could. The two of us could have faced this angry world at eighteen together. I followed Nix.

That's why I was mad, mostly. I think. The loss of her scared me. And I was shit at being scared. When she left, I never got to put down this wall I built. I had a persona to keep up. Unless I was with her. We'd been havens for each other.

I followed through on the plan and was a lookout for Nix. I alerted him when his meeting with Feybi went too long. Nix was intense about this guy. He was taking everything about this job personally.

All of a sudden we heard gunshots in the distance.

I knew it was T. Just like I knew it was her between the cars under the toll bridge when we were kids.

My stomach was a ball of nerves. I'd fucking let her go into those woods because I was pissed. Because I couldn't process a change this big that quickly. I scanned the path we sent her down and she was already headed at me, head down, arms pumping. She was either great at hiding injuries or she was completely fine. I slowed my bike and held out my arm. She latched on and swung her leg over the seat. I gunned it once she was holding on tightly. Nix followed us, making sure there weren't any tails.

T threw her gun over the bridge into the water and then put her helmet on.

I was going to take the long way to keep us safe from Feybi's men who were most likely following us.

"You okay?"

"Yeah. I got clean shots off."

She had her arms wrapped around my waist hard. I was guessing her adrenaline was still coursing through her.

"You still good at shooting?" It was out of my mouth before I remembered we had all this tense shit between us.

Her responding laughter was a home I hadn't visited in far too long.

Her happiness trickled through my ear and down my spine like medicine that healed me. I started laughing as well.

She hugged me harder. On purpose. As a welcome.

I put my hand over hers. We didn't have skin-to-skin contact, but it was the best I could do to hug her back.

"I got way better at shooting than the night they tried to kill you. I missed you, Animal."

Tears welled up in my eyes, I blinked them away.

To be missed.

It was all the Hallmark cards and Christmas songs talked about.

We were nearing the drop-off point where the hookers were. I knew my T wasn't a hooker because of the things that happened to her so long ago. Before she could take off her helmet, I let her know.

"You're still my family, T. I'll be back in a few hours. I hope we can talk." She got off the bike and nodded, then took off the helmet.

She turned from Nix and me and gave us the middle finger as she walked away.

My brother would never know that T and I were previously acquainted. I didn't like keeping things from him, but T's story was hers to tell. I wouldn't out her unless she wanted me to.

Nix and I headed back to his house. His place where I had a room. I hoped that T would stay in town. I wanted to get her alone and find out what the hell had gone on. She seemed to still feel at least a little something for me.

22

I followed Nix home after dropping T off at her street corner, I turned around and left. I wanted to see her in person. Where I wasn't pretending not to know her.

When I came back to the corner, Helena and Debra, the hookers, pointed me in the right direction.

T was in the back corner of a dive bar where pimps and hookers met up to talk business.

She was sipping on a water bottle. I nodded when I saw her then, and she bent her head in acknowledgement. I made sure to look around and assess the situation. I had to make it clear to every man in the room that

I was not to be messed with. I managed to do it with a smile.

A few of the hookers tried their luck with winks and come-ons. I didn't have to pay for sex, but I was polite to them.

"Can I sit here?" I pointed at the chair across from T.

"The seat across from me always belongs to you." T set her water bottle down.

"Really?" I ran my hand through my hair as I sat. "I thought maybe I'd never sit in my spot again."

I put my sunglasses on my head.

She returned my gaze briefly and then it darted all over the room.

"Care to tell me what happened? Every night before I closed my eyes, I wondered if you were dead. Until Merck showed me a picture of you checking on your mom." I rapped my knuckles on the scarred wood.

She picked up her water bottle and took another sip.

"You get addicted to something, T?"

I watched her body then for tells. Because lies could be tucked in words, but not in reflexes.

No tremor. No flinch.

"I'm not addicted to anything."

I watched her swallow. She was obviously uncomfortable. I was making her that way. I reconsidered my approach. I was handling her like an enemy.

"I'm sorry. I shouldn't have accused you of that. You've been to your mom's? How's she?" I rubbed at my lips. I knew she was having some issues. It was medication based and there wasn't anything I could do. I was still watching out for her.

She shrugged off my apology. "She's not well. Part of the reason I'm home."

"Anything I can do to help?" This should have been my opening question when I first saw her.

"No. Thanks, though. It's...good to see you."

The shyness peeked out. I recognized it. When we were kids, if I kept testing her, I'd eventually get a smile and even a laugh out of her. That's when I knew I was truly funny, when she forgot to be demure and would snort laugh at something I said.

"Same here. You look beautiful. Badass. But super pretty. You glowed up." I tried my grin out on her.

She blushed and I thought I saw a glimmer of happiness.

"You packed on some muscle and height. That all happened how quickly after eighth grade?" She closed one eye while she looked at me.

I sat up straighter and flexed my biceps. She laughed.

"It took a while. The height came before junior year. Sister Mary was complaining all the time about how she could barely get the tags off my jeans before I needed a new pair." I drummed my fingertips on the table.

When we had eye contact again, I saw her brown ones sparkle with delight.

"I was like a long string bean. But then soon after—the muscles." I worked out now to maintain, but Nix always complained how few reps I needed to stay ripped.

"How's Merck?" She rubbed her hands on the table like it might be a Ouija board.

"He's good. Shot up the ladder at work." I bobbed my head.

"Did it work out with you? Ever?" She flipped her hair so I could see her whole face. My favorite version of T. The betrayal was layered just under our pleasant conversation. Heartbreak. Bitterness, maybe. But still, her face and voice took me back to a purer time.

"Like adoption wise? Nah. It was too complicated for him and eventually for me. He'd drop by two or three times a week to take me out of the home, though. Made sure I went to baseball games and concerts and stuff." I touched my phone thinking about sending the old man a text.

There was silence then. The past crowding out the common conversation. "I never stopped looking for you." My voice cracked with the emotion of it. I stopped talking and looked to my left. The hookers and pimps were minding their business, but all at once I wanted T and me out of there. I wanted us both to feel too important to stay in this environment.

She started and stopped her sentence a few times before squinting at me. "This is not the conversation I expected to have today."

"Me either." I didn't let her off the hook, though. "But still."

23

He was devastating. Just being near him was like getting pulled into the sun. I knew it was probably bad for us both, but my heart was set up like a clearance sale. No returns, no refunds.

Animal was more beautiful than ever. When we were kids, I was his friend because I watched him look out for everyone else. If a teacher dropped a pencil, he picked it up. If he saw a kid being bullied, he stopped it. Sometimes with fists, but mostly by just talking everyone out of the situation. He was like a magician.

My observations as a quiet person had paid off. I remembered seeing him lose his cool with a math teacher long ago. She couldn't understand how it was possible for Animal not to do his homework.

But I'd watched Animal at night before when we were still in middle school, when his fosters threw him out on the street. He'd banged on the door, yelling for them to at least give him his work, and they'd refused.

I knew about Animal, but I was a creature of the night in my head. A bat.

A fox. Mostly an owl.

I could see everything around me, and I stayed awake all night a lot of times.

He wasn't being disrespectful to that math teacher. He just wanted someone to understand. I got him and the struggle to hand in work when you were trying to survive first.

That recess I sat near him. He was jovial to everyone on the pavement, but I could tell when he saw me. Like a magnet, he was drawn until we clicked together.

I'd told him I liked his shoes, and he said he liked mine.

That same man was in front of me now. His potential was limitless. It had been then as well.

He was angry that I'd left, and I had shame with that. What he didn't know was I'd be back until death parted us.

I'd traveled all over the country, and I'd never felt the magnet again— like I did that day.

Later, when Nix left to work for the Feybis, I knew Animal would need a person to be with who didn't have expectations for him. I slid into that place. I belonged there.

24

Animal

The year I spent with Nix in Feybi's organization sucked. I tried to understand his reasoning. He'd lost his will to live when Becca's mom asked him to leave her alone. Granted, I was glad he was still alive after the scare we had when Becca killed his horrible father, but Nix took things to the extreme.

I saw the future, though. I knew my man would get out if he wanted to. And he had to want to. Whatever punishment mechanism made sense in his skull-flavored mind wasn't something I could figure out. Like I didn't know where his finish line was. I hoped he would recognize it when it came.

I started to build. In that time the material was already on site, so to speak. I knew how to collect people. The bruised and battered. The ones that needed to have a place. T came around. It's what she did. It reminded me of when we were kids and had each other's back. I was guarded. Not with my words, but with my heart. It wasn't that she'd left, but that she returned and didn't tell me that was the deepest wound.

She was getting back in, though. In her head, I think she was doing a penance. In the time away, she had honed her skills for survival to a deadly edge. She didn't talk about how life was hacking the world on her own as a teenager.

She didn't want for money, so it seemed. She learned how to make it. She never shared with me if she finished school, and I didn't want to open the door to that conversation. Because I had my degree, I didn't want her to think I was judging her if she didn't have one.

Nix was highly inaccessible. He checked in, but shut down. He'd submitted to the Feybi top soldier mentality as far as I could tell because he'd be able to get me a message if he wanted to. He could hack anything if he wanted to.

So while he improved the Feybi organization, I was creating one to take it down. It was okay, because he'd run it with me once he came to his senses.

T became my go-to person. She was still quiet and apprehensive, but listening all the time. While I tried to hash out solutions to problems like the docks being run by the Kaleotos, she would file it away, and two weeks later I would hear a rumor that things were settled. Sometimes it was as simple as police activity increasing in the area. Other times places of businesses were burned to the ground. After about three incidents, I addressed her.

"So the docks, Kaleotos' restaurant, and the drug deals over at the Duggerton—those were all problems that sorted themselves out."

We were in my office in my house. It was temporary. As soon as Nix was back, I was going to his place. I didn't like being there when he wasn't.

T was wearing tight jeans, a baggy T-shirt, and a hoodie. Her style hadn't changed that much since school. She didn't wear the black eyeliner as thick anymore, though. Her hair still swooped over one eye.

She was sitting on my couch. She didn't look up to acknowledge the fact that I was talking to her. I watched as her pinkie twitched.

"I'm thinking it wasn't a coincidence." I waited until it was awkward for her not to make eye contact.

She finally looked up. "Things happen."

I snorted. "Things that I specifically bitch about mysteriously resolve themselves in my favor? I find that hard to believe, T."

She shrugged.

"And Smiley tripped into the river the night you left me. Just coincidence, huh?"

Most foot soldiers would be quick to claim responsibility to the man in charge to make sure they got props when it was time. But she wouldn't even admit to the murder she committed to tie up loose ends before she left town back in the day.

"'Fess up."

I wanted to know if she was going rogue to do these things.

"I just see a solution and implement it. If it works, it works." She shifted in her seat.

"Listen, I appreciate you going and getting shit done, but you have to keep me informed. If you're out there putting yourself in danger, I want to know. I don't like losing track of you."

I watched as she tilted her head down. I heard the double meaning of my words then. The argument we never really had.

That she knew where I was and how I was doing, but I never knew where she was so long ago.

"I'm sorry." The apology was for now, and maybe then.

I didn't like to beat a dead horse. But I apologized just like that if I accidentally stepped in front of someone in line. I wanted more for what we'd been through. What I thought our relationship deserved.

"You still haven't told me why."

"It's embarrassing." She was finally admitting there was a reason. "Sweetheart, you knew that my fosters would shoot up the check they got from me, and I was okay with that so I didn't have to move again. You know I hate snakes. We've shared too much shit to be worried about embarrassment."

"You remember when I told you I only love once?" She was so far behind her hair that I knew we were about to get real.

"Yeah. You were loyal to your mom no matter what. She was the only mom you would ever let yourself have." I tapped my fingers on my desk.

She raised her face and her hair fell away. Her eyes flashed.

"Not saying you were wrong about that. But that last foster mom for you would've been a real decent choice. I know it costs you to be that way. And I respect it."

The flare of anger in her eyes simmered down.

"I did come back to talk to you in a thrift shop dress. I figured I'd show up and it turns out it was prom night, you know? And when I got there to say hi, I saw you on your way in." Her voice got so quiet that her sentence disappeared.

"I went to prom with two chicks..."

"I only love once, Animal."

Oh shit. That's what it was. She was in love with me. All I could say was, "Oh."

Because I loved T. She was—well, is a beautiful woman. But I wasn't *in* love with her. She was family. I wanted to keep her behind me. Protect her.

I pictured the scenario at prom. Her arriving and me somehow missing her. I'd just found out from Merck she was in town from time to time and not checking in with me. And I was pissed and in pain.

But for her, in the sidelines in her thrift store getup made my heart want to punch myself in the balls.

I wanted to tell her I would've dumped those girls in a hot minute to take her to that dance, but something stopped me. She loved me. And that changed the script. Because I wasn't about to lie to her. I wasn't going to try to fake it for her either. She didn't deserve that.

She gave me a hard nod, hair curtain fully engaged. "I have to go."

She had revealed herself and now wanted to bolt because she knew I didn't feel the same way.

I had to move fast, because she was fast, but I was able to catch her by her arm and hold the door closed.

"T."

She wouldn't face me, so I was talking to the back of her head while I held on to her lightly.

"I didn't know."

Because we weren't face-to-face, I guess she felt like she could talk to me, finally. "Everyone falls in love with you. It's what happens. You're you. You fill a room. You are…something else."

"You're not everyone. I'm so sorry. I could never lie to you. I love you. You're my girl."

"Don't. I already know. I'm not the one for you. I just want to be here, do what I can to help. Make sure that no one hurts you."

She pulled at her arm a little, asking me to let her go with her body language.

Instead, I moved her gently so I could look at her face. She wasn't crying—just defiant. Her truth was out.

"You already did that. I've not forgotten the day you saved my life, T. You killed for me. I can't lose you. I mean, again. You have to be in this life with me." I let my hands drop. I wasn't going to force her to stay anymore.

"You'll never lose me." T tucked her hair behind her ear and then reached up close to my face. "And you've saved my life more times than anyone can count. You just didn't know it."

She put her palm near, but didn't touch me.

I leaned into her hand, forcing the contact.

"Don't misunderstand this. I've known. It wasn't both ways. The way I feel about you isn't the way you feel about me."

She curled her hand, almost making a claw, but not hurting me.

"I didn't come back trying to get with you like that. But I see how you're doing stuff here. Putting everyone else first. You needed to know how I feel because when push comes to shove I'm here for you. When crap goes down, I will look to you first. Take care of *you* first. No one else has priority. Not Nix. Not Becca."

Her hand opened and the soft touch of her palm cradled my face. "And I know that's not how you think. But call me selfish. I can't be any other way. It's how I'm wired."

She was shredding me open with her loyalty. The truth of it all.

"T, I can make it work. Let's try. I can try. You know you're my wife in my head. Nix is my man wife and then there's you."

She whispered, "Man wife."

Her ghost of a smile made me more determined. "Let's try."

She took her hand away to reach for the doorknob behind her.

"Animal, don't you get it? You deserve to feel how I feel about you. It's really big. And it's going to be for someone other than me." She completed the smile that my joke had started and left the room.

I hung my head and felt like a giant asshole. How could I not be in love with this girl? I loved her in my head and heart. Was I not feeling it in my soul?

After I sat back down at my desk, I banged my head against the back of my desk chair.

25

He knew. It was freeing and devastating in one fell swoop. At least I could tell him what I was doing, unlike my mother. She just had to think I abandoned her. Animal was mentally healthy and could handle knowing about my love. It wouldn't affect his decision-making.

I walked down the steps, half-hoping he would chase me. The part of me that loved to see beautiful things happen wanted a moment like that. The Cinderella moment. The kiss that people wrote songs about. I straightened my spine. I was braver than the pain. Tougher than the hurt. I inhaled. I could be near the people I loved. That was enough for a girl like me. I could make it enough. I'd spent years making the wishes in my heart so small I could barely hear them.

26

T acted like she hadn't said anything to me about her feelings. When I broached the subject, she brushed me off. When I brought girls home, she was gone. It seemed like she knew what I was planning before I planned it.

She watched out for Ember. T told me she loved me just so I would know, not so anything would change.

Nix was getting bolder in the Feybi organization. Rumor had it that he'd made himself a right-hand man. Something would happen soon, I could tell.

After, I found out Becca had switched professions to a tattoo artist and had inked half of her face in a skull tat in honor of Nix, even though she hadn't laid eyes on him in so long.

The night I was bringing her to him, Nix left the employ of Feybi, murdering the old bastard on the way out.

T and I had prepared and started our defense and offense in the same moment.

Basically, we had designed my organization to be a place where people could find protection. We had ways to make money. Nix's philosophy of saving people was the cornerstone. Hookers found that their pimps beat them less because we had a way for them to check in on an app with Debra and Helena's crew. We had merchandise that we moved, and Mary Jane was a big seller. We were trying to move the harder drugs out of town, too. It was a big task, but the people we had were professionals. We were handling business with a slant. Things that were considered impossible to try were attempted.

The men and women who worked for the Feybis and the Kaleotos were used to getting shit on. With me, I was honest. They got paid for what they did. I wasn't cutting people's balls off. Instead, I gave them time and opportunities to figure out their lives.

We weren't saints, but we weren't assholes either. And the approach was taking the snot out of the existing structures.

After I got Nix and Becca back, we all moved into his house. T would stay sometimes, but we had to lock shit down now because our lives were getting more and more dangerous. Even our allies could be enemies in this business, so she had a hard time staying when the doors and windows were closed.

But my process continued to mature. Meetings. I spent time studying police reports, watching sales of property. I poached men from both warring families in Midville.

I was the Amazon to their mom and pop store. Eating them alive at a game they thought they knew how to play.

I hit them with a combination of theatrics, knowledge, and sheer personality.

Soon, guys were coming to Nix and me, sniffing for jobs.

T would vet them for me, and she was never wrong. Her silence made her a weapon. She just knew where to hear stuff.

I was going light on him while he had his honeymoon period with his honey. He'd reconnected with Ember, and my boy was happy for the first time in a long damn time.

But he saw what I was doing, how I was helping, and he wanted to be a part of it. The way I was running shit was something he could get behind. Of course, I wasn't surprised because it'd been his modus operandi that was the handbook.

But that was where we stood. I'd been to Meme's earlier in the night to meet some ladies that had been itching for a date. As I got dressed, I noticed that T had made herself scarce. I was looking forward to talking to Nix about the whole situation. And soon.

But not that night.

27

Animal

Meme's was busy. The Day of the Dead theme had stuck, but people weren't as riled up about it as when they first implemented it.

I was there for the usual. A nice group of beautiful females to teach how good they could possibly feel. A few of my repeat offenders were here tonight as well. I went to my table near the dance floor.

I had a formula. Let the ladies see what I was offering, give them a big smile, and wait. My reputation preceded me. Turns out, girls talk. They shared even the most intimate things. They also knew there was no competition. Everyone left my bed before morning. I was an experience. A thrill ride.

The music was good tonight—another holdover from the Day of the Dead event. The owner learned that more than just alcohol and two girls in tight clothes were required to make a place a success.

I bought the four girls hanging near me a drink. I could do four, but preferred three. Never less than two. I'd rather go home alone than do the one-on-one thing.

When the bass dropped on the song that was ripping through the bar, the front door opened.

Some people just have a light around them. A pull. It exists in varying degrees in most. In some, it is undiluted. I'm one of those people. People were drawn to me. If not their physical bodies, definitely their gaze. The way I moved. How I laughed. I was used to it. So was the woman who walked into Meme's. I'd never seen her before. New.

But it was more than that. Her face was stunning, her movements purposeful. She scanned the club like she was looking for something. Then she dropped her lashes and smiled.

With alcohol involved, there was no way she was going to be alone for long. My girls orbited me, and I didn't want to be rude.

But this girl. Something about her stood out.

"Why so serious?" Jelissa snapped her fingers in front of me. I captured her hand and turned my attention to her face. "Sorry." She was immediately regretful. "I didn't mean to snap. You were just so—focused there."

I nodded at her so she would know that she was forgiven. She was also not getting in bed with me ever again. But she'd learn that later.

I entertained my girls, but kept the super lit girl on my radar, sneaking peeks every once in a while.

The men trailed behind her. If they had any shame, they'd dropped it to try to get her attention.

I slid my sunglasses off my head and hung them off the collar of my shirt.

The way she was looking around set off all kinds of internal alarms.

Her overwhelming presence almost camouflaged it. I knew she would find me soon, because I was never easy to miss, even in a crowded bar.

She weaved her way onto the dance floor. She pity-talked to a few of the fuckers that were following her around, trying to get her to give them the time of day.

Her skin was a beautiful honey color. Her hair was past her ass. Her body was insane. But it was more than the package she was in. It was the control she had on the situation. She knew she was starting a fire in any room she walked into. She was ready for it.

When her light green eyes met my gaze, I was waiting for her.

I felt the zip from my head to my balls.

She lifted an eyebrow like we had a running joke. And we did. The pull. The way to change a room. It seemed almost orchestrated. Like there was a scriptwriter for this exact moment. Maybe it could even seem tactical.

I raised my glass of water in her direction, acknowledging the show I was watching.

She started dancing a little. Just enough that taking my eyes off her was impossible.

This girl was even better than I thought. Sweet hell she could dance. I could as well. The ladies loved seeing this giant body move so effortlessly. It took practice to make sure I never looked out of place on a dance floor. But I had put in the time.

When I gave my shoulders some movement, I watched as delight caused her head to tilt back.

I felt like my heart was heating up. Having her in my line of vision was like having a set of firecrackers going off in my head.

I knew she would (because they all do), but I was still excited when I realized she was dancing to me.

There were exceptions to every rule. And mine with the ladies around me were about to be bent.

She danced up to me, and Jelissa and Marin parted the tight circle around me to let her in.

Two of the men behind her were shouting at her like carnival barkers, "Can I get you a drink?" "What do you want to drink?"

She wrapped her hand around my cup, her nails just a hint longer than her fingertips. They made a clacking noise on my glass.

"It's okay. I've got *his* drink." She claimed me in front of our spectators. I let go of my glass with a flourish, like it was obvious that she and I would share a glass.

"I'm guessing water." She brought the glass to her mouth.

I narrowed my gaze at her. She didn't register surprise when she was right, just guzzled it back.

When she was done, she set it on the table. Then she took my giant hand in hers.

She twirled around and dragged me to the dance floor.

I heard my circle of girls starting to complain, but I was following this girl wherever she took me.

Her red lips were turned up in a smirk when she whirled around and started dancing.

So that's how it was. We weren't finding out names or making small talk.

We were just dancing.

And she was magnificent. Maybe she'd had professional training at some point, because I could hold my own with most, but not her.

It seemed that it wasn't fair for a girl this hot to also know how to dance.

Talk about stacking the cards in her favor.

Her black dress and strappy heels were not complicated, but the way the dress was scooped in the back gave me hope that if I was close enough I could peek down it.

She wasn't wearing a bra. Shit. I realized that as I tried to see her ass. This wasn't slutty, though. She wasn't begging for anything; she was

confident. Her competence with dance made my proficiency look more elaborate than it was.

There was no one better in that bar that night than she and I. We knew it. Watching us dance was a gift the customers didn't earn, but they were getting.

I quickly glanced around and realized I was right. All eyes were on us. I could handle the attention. At six foot eight, I was used to it in spades.

But the lady who was currently rubbing on me had that and more.

The two of us were rock stars and movie stars all at once.

I got the sense that she was temporary. Her gaze would flit around the place at moments and I knew I was a prop. Because of what I now did for a living, I realized I had to find out what she was up to. She didn't need to come to Meme's to get laid. Certainly a girl like her would be able to get whatever she wanted out of life—sexually anyway.

I pulled her against me. She braced herself with her hands and gave me a practiced come hither look.

She could flirt with the effectiveness of a nuclear bomb. My dick literally wanted to learn how to talk instantly.

"What's your name?"

She smirked. "Poison?"

"I wouldn't doubt it. Dropping all that sex appeal on these fools like they deserved it. Now, what's your name?" I didn't try to cop a feel, though I could tell she was fit from where our bodies touched.

"What's yours? Tit for tat, sweetness."

Her use of my common term of endearment caused me to suspect her even harder.

"You already know my name." It was a guess. A pretty self-absorbed guess.

"And you don't know mine? Does that mean only one of us does our homework?" She started to sway, encouraging me to make this faceoff look like a dance.

I rocked with her. "Feybi or Kaleotos?"

She rolled her eyes. "You think local. Don't do yourself a disservice." I stopped rocking.

"There are bigger fish in the sea, Animal." Her eyes flashed with reams of knowledge I didn't have. Yet.

"What's your name?" I was getting that out of her.

"Albany."

"That's a city." I looked around the club to try to place who she was here with.

In the corner I saw T. She nodded when my eyes passed over her.

Always watching. Always making sure I was safe.

"It takes a city to hold me."

She was fire in my arms. Burning anyone that dared to try.

"You here to get me killed, Albany?" I twirled her and pulled her so her back was against my chest. I put my arm across her like a seat belt, my hand holding her jaw.

To the Meme's patrons, I was putting the moves on her. To anyone with the right background, they knew I had her in a very dangerous hold. Easy to snap her neck.

I brought my lips close to her ear. She smelled like vanilla. A clean scent in this bar that was thick with manufactured flavors.

"You'd be dead before I hit the floor," she whispered as if she was suggesting a rendezvous instead of my demise. "Which would be a shame. I've got to say, you're quite the snack."

"Say what you came here to say." I wanted to keep her flirting with me forever and not have it tainted with this life I was in now. But T was right there, too. And as amazing as this girl was, when it came to T, I wasn't about hurting her intentionally.

"You've captured people's attention. They want to talk." She started to move against my dick.

"How much does it cost to have a girl like you come in here to pass a message?"

She laughed. Despite my hold, she turned so her chest was against mine again. "I'm beyond money. I work for power. And I think you do, too. Meet my people. It's worth it."

"No." I dropped my hands and took a step back. She stopped moving the instant I did.

"That's a mistake." She flipped her hair. There was a layer of wisdom under the come-on.

"Not where I'm standing. If I let my dick make my choices, then everybody's going down." I turned my back on Albany.

I walked to the circle of pouting ladies that cheered when they saw me return.

I felt Albany's attention on the back of my neck. It took everything I had in me not to pivot and give her a glower. I wanted to pull my phone out and warn some people to follow her.

When she was gone, I felt the energy of the room change. I shifted so I had my back to the wall. Albany was gone from Meme's, but so was T.

I pulled my phone out and texted her.

Following?

Her answer was fast.

Of course.

I reviewed the conversation I had with Albany. A whole extra layer of evil was out there that I wasn't aware of. My phone buzzed again.

Do your night. Do those ladies. Don't let them know she rattled you.

I responded.

I don't want you to do this alone.

I'm already gone.

I was in the middle of typing out a reply that was very boss-like to her. I didn't like that she was telling me to go sleep with these chicks I had around me. We didn't talk about that stuff. She and I.

Maybe trust me.

I deleted what I had and amended it.

I trust you with my life. Promise me I can trust you with yours.

She sent the middle finger emoji, so I knew she was at least feisty.

Okay. Keep me posted.

I ordered another round for the ladies, entertaining them while I thought of a million other things.

28

I was sitting in the chair in my room. Each of the three naked women on my bed was passed out. Satisfied. I flexed my forearms and twisted my fists until I could open my hands and stretch out my fingers. I still had my silver rings on. A request from the brunette. She liked the jewelry. I felt a smile form on my lips as the redhead started to snore. Super satisfied. This was the second night where I had to entertain. I had one text from T saying that I had to keep going as if nothing was happening. So it was another evening of entertaining, like I normally would.

If sex were the Olympics, I'd have a platter of gold medals.

Maybe a bucket. My phone buzzed and I glanced at the screen. Only very few texts could come to my phone right now that I would answer.

It was from her, so I stood. I turned my back on the buffet of living porn on my bed to tilt my head over to the glowing screen lying on the side table. From T.

I'm at the old mall.

And that was all she had to say. I'd been waiting for an update from her. I flipped the lights on in the room. I started tossing the various scraps of clothing from the floor onto the naked torsos.

"Ladies! The time has come. You have all come." They started to blink and sit up. "Marin, you came, I think, like five times."

The redhead was the most confused. I clapped my hands loudly. "I got business, and you know the rules. No one stays overnight. Even if you can wrap your sweet, sweet ankles around your own gorgeous neck." I gave the blonde a kiss on her shoulder.

The brunette tried to reach between my legs and I sidestepped her. It took more cajoling than I wanted, but eventually, I hustled them out the front door to the waiting Uber.

After they pulled away, I heard a snicker.

I looked at my reflection in the mirror. Nix was just to my left.

"Brother, you should be in your room living the dream. Why you got your sweet ass down here creeping on me?" I scowled at the refection like I was ready to fight him.

"Three? How many is it gonna take?" Nix raised one eyebrow with his question instead of answering mine.

I turned on my heel so I could look at him in the flesh. "I've got needs. And I have to do my part to make sure those ladies know what it feels like to be properly handled by a man. So many fuckers out there being pumpin' chumpers, I got my work laid out for me."

"Sure enough." Nix gave me one of his rare smiles.

"I got to go. T just texted." I pulled my jacket out of the closet by the front door and shoved my feet into my giant boots.

Nix was instantly on point. "You need me?"

"No, baby, I'll let you know." I put out my fist for a bump.

Nix ignored it. "I'm watching you. You can't bubble wrap my shit forever, Animal."

I gave my fist a pointed look. He tapped it with his tatted knuckles.

"I got you. Let me see what I'm packing." I had guns in my black SUV, so I didn't have to take anything from here. "Just keep your lady safe, feel me?"

I didn't wait for his answer as I took to a light jog across the foyer. I felt another buzz in my pocket and moved even faster.

I took my SUV to meet T in the parking lot of the old mall. She was still in the clothes from last night, and she looked tired.

I hit the unlock button and she climbed in the passenger side. I handed her a bottle of water from the cup holder, and she swigged it.

"You all right?"

T winced and nodded.

"So that chick had a car waiting for her outside of Meme's. Actually, a few cars. They trailed one another like she was the President."

"Okay." My mind was racing. Was one of the families

trying to make a move on Meme's? Claim the territory? I could shut that shit down. I pulled out my phone in honor of her news.

T covered my hand with hers "No. Not yet. Hear me out." She was reading my mind again.

After turning in the seat, she folded her legs up and pushed her back against the door so she could look at me directly.

"I followed the caravan. They took the long way home, making sure they weren't tailed. When they were comfortable, the lot of them pulled up to a place not far upstate. The gate sign identified it as Breston Pharmaceuticals." She let me digest the information.

"She's from a pharmaceutical company? What the hell are they doing sniffing around me?" I was stumped. I mean, everyone had heard of Breston. They were on the back of most of the bottles in everyone's bathrooms. They also owned a national chain of pharmacies. Maybe international. I'd never paid that much attention.

"They are mammoth. Far bigger than they let on. I researched them from my phone. She never came back out, by the way, but they had caravans coming in every half hour or so, all night long."

"I wonder if that's business as usual for a pharmaceutical company. I mean, I guess it's just legal drugs. Business has to be good." I set my phone down on the console.

"So, what do they want with you? That's the question we need to worry about. She came in and went straight for you, both barrels loaded." She hugged her arms.

I leaned over and turned the heat up.

She continued, "If I was setting up someone to get information or cooperation from you, I'd have sent that chick, too. She's like napalm. Overly effective."

I gave her an amused look. "Really? You planning on saucing me out soon?"

She gave me the finger. "That's not even a thing people say. And yes, I think about it. I plot conspiracies. I plan your death. I kidnap you in my head all the time."

Now I lifted both eyebrows at her. "Wow, we need to get you some better hobbies."

She ran her hand over her face. "If I've already thought about it, I eliminate the element of surprise in those situations."

I nodded when I realized her reasoning was sound.

"You do it, too. That's how we get jobs done. You probably haven't put it in that morbid of a context." She yawned. "Any of the sluts from last night new girls?"

I didn't want to talk about last night with her. "Yeah. Two of them actually."

She rubbed her temples. She was clearly exhausted. "Okay, let's go back to your den of sin and see if they took anything. You have cameras rolling during your slippery hole and stick party?"

"Damn, T."

"What? You're a well-known pied piper of dick. I'd send some hookers out to act like sluts and get into your room if I was out to get you, too."

I put my seat belt on and looked at her. "What'd you drive to get here?" After I heard her belt click, she answered, "I jacked a car. It's in the river now. So I walked from there to here."

"You'd send me hookers? Am I that gullible?" I put the SUV in reverse. "Only about your own safety." After we were rolling, she used the electric controls to tilt her seat back.

She mumbled, "Attention can feel like love if you're scared."

Then she fell asleep quickly. In repose I watched as she let down her guard. She was beautiful. Perfect lips, skin so pale she'd burn easy in the summer sun. I felt my heart swell looking at her. I was glad she'd come back to Midville. Having her here and knowing I was messing with her head wasn't easy, but it was much better than wondering if she was alive somewhere else.

Her steady breathing told me that she was now out. The sentence she'd uttered rattled around in my brain all the way home.

29

Animal

I had to wake T when we pulled into the driveway. I knew she was never completely relaxed—unless she was in my company. She was groggy but able to function.

T and I walked in on Nix and Becca kissing against the wall. It was cute how much they were into each other. I knew Nix was still on cloud nine. That his stalkee was very willing to be stalked. We greeted them and I teased them about getting back down to business as T and I jogged up the steps.

After we stepped into my bedroom, I realized she'd never been here before. Despite the chill, she went to the closest window and opened it.

"Let's air this sucker out a little." T turned around and frowned at my room.

Ember came to the doorway and said hi to T.

"About time we got some fresh air in here. Those girls better cut back on the perfume and sweating and stuff. I can smell it all the way down the hallway."

I shook my head. "That's the guest room. You're in the *guest* room. We're still getting you back to your place with Aunt Dorothy." The things I stored here weren't too incriminating; my phone was always on the charger running the playlist for the ladies, so I would've noticed if it was missing.

Various sex toys were scattered around and plugged in. They were all covered with condoms so that the ladies didn't have to worry about catching things from one another.

Both Ember and T gave the toys a scrunched up face.

"What? When there's three, I gotta be creative."

Ember kicked at one with her socked foot. "You know, if I was a psychologist, I'd say that you have to fill this room with girls because you're terrified of being intimate with just one."

T snorted. "Nailed it."

They fist bumped each other.

Ember continued after the touch of sisterhood, "Don't worry, handsome. When I finally make an honest man out of you, we can have lots of naked therapy sessions. With just us." She gave me a huge wink.

"Ember, get out of here. T and I are trying to do something." I pointed toward the door.

She laughed but obeyed, closing the door behind her.

"Punk ass kid." I sat on my bed and opened my end table drawer.

Nothing too incriminating there either.

T was at my desk, rifling through the papers I had there.

She held up a packet that was stapled together. "You keep notes on the meetings?"

I got off of the bed and walked to her, looking over her shoulder to scrutinize what she was examining.

"Yes, I write the minutes of the meeting while it's still fresh in my head." I pointed out the deals of the Feybis and the Kaleotos' recent agreement.

"This is not too intricate. Still information I wish they didn't have." T flipped through the document. "You're like a PTA mom."

I turned from her and scoped the rest of the room. Nothing else, really.

T put the paper back on my desk. "So we have to assume one of them at least was a plant. And that they saw everything on this paper. Where does that leave us? What information do Breston and Albany have on you now?" I put my hands on my hips. "They know I'm in charge. And that I made the Feybi and the Kaleotos families my bitch."

"Yeah, they already knew that, so we should be okay." T headed out of my room. I had some cleaning to do in here, but I closed the door and followed her to the kitchen.

Ember, Nix, and Becca were all eating salads.

Nix pointed at the fridge. "I made an enormous bowl. There's plenty for you two."

T and I pulled out bowls and drinks. After we were settled around the table, I looked at all the faces present. I was happy with this. My people. Here, having dinner. It made me beam.

Nix looked up from his salad and caught me.

He used his fork to low-key point at everyone at the table and then grinned. We were on the same wavelength.

We had it all right now. Surrounded by people we loved and considered family. If I had Merck tucked in somewhere here, it would be complete.

30

I didn't like Albany. I didn't like how she looked at Animal. And I didn't trust her. She was the kind of woman who scrambled men's minds. The way she walked was just a calling card to the kind of sway she could have over clear-thinking guys. And she would claim I was jealous, and honestly, I probably was. When Animal's head had snapped around and followed her at Meme's, I wished it were me. I could sense bullshit and Albany had it in spades. She used what she had to convince people to do her bidding.

Her family was rich—I knew that. They could be powerful,

with billions in the coffers. They could buy any politician they wanted.

So what did she want with Animal? Besides the obvious.

I followed her in a black sports car I borrowed from Wardon, one of my soldiers. He wasn't Feybi's or Kaleotos'. A professional driver drove her to a Starbucks. I parked and went inside.

I expected her to flirt her way in and out, and because I didn't have a dick, she wouldn't notice me.

But I was wrong. I took a seat in the corner instead of getting in the ordering line. On her way out she spotted me. A knowing smile spread across her face. She sat at my table without being invited.

"You're Animal's friend." Her pink lipstick was perfectly glossed, her hair nearly as shiny. This lady was really good at being a girl.

"And you're not." I knew I'd have an edge. No one could accuse me of being friendly, and I wasn't starting with this bitch.

Her sneer grew wide, revealing her perfect porcelain teeth. "Animosity already? Usually I have to sleep with a lady's man before I get this kind of vibe."

I shrugged. If she wanted to truly fight, I would put her to shame. I could take down three men twice her size.

"Your confidence is sexy. Do you know that?" Albany took a sip of her coffee and then hissed. "I always do that, like I don't expect to be burned."

She patted her mouth with a napkin.

"Seems like a motto you live by." I gave her a hard stare.

Albany laughed. "You've got me down, huh? That's awesome. Does he know you're in love with him?"

Biting and quick, she was faster than I gave her credit for.

"He knows." No use in lying if my feelings were that easy to read. “That’s a shame. He’s still putting it to other people. How do you live

with that?” Albany opened the lid on her coffee cup. “I’m going to let this cool.”

“I just protect him. That’s all I need.” I had no prop for my hands so I folded them on top of the table.

“Commendable. I hope he’s worth this devotion. Because you’re gorgeous. I mean, there’s a certain tomboy capable thing you have about you that’s at odds with that gorgeous figure. You could even model, I bet.” Albany pulled out her phone and snapped a picture of me before I could stop her. She flipped the phone so I could see the image of me glaring at her.

“Hot, right? A picture that could launch a thousand erections.” “Delete it.” I tapped my finger on the table. She wrinkled her nose as if she was being cute.

“My phone, my property.”

I assessed her for a second before I snatched the phone out of her hand. I slid it under the table and put it in my hoodie pocket.

Her chipper demeanor fell away. She ran her tongue over her teeth before clearing her throat. “I need that back.”

“No, you don’t. You need to respect people’s private space. This’ll teach you that lesson.” I put my hands in my pockets, my palm stretched across her screen. Nix could do some work with it.

Albany stood slowly, as if she thought if she gave me enough time I’d change my mind. “I really hoped that we could be friends. Trade makeup tips. Fun stuff.”

I looked up at her, not changing my demeanor at all. “Save your hope for unicorns and rainbows. I’m no one’s friend.”

I stood, my chair making a scraping noise behind me.

A fake smile started to form on her face. She put the lid back on her coffee like there was no rush.

"You know, I have plenty of pictures of you. Some more flattering than others, if you know what I mean." She ran her red fingernail around the top of her cup.

I looked away from her and tried to get a good canvass on the parking lot. I was betting there was security for her here now along with the drivers.

I wouldn't show fear. I turned toward her.

"You know what, T? I think I'm going to pay you back by sleeping with Animal. Whatcha think about that?" She gave me a campy shoulder shrug like she was a '50s pin-up girl.

"Animal can put his dick wherever he wants. He likes to play with fire, and I'm betting your crotch is all lit up with STDs." I gave her the same cheesy shrug.

Albany turned and walked out like we'd just had a great meeting.

She was crazy. I felt my heart flop into a pile because I knew that even with a warning, Animal might just give her what she wanted.

31

T had warned me. She said that Albany wanted me in the worst way. She'd been right.

At my last meeting with a supplier, she was waiting for me, back against the purple Hummer. She wanted me to hit it, and I told myself that I could handle her. It would be a great way to figure out what she knew, so I took her home with me.

Now, I had her in my bedroom. All the sexual tension and back and forth were about to end. After I closed the door, I realized that Albany was the first girl I'd had alone in a long time.

I missed T in that second. I knew it wasn't meant to be. T

loved me, and I'd never mess with her head by sleeping with her, but I didn't feel as comfortable in a room alone with Albany.

"I've heard the rumors, Animal." She trailed her red nails along my dark gray bedspread. "And the things you know how to do here. Gotta say, it makes a girl curious."

She shed her dress while she spoke. "I've had the worst luck with lovers lately." She was in a black bra and panties and an old school garter situation. Her heels were high. Albany had the body for it. "The men I'm with say I'm too bossy. But I swear, they just don't know how to take the steering wheel, you know?"

"How'd you get the name Albany? It's a place." I folded my arms in front of me.

She sat on the bed and pulled her legs around so she could put her back against my headboard.

"My parents gave it to me. I'm assuming it's where I was conceived." Her heels were piercing my bedspread. This lady was trouble. I knew

that. I kept my eyes on her as she took off her bra.

Everything about her screamed pampered. Manicured fingers, matched manicured toes—which I discovered when she kicked off her heels. She arranged her legs to show off how long they were.

Her breasts were spectacular. They were enhanced, obviously, but a lot of money had gone into them.

"Do you just stare at them? The women you bring here?" She rolled her shoulders and touched her chin to one. It was like she was posing for an erotic photo shoot. Practiced.

"Intimidate them with your big size?"

I was hard. That was a given. She was half-naked and baiting me on my bed. Hell, I'd brought her here. I knew what I was going to do. Pushing aside the guilt I had, I stepped to the foot of the bed.

"Maybe I need to be tempted a little more." My voice was husky.

This was a mistake, but I was about to make the hell out of it.

Albany licked her lips. The only thing that was missing was the camera rolling. The practiced motions of disrobing seductively should have been a warning sign.

But I wanted to try her. To demand she do things my way. To make her pleasure beholden to my whims.

I rubbed my bottom lip with a fingertip. "Do they just jump on you, Albany? Do none of them make you work for it? Just show them a pretty, magic pussy, and five minutes later, they dub you a princess?"

"Oh, I have to earn it? I think I'm up for that." She pushed herself to her knees. "Are you up to it?"

After getting on all fours, she crawled toward me until her mouth was as close to my dick as she could get.

"Do some girls run out of here screaming when they see what you have to offer?"

I took my finger from my lip and ran it from her temple to her jaw. "Never yet. Some cry a little. But by the time I'm done ringing your clit like a doorbell, you'll come all over it. Just like they all do."

The challenge flashed in her eyes. She was competitive. She wanted to be the best I'd ever had. Her raw sexuality was on her side. The way she moved, the innuendo in her sensual-ness was a calling card and a sledgehammer all at once.

"I've never had any problems getting what I need." Albany wiggled off the bed and stood topless close to me. The tips of her nipples brushed my shirt.

I touched her lip and she licked around my finger before sucking on it.

I let out a laugh. "Remember, I usually have tons of company. Can you compensate for that?"

Maybe I was being cruel, but both she and I knew we weren't in this bedroom to start a relationship.

After gently biting my finger, she pushed it away and took a step back.

I'd pressed her enough that I expected a show.

I turned and sat on the bed.

The dancer in Albany came out. "Put sexy music on."

I spoke to my phone, it cued up a playlist for just this purpose.

Albany started to move, and the dance floor had been just a notion at what she could do. She worked taking her panties and garters off into a maneuver when she'd dropped low. And then she danced. Naked for me.

There was no denying she was a gorgeous woman, and she was trying really hard to be the best I'd ever had.

After she went to her knees in front of me, I dared her, "Show me how you touch your pussy. Make yourself come."

Flustered, she stopped for a second. I lifted an eyebrow.

"You want to know what I can do to you? I need to see your limits first. Because what you think is too much will be my starting line."

I tapped my foot to the music. She flashed through all the emotions. Apparently, she'd never gotten through that whole show without getting nailed, but I could watch for hours. I knew how to pace myself. I wasn't an amateur.

Albany tried to flip the tables. "Well, I can't do anything to me if you're not touching yourself."

I put my hands behind me, kicked out my legs, and crossed

my feet at the ankles. "No. This is a test for you, not me. I know what I like. I need to know what brings you to the edge."

Albany tried to stand, but I shook my head. "Do it on the floor. No comfort. Just pleasure."

I saw the goose bumps form on her naked skin. As she lay back on my floor, I looked harder between her legs. She didn't have any hair, and it looked bare enough that I figured either she was a very regular waxer or had medically removed the ability to grow it.

Albany started in on herself, but it was a show. She was giving me porn.

This was what she thought I wanted to see.

I eased off the bed and kneeled next to her. Her pouting lips and writhing was an act.

I put my mouth close to hers. She anticipated the kiss. I spoke quietly, knowing she had to hear my voice deep. "This is not you. Show me what you look like when you're alone. Show me what you like, not what you think I like. Impress me."

At first she was insulted. I waited her out. "This is what I like."

"No. You don't like it like this. You've practiced this in a mirror. I want to know what happens to you when you've spent a night dancing with me. And you've gone home alone, but you're thinking about me and what my mouth could do. How long my fingers are."

Her nostrils flared. I kept talking. I was asking a lot and not giving her any prep.

"You're used to being in control of the scenario. But not this. You don't know what I'm going to do."

She started touching herself with less theatrics. Her pupils started to dilate.

"There we go. Show me what your hands do." I put my right hand gently around her throat.

She went from a delicate two fingers to three fingers inside herself. And, of course, she was rubbing her clit. I put a gentle pressure on her neck.

"Touch me more," she commanded.

"No, baby, I'm watching. I'm learning." I released my hold on her neck and shifted to a better view between her legs. She liked it rough, undoubtedly. The pressure she wanted was direct and in a circle.

At the foot of my bed, I had a small chest that held my favorite sexual weapons. The poor thing needed just a bit of help. She only had two hands, after all.

I got two clamps out and leaned over her.

"How about this?" I pinched the clamp open and closed it on her right nipple. She gasped and her eyes rolled into her head. I pinched the second and clamped it down.

Her ass was moving, rubbing into the carpet. I could hear her getting wetter with every pump of her fingers.

She liked the clamps. I resumed my position to watch her.

Albany lifted her head and made eye contact as she got close to her peak. And then she was there. A pretty orgasm. Her muscles tensed, and she certainly was lost in the pleasure of her body. That was her limit.

And I was about to test it.

I reached into my chest and grabbed a vibrator and a dildo. I quickly rubbed both with lube.

Albany was on her comedown. A very controlled orgasm. She didn't even curse. That was about to change. I pressed her clit hard with the vibrator, making sure I mimicked the direction and pressure she seemed to favor.

It was like I touched her with a live wire. Her legs kicked out.

"Oh! God."

Instead of coming down, she was about to get ramped up.

"See, baby. You're not done. Not even close. You're going to pass out on this floor by the time I'm done giving this pussy the sexual Willy Wonka acid trip of its life. Buckle up."

I inserted the dildo, one inch at a time. I pressed the vibrator harder.

Albany lost her demeanor. She'd never turned herself into a carnival before.

She reached out and tried to grab the carpet. I moved the dildo in and out of her, going deeper with every thrust.

I made sure that my pinkie was well lubed from the vibrator's excess and slipped it into her asshole as well.

The veins in her neck began to stick out. I slapped the clamps off of her nipples.

"Sweet fuck. Oh God. This. Yes. Stop. Don't stop. I'm coming."

I felt satisfied as her voice got deeper and her words began to slur together. I pushed the dildo deep and went back into the trunk for a condom. I unzipped my pants and pulled out my dick. After rolling on the condom and pinching the tip, I watched her fairly crazed eyes land on it.

"Oh no. That's too big. Too much." She started to move away. I pulled the dildo out of her and tossed it aside.

She curled her shoulders around herself. She was scared of it, and I was proud.

"It won't hurt you. It'll ruin you, but you'll beg for it the whole time. Promise."

Albany's skin was all pink on her chest. I reached between her legs and inserted two fingers. I used the come here motion to stimulate her even more. Her fear fell away, and I watched her nipples perk up even harder than before. I pulled out my fingers just enough that she would have to scoot closer to my dick to get more friction.

I used the lube to prep myself. Because as turned on as she

was, I was a lot.

When she was close, I stood, sliding back on my bed.

She barely had the strength to get to her knees. I watched her wobble. Albany panted. I knew my smile was slightly evil. "I usually have three women sucking this dick because it's so goddamn big."

Her throat moved while she swallowed, eyeing the prize I was talking about.

"You impale yourself on this monster. I'm barely turned on. You better make me come as hard as I just made you come."

The competition rose in her. She was haunted by all the other sexual experiences that had come before her in this room.

I put my hands behind my head.

Albany had a renewed sense of vigor. "Should I make you masturbate, too, so I can take notes?"

"Nope. This is a pop quiz. Do your worst, baby."

The confidence was gone in her stride, but it was replaced by sheer determination. Albany had to stand to position herself, feet on either side of my hips. It was like watching her lower herself into a shark tank, she was so jumpy about it. When she got to the tip, the lube helped me get into her. And God bless America, she was tight as hell.

She slipped. She took the next seven inches of me in a free-fall before she could catch herself.

She let out an almost painful moan. I had doubts that she could get all of me inside, but I was really interested to see her try.

It was a mix of pain and want in her moans now. This wasn't the practice drill she was used to performing for other shitheads.

We were getting to that place I knew how to take a woman. Multiple women, actually. Where she was on the next level.

Where she realized that the other sex she was having was just the pre-game for this. Handling what I had, combined with the size of my hands, my fingers became a realization that there was more in this world. For her. Between her legs.

As I watched her get all of me inside, I complimented her.

"Fuck yeah."

"I don't know...if I can move." She hesitated to do any more. I had her stretched.

"Grab the lube. Try, Albany. Other ladies manage."

I snagged the bottle off the bedside table and handed it to her. She did her best, truly. She lifted herself up, awkwardly trying to add moisture to my shaft without releasing me.

Once I saw she was properly lubricated, I started a very slow roll of my hips. Just the tiniest movement in and out.

She started squeaking and wincing. I put her out of her misery and started to thumb her swollen clit.

And then the magic started. She was so full of me, I was changing the shape of what she could accommodate.

"Oh. Oh. Oh."

The full body spasms were starting in her. And I was barely moving. This was a result of the deeper orgasms she was experiencing. I knew how to get both. Usually, I started speaking to the lady, encouraging her. Imprint the sound of my voice with the sensations rocking through her.

It had been enough playtime. She had a big presence, but she was small. I held her hips, keeping myself deeply inside her as I flipped.

She screamed a little, then settled back, realizing I was in control now and she didn't have to try hard to make it all work.

"You ready?"

As demanding as I was, I never wanted a girl to feel like her opinion didn't matter.

"No. But yes." She put her hands on my chest and dug her

nails into my pecs.

"I'm about to change everything you know and your sexual tastes for the rest of your life. I'll ask you again. Are you ready?"

Her eyes grew wide, but she nodded her consent.

"Grab the headboard. And maybe start praying." I waited until she did as I said, wrapping her hands around the bar detail on the furniture.

She arched her back as she panted, like she was at the top of a roller coaster with no restraints.

I slipped my hand under her ass and lifted her so I could use all the motion I had in my hips.

And then I started like I had to, slowly. I added even more lube. Deeper.

Faster. I watched as her fingernails dug into her palms.

I pinched her nipple and then ramped up. The guttural cursing started. People would think I was turning her into a demon if they walked in on us. The way I combined the talent with the force and sheer size was why there were usually a few sets of eyes on my ass waiting eagerly for their turn.

I went to my knees and put her ankles on my shoulders. She was tight around me. I was the size she would crave as long as she was the proud owner of a pussy.

I stopped and she went boneless, but her eyes had the tint of an addict. "Is it over?"

"No."

I pulled out another vibrator. This one plugged into the wall because it would take something this fantastic to make her feel it over what my cock was doing.

I pressed it to her clit and flipped it on. I could feel the deep, low vibrations in my balls. It was a strong vibe.

She tried to move away and let go of her handhold.

"Hold the fucking bars. Don't you let go."

She did as I commanded. Albany was sweating now. I'd left

the lights on, so I could see all of her. No secrets.

And then I took what I needed. I knew she was ready inside, and I went for it. All the way in and out so I could get to my finish.

She started convulsing as she screamed. Her pussy had gotten wetter, suddenly soaking the bed.

I yelled at her, because I was concentrating, "Grab your tits!"

Albany got two handfuls and punished herself, letting my intentions become her consciousness.

I flipped her again, bending her legs to help myself get her to my favorite position. Setting the vibe in the center of the bed so it would stay pressed against her, I humped her from the back, my hands on either side of her shoulders.

Not worrying anymore about her, I made her a destination as I came hard inside her.

She was gasping, her head hanging over the edge of my bed.

I flopped to the side. She couldn't move. We both struggled to catch our breath. After we had cooled, I looked her over.

My handprints were all over her. Her sensitive skin was a hot pink near her erogenous zones. Her hair was stuck to her forehead. She was beyond satisfied. I watched as she went from attracted to me to infatuated with me.

Her eyes took on a glaze.

Eventually, she tried to sit up, like she might be done for the evening. I started to laugh. I took my condom off.

"Baby, you're not nearly done. I'm just getting started." I pointed to my semi. "Suck this clean and bring it back to life. You have to be as good as at least three pussies tonight."

She staggered when she stood, but she bent at the waist and took the tip of my dick in her mouth.

And round two began.

32

I was in deep in my research of Breston. Animal, Nix, and I needed to be well informed. It was how Animal and I conquered the other warring families.

This was far different. Breston, Inc. had no bad public relations. Which was unusual. It seemed to me that they had money to cover any sins. They had pharmaceuticals, but you never saw the long, boring commercials from lawyers promising to pay money if you were hurt or injured from something Breston produced.

I took notes on what I could find. The owners, which started a few generations ago in the business, had the kind of money that made them the people who signed the rich people's paychecks.

Albany was the second child. The first was a boy, Royce Preston Breston III.

Albany's father was near sixty years old when she was born. Her mom was famous for her hourglass figure and low standards.

She was Breston's third wife.

The old man was eighty-five now and still seemed to have all his piss and vinegar intact.

Why he wanted Animal, I wasn't sure.

I spent hours in front of two different computers. I hadn't checked the surveillance cameras in a long time. I knew Nix always had one eye on them, so I wasn't worried, but reviewed them anyway.

That's when I saw her. Albany holding Animal's hand like he had put a diamond ring on one of her fingers on the way into the house.

She looked right into the camera and gave a sarcastic wave.

She knew I would see it. I searched the rest of the footage until it was live. She was still in the house.

I went calmly to the closest gun and loaded it. I checked the chamber and released the safety.

I crouched down on the balls of my feet while I tried my best to talk myself out of going up there and shooting her.

Waves of pain hit me until I finally sat flat on the floor.

She'd gotten what she wanted: Animal in bed. I picked myself up and unloaded the gun.

Love was pain where I was from. And I was in so much love I wanted to die.

33

Albany didn't know about my rule. Girls didn't get to wake up in my room.

I reminded her.

Usually, I took pleasure from giving pleasure. I thought of it as a master's class in their own sexuality. That I was setting the bar for how much they should reach for their own orgasms.

But this was different. It was more of a hate fuck. I didn't feel good about it. It wouldn't happen again.

Albany was holding her high heels and her new phone. I'd called her an Uber and her hair was a wreck.

Out of the corner of my eye, I saw T pad into the kitchen in her pajamas, not turning on the lights.

Shit.

I didn't want her to know about this. I knew we weren't together, but I didn't want to hurt her either.

I showed Albany the door. She tried to kiss me. I turned my head so that she got my cheek instead.

I didn't kiss. Not when I was doing this. Not when it was a festival of sin in my room. When I closed the front door, I took off running because I knew T would bolt. I cut her off in the hallway, stretching my arms open so she couldn't go past me.

T spun on her bare heels to avoid running into my chest. "Dammit." "Whatcha doin' up, princess?"

She wasn't the kind to back down, so she faced me and folded her arms in front of her chest. She had soft pj pants and a tank top on. Her hair was swung over one eye.

"Don't call me that." She pursed her lips and wrinkled her nose.

"I call you that all the time." I dropped my arms, point made-- we were having this conversation.

"Not when you smell like her." She didn't look in my eyes, but leveled her stare at my mouth.

Not ten minutes earlier Albany had been sitting on it while she sucked my dick. I took a step backwards.

I probably did smell like sex.

I heard T professing her love for me in my mind all over again. "I'm sorry."

The bravado was dropped. The chip was off my shoulder. My walls down. Young Animal was talking to young T all over again.

Her hard demeanor softened. "I know you are."

I grasped at straws. "How about I set you up on a date? I know a couple of great guys."

She blinked three times in a row, offended. “I don’t need dates. I turn them down all the time.”

My intentions were coming out all wrong. “I just want to see you happy.” After massaging her temples, she addressed the elephant in the room.

“*This* is as happy as I get.”

She laid it down between us. She loved once. And I was that once. So she only allowed herself to feel what I gave her. Which was friendship. God, more than friendship. Family.

My T.

“You’re better than what I do to the women up there. You’re 110% better than that.” I pointed in the direction of my bedroom.

After snorting, she rolled her eyes. “You’ll never get it. Your dick could fall off.” T advanced on me, pointing at my crotch. “I don’t feel the way I do because of this.” She flicked me on my bare chest, right above my heart. “It’s for this.” She looked up at me then. Young in the dim light thrown from the kitchen. “Can I go?”

“Of course.” I pressed against the wall and let her by. I watched her walk down the hall and then up the stairs, two at a time.

I was another person for her. She told me a long time ago that her mom wasn’t strong enough to be her mother, but that T was strong enough to be her daughter.

That’s how she saw me—I was betting. She was strong enough to love a man who tore her heart open on the regular because she knew none of these other women were staying. But she always would.

I looked at my feet.

I heard a low hiss.

“Bones. What are you doing up now?” My brother was shadowed in an alcove behind me.

"Getting my lady a drink 'cause I dehydrated her." He stepped closer.

"Wow, Albany's got a calling card." He waved his hand by his face.

"I didn't realize the whole damn family would be down here cooking Thanksgiving dinner at four in the damn morning." I followed Nix into the kitchen and sat at the island on a stool that creaked.

Nix filled up four glasses with ice and water from the fridge dispenser. He put two in front of me.

"One for you. One for her." He motioned in the direction of T's room with his chin.

I took mine and drank deeply, draining the whole thing.

"She doesn't want me up there now. I hurt her. Deep." I hadn't told Nix about the feelings that T had caught.

"She's something else." He wasn't interested in passing judgment. I knew he respected T as a professional. Trusted her. It wasn't something he did lightly.

"She's T." Stating the obvious.

"Yeah. You got stuff you're avoiding. You know it, and I know it. She's not just an employee." Nix drank.

"I never said that." I ran a finger down the condensation on the empty glass.

We looked at each other and silence came over us. I knew what he was trying to broach. It wasn't something I was interested in dealing with right now. I wasn't horny for Albany anymore, and I was grateful for that. I'd had the fruit she'd dangled. It was an empty feeling now, and I liked to be alone. Even as much as I loved Nix, there was a bit of a process I needed to go through after I was done with the ladies.

"I'm not trying to tell you how to live your life. It's not something I do. But that girl?" Nix pointed with his skeleton tatted finger toward T's room. "She's a game changer."

I watched hesitation cross his face. "Sweetness, say it. Tell me what you just thought. I can take it."

Nix clenched and unclenched his fist before responding. It was distinctly a battle for him. I wasn't sure if I was winning or losing with his next statement.

"If you aren't going to bring her in, then you should let her go."

I wasn't expecting that. My man—he'd light the whole world on fire for me—Nix was telling me I was doing T wrong.

I looked at my feet and let it sink in.

"Hey, I'm not trying to bring you down. I'm just saying I know how to watch. I've done it before. With Becca I watched. But at least I had the distance and a screen protecting me. I didn't have to be judged on the daily and found wanting. You know? T's here all the time and has to see what you're doing. She's got deep feelings for you. She's a stronger man than me."

He tossed me the joke at the end. To try to wash the salt from the wound. He was right. Goddamn it all if Nix wasn't right. Keeping her here was selfish. Damn near torturous.

After pushing the water toward me, he advised, "Maybe wash your face and go take her this. Talk to her. You both deserve it."

I twisted the glass in my hand. "Okay, I will."

Nix touched Becca's water glass to the one he'd poured for T and walked past me to go back to his lady.

I did as he recommended and spent some time at the kitchen sink cleaning up, then I took the glass to T's room. The door appeared to be closed so I rapped on it. It swung open from the force. The window was open, but that wasn't unusual. T was gone, though. I walked into her room and set the glass down on the side table. Her bathroom was neat and empty.

It was this way with us. She needed space to think. To breathe.

I missed her. I wasn't sure what the hell I was going to do. If I could let her go again...

34

I knew he didn't really want to hurt me. Not really. But it did. Maybe he had to punish me for loving him like I did. I didn't have Albany's tricks. She could attract a whole room. I never developed the talent that some girls had. The way they could rope in men like a fishermen's bounty with dynamite.

This was the outcome for loving like I did. There was no plan B. I'd bury myself in the disappointment and power through. I knew how to do it.

I walked down the path in the backyard late at night. I took this walk when I needed to be away from walls. From people.

I heard the twig snap behind me and I stepped quietly behind a tree. I had my blade with me and my focus narrowed to a point.

Instant defense. Automatic offense if it was required.

I took a peek. It was Ember. She looked spooked, but she still kept walking down the path I had taken. She was following me.

"T?" she whisper-yelled.

I stepped out. "Here."

Ember jumped a foot in the air and put her hand on her chest. "Fester shit!"

I started laughing because it was the last curse I ever imagined coming out of her mouth.

She started laughing with me, possibly from the jump scare.

"*You* were following me, and *you're* scared?" I watched as she made sure that it was really me in the dark.

"You were creeping out in the middle of the night. I wanted to see what was going down." Ember looked over her shoulder.

"Why are you up now? You should be in bed." I moved my hair behind my ear. I liked Ember. She had a fire about her. And she seemed a little lost. Reminded me of me.

"I couldn't sleep. I saw that Animal brought just one lady home and I was curious."

I was, too. Albany had stirred something in him that allowed him to be alone with her. It terrified me.

Because I could handle him being a ladies' man. None of them threatened my place in his life, though I hated the intimacy I didn't have with him. But one girl? That could be an issue. I didn't know how I could make that okay in my head.

And Albany of all people. It was a slap in the face and in the heart at the same time. I could rail at the way it was, but I knew the day I watched him walk into prom with two girls, and continued being devoted, I was in for it.

So in for it.

Ember was no fan as well. "I mean, usually he's got a herd of them with him. Like, what goes on up there? Does he pack them all on at once like a giant slut kabob?" She made elaborate hand motions.

I felt my jaw drop. "Slut kabob?"

"Yeah. Well, that's what I call them in my head." She shrugged.

"I like you, Ember." I rocked on my heels.

"So, where are you going?" She looked past me as if there was something waiting for me down the end of the path.

"Just getting out of there. Clearing my head." I put my hands in my hoodie pockets.

"Oh, okay, let me let you have at it then." Ember looked disappointed.

I considered her for a few seconds. She was trapped in this humongous place with people not really in her age group. Animal was busy trying to get her back home, and I understood that. It was to keep her safe. But still, I knew what it was like to feel like I didn't have a place that wanted me.

"You wanna come?" I pointed over my shoulder.

"Sure!" Her eagerness made me glad I asked.

We walked in silence for a short time before she started in with questions. "So, I know Nix thinks you're pretty kick-ass. Do you want to do this forever? Like be here with the guys?"

Ember was keeping up pretty well.

I answered, "I don't know. I don't think of forever much. Tomorrow, yes. Next year, sometimes. But forever isn't something I'm too sure I'll see." I held a long branch so it wouldn't slap her in the face.

"I feel like I think of forever a lot. I wish I knew what will happen." She took the branch from me and continued to follow.

"What are you trying for?" I was curious about her. I knew Ember was still taking college classes, but she was at odds with her aunt who had raised her.

"Well, I think my plan of getting Animal to fall madly in love with me has failed. I don't know. I feel like I just want to get to know Nix. But he's got his new relationship so I don't want to interrupt. I think I want to go into communications. Maybe be a newscaster or a model or something." Ember slowed her pace. "I really like taking pictures, and people say I'm pretty good at it."

"That sounds like a ton of different opportunities to be amazing in the future. Maybe just figure out how to get that degree," I offered. It seemed like good advice.

"Yeah. I just feel unsettled. Like I'm missing something." She trotted to keep up. "So I know you're a badass, but how'd you get that way?"

"Like, with fighting and stuff?" I was trying to figure out how much I should tell her. I mean, she's nineteen, a full-grown adult.

"Yeah."

"Well, I grew up homeless, pretty much. And I had to figure out how to fend for myself. After being on my own, I wanted to feel safe, so I made sure that I did. I took self-defense classes at first—because they were free— then I sort of sought out new experiences that would add to my bag of tricks."

That was a seriously glossed over summary. I left out all the freezing nights. The dangerous situations. How incredibly lonely it felt to stay true to my mother the only way I knew how.

Ember hauntingly resembled the two old, fuzzy pictures Nix had framed in his house of his mom. Pictures didn't capture vivaciousness. I wondered if that had been the same for his mom like it was in Ember.

She would be like Albany someday. Able to bat her eyes and have the men run to her. I hoped she found her soul mate before that happened, because it had to be confusing to come into your own with that much power over the opposite sex.

"You've fought for everything you have, huh?" Ember saw through to the parts I'd edited out.

I changed the topic. I never liked talking that much in general, and certainly not about my past. "What about you? How's life with Dorothy?"

"It wasn't hard like it was for Nix. I mean, he felt like he needed to hide his face from the whole world and himself. But it wasn't easy. Dorothy wants a lot of stuff she doesn't have. I think she lived to show me off as a daughter and then write me off after the doors closed behind us. She wasn't my mom." Ember grew quiet.

We were as far as I intended to get, so we turned around to head back. "What's Dorothy doing now that you're here?"

Ember sighed. "She's pissed. She wants me back at the house. And I feel like that's part of my responsibility, but it's way, way cooler here. I mean, this house. The vibe of it. It's really great."

I was sure there were worse influences out there in the world, but a house with a gun range and full-scale surveillance was not a Disney playhouse either.

"You got to do what makes you happy. I think anyway." That was the best I could offer, if that was even what she was asking for.

"Yeah, I'm trying that. My aunt has said some real strange things lately. Almost like she wants me to get married or something?" Ember followed me back onto Nix's property. The lights were on and Nix was standing on the back porch.

I waved and the man nodded in my direction. Ember gave me a confused look. "What the hell?"

"He's got cameras everywhere. And most likely tracks your phone." "So, he'd be okay if I went out for a walk in the middle of the night?" "Well, technically, it's morning and I think he was watching me as well. He knew you were with me and that I'd keep a lookout." It was the truth. I figured he'd known.

Nix basically raised himself to be a stalker; he probably did it without even thinking about it.

We walked in the back door, because the sneak part had been completely eliminated. Nix met us on the back steps.

"Hey."

I waved to him and moved past. His conversation with Ember was sweet. He spoke to her in a very respectful way, asking her to let him know if she was heading out—no matter what time.

Soon they were out of earshot. I wished I'd had a brother like Nix. He was supportive and understanding, but still protective.

I wondered if letting Ember have a relationship with Nix was actually the right move. Especially if her aunt was starting to act all medieval about weddings. I'd have to mention it to Becca. I knew she'd complained a few times about the pressure her mother used to put on her about getting married before she'd added her skull tattoo to her face.

I wished my walk had settled the restlessness in my heart. I avoided Animal when I saw he was in the living room and went to my room alone.

35

Animal

Nix told me when the girls got back from their walk, and I left the living room when I realized T had deliberately avoided me. After that, I stayed in my room, cleaning it. T's eyes pierced me when she saw through me. It was a burden I didn't deserve, knowing that she loved me.

I stripped the sheets off my bed and replaced them with fresh linens. The whole scene with Albany didn't sit right. I shouldn't have succumbed to her. I'd listened to my base instinct.

When my room was straight, I sat on the bed and ran my

hand over it. I wanted T here. I was lying to myself thinking otherwise, and I hated when I was a punk like that.

I wasn't ready to be that intimate. Sex was one thing. But to bring T here —she would be forever. How could I still be everything Nix needed if I had a partner who was...well T? She deserved to have the white picket fence. A normal Friday night with a bottle of wine and Netflix.

The farce was an enabler. I avoided getting like that with her to keep her safe and to keep my heart locked.

I didn't sleep that morning. I just flopped backwards and stared at the ceiling. I'd had sex for hours, but I wasn't even close to satisfied.

36

What I knew about Albany and her role in Breston increased. My focus was sharpened every time I pictured her waving at the camera before going in to fuck Animal.

He was out of the house by the time I was ready to go to the kitchen for coffee. Nix was gulping down a bottle of water, drenched in sweat. It was a fairly common sight. He worked out a great deal. Sometimes we would go on a jog together. I didn't say much, and he was happy to be quiet. He was a comfortable person to be around—once you got used to the skeleton ink.

"I need to get some deeper intel on her."

I didn't have to describe who it was. Nix knew I'd be after Albany. I didn't take seeking revenge lightly. Neither did he.

He put the cold bottle to the side of his neck. "I was going to show you what I'd come up with so far, if you want."

I put my index finger in the air as a way to indicate that I was interested. "Can I grab a shower first? Or is it urgent?" Nix turned his hips toward the stairs.

"Not urgent. Just important. Becca's at work, right? Where is he? Where's Ember?"

Nix clicked his tongue, letting me know I was right about Becca. "He's following Ember. She was going shopping."

"I'll meet you downstairs."

Nix was a hacker and a computer expert. I wasn't a slouch, but he was savant level accomplished.

I sat in the recliner that faced the few claw machines he had set up for Becca to play on when she had off time. Apparently, she was addicted.

He was down in less than five, the tank top and sweats damp in spots that let me know he didn't dry off completely in his haste to get down here.

He parked himself in front of the computer and pulled up some passcode protected files. "Breston is a fairly clean enterprise. They're wildly wealthy.

They have their name on everything from shampoo to prescription Proloc." I knew that much. They were a name brand and produced the latest antidepressant. Ironically, they made the drug I hated so much when I was teen. It was eventually recalled. Hell, they made my deodorant.

"Seems like Breston Sr. is in charge. And he's been grooming his son to take over the business someday. Of course, there are so many more people involved in that place. It's too extensive for one person to manage."

"So, why are they messing with us? With Animal?" I sat forward in the chair.

Nix put his index finger on his bottom lip. "I haven't figured that out yet. There's some chatter on the sites I visit, but whoever they have on their side's very good at hiding trails."

"Better than you?" I was curious if he'd admit defeat.

He looked slightly amused. "Depends on my motivation. How worried are you? Is this because they slept together, or do you have a new concern?" Maybe it was just that obvious—my devotion to Animal. I was like the dog that lies by the owner's gravesite forever. Pining. Loyal.

"He sleeps with a lot of girls. I handle it. But there's something sinister about her. I don't trust her. She has too much invested in this whole scenario, and I'm not sure why. She's tripped some signals for me. Do you not feel it?" I stood and cracked my knuckles. Albany just made me want to hit something.

"I don't like it either. He's trying to keep me out of shit, but I think we have to make sure he's protected. Sometimes when you're the king of the hill, you can't tell when someone's digging a tunnel underneath you." Nix turned back to the keyboard. "I'll find out as much as I can."

I stepped closer and squeezed his shoulder. "Thanks."

Maybe it was a personal vendetta now, but I could see her poisonous colors seeping out.

37

"Baby girl." I rolled up next to her in the Hummer as I turned down my music.

Ember's megawatt smile was blinding. "Hey, future husband." She had her headphones in and was carrying a bag from a local boutique.

"You up to trouble?" I checked in my rearview to be sure I was out of traffic.

"Every day I can be." She slid her sunglasses into her hair. She was rocking a high ponytail and bright red lips today.

"How about I give you a ride?" I leaned over and popped the door open.

"I only get in cars with strangers if they have candy." She licked her lips and I rolled my eyes.

"Get in, jailbait." She put her bag on the floor and climbed into the passenger seat.

"I'm perfectly legal. Legal to date. Legal to marry. Legal to..."

I put my hand over her mouth. "Stop. You're the equivalent of my younger cousin."

She kissed my palm with a loud swack and pulled the door closed.

I put the Hummer in drive and eased back into traffic. "Where you headed?"

Ember ignored the question and started opening the various compartments in the vehicle. I took breaks from watching the road and navigating traffic to keep closing the doors on her.

"You'll blow your head off if you open the wrong thing. Hands in your lap." I pulled one of her nosy paws off the console.

"Can I put them in yours instead?" She was laughing already at my headshake. I knew she was teasing me, but I sensed a little bit of a crush in her, too.

I was old for a girl like her. And Ember had oats to sew yet.

"I was going to hang out with Jet and Finn at that Speakeasy Coffee Shop." She finally stopped fidgeting.

"They in school?" I clicked the blinker on, heading us in the direction she wanted to go.

"Nah. Jet thought about it, but never filled out the forms he needed to." She pulled her phone out and started texting.

"Sounds like Jet's a deadbeat." I passed judgment.

She snorted. "Well, maybe he wants to be in your line of work."

I glanced at her. That wasn't an off-the-cuff remark. She was seeking.

"Ember, I have a degree. And I want to get more. I think Doctor has a nice ring to it." I circled around the block, even though we were near the coffee shop. I'd wanted to have this conversation with her for a few weeks since she'd moved in.

"Damn. That's great. Good for you. You're a little bookworm. That's so cute." She blew a bubble and snapped it.

I looked over my sunglasses at her. "Nothing about me is cute, baby girl."

She gave me her full pout. "Promises, promises."

"You're trouble. You're living in my house, under my roof—for now. I need you to go back to school. The commute is reasonable. I don't want you wasting these years." I pulled into the coffee store parking lot and wrangled the Hummer into two spots. I pushed the lock button to reinforce the fact that we weren't done having this conversation yet.

"Really? I thought that was my brother's house?"

I pulled my sunglasses off and dialed Nix, setting the phone to speaker. I put my finger to my lips to encourage her to stay quiet.

"Yup, brother?" Nix answered the phone.

"Baby, who owns the house we live in?" I watched Ember as we both listened to Nix's reply.

"Joint custody. You and me. Unless you want it. Then it's all yours." Nix sounded like he might be at a gun range, with low pops in the background.

Ember clouded up at me and spoke, "Nix, I think you'd just agree to anything Animal says."

Nix laughed. "If Animal tells you something, just know I agree one hundred percent."

"Later, Bones." I ended the call and slid the phone into my pocket. "You happy?"

She huffed, "Yeah. Fine. I'll see if I can make up the work I've missed. Or at least enroll in some late starting classes."

"Another thing." I hit the lock button again as she reached for the handle.

"Come on!" She slapped the window.

"You're going to have protection. People know you're with us, which means that you need to be protected." I used my phone again to send a text to T. With as sexy as Ember was, I wasn't looking forward to setting up one of my men as her bodyguard. And T was literally the best I had. "She'll be here in five."

I watched Ember perk up. "T?"

I nodded.

"Oh, that's cool. I'll take that in a heartbeat. Can she take classes with me?" Ember was excited.

I frowned while I thought about it. If T hadn't graduated, I could find out what it would take for her to be enrolled. I knew she was intelligent, but I also didn't want to insult her with the offer. It made sense, though.

"You like T?" I folded my arms across my chest.

"Hell yeah. She's awesome. And she's not a chatterer. Like when she talks, it's real shit. I like her. I hope she doesn't find me too annoying?" Ember bit her bottom lip.

"I've known T a long time. She dislikes assholes. And you're a pain in the ass, but a nice one." I looked around the area and saw Ember's two friends in the coffee shop looking out. Jet had spotted us, but was pretending like he hadn't.

He was a young kid, but had street smarts. If he weren't involved with Ember, I would've probably dangled a few carrots his way to see if I could get him in my employ. If he was hanging around her, the less trouble he got in, the better.

I watched as a familiar Lincoln parked across the street. I

looked from Ember to the old man and back as he got out of his car.

This wasn't my intention, not today. Merck was crossing the road with a massive grin. Father and most likely daughter were about to meet, and there was no way of gracefully stopping it. Sometimes fate decided.

38

Animal

I told Ember to stay put and opened my driver's side door. I met Merck with a big bear hug. He aged well. Just looked a smidge wrinkled, hair a little thinner—but he was a good-looking guy still. We greeted each other and caught up quickly. I walked around the Hummer with him so we were standing on the sidewalk. I glanced around and saw T. She was waiting until I beckoned for her, seamlessly slipping into the look out task, keeping watch over me.

I could make out Ember's silhouette in the dark, tinted windows of the Hummer.

Merck seemed to be following my gaze. "You're lucky

you've got a cop on your side, because that tint is illegal, young man."

He was joking with me, the laughter coming easy. I wondered if Merck knew Ember was living with me. How much did he keep track of the little girl he was pretty sure was his?

I stepped to the side to block his view. "What've you been up to? I haven't seen you around?"

"Took Kinsey to see her family out west." His eyes took on the dull glaze that they usually did when he spoke of his wife. I believed in loyalty, but Merck's devotion to his loveless marriage was something I couldn't understand.

He might not know that Ember had left Dorothy's. Or maybe he assumed she was in college.

"Um. Hey, just a heads- up..."

The door behind me snapped ajar. I watched as Merck's jaw fell open. Nix had mentioned that Ember looked so much like his mom it was eerie at times. I heard him whisper Elise's name.

Ember slipped under my arm and kissed my cheek. "As much as I like being your prisoner, I have people to meet."

I didn't look at Ember but watched as Merck registered it all. That Ember was in my Hummer. That she was here. I saw confusion at the familiarity Ember and I had. I pulled her against my side when she went to move away.

It was time they met. "Ember, meet Merck. He's family to me."

I watched in my peripheral as Ember turned her face to his and put her attention on him. Pain and ache flashed in his eyes.

"Hey, Mr. Merck. Any friend of Animal's is a friend of mine. It's nice to meet you." She held out her hand for a shake.

Merck looked from her face to mine, and then down at her

hand like it was a snake. Ember looked from me to Merck as her hand hung there awkwardly.

I was just about to smooth the moment over with a joke, when Merck held out his hand and gently took hers in his.

I watched him swallow. He swayed a bit on his feet. T was behind him, just off to the side, as if she was waiting for a bus. But she knew what was going down. She'd put it all together.

He said nothing. Ember giggled, pumping his hand once. "Okay. Catch you around."

She slid between Merck and me and turned her back to him while she gave me a *what the hell* stare.

T watched as I nodded in Ember's direction. That was all I had to do. T would stay on Ember until I told her otherwise.

I stepped next to Merck and put my arm around his shoulder. "Hey, let's get in my vehicle."

He nodded at me, his face completely conflicted. I opened my passenger door and he got in.

After I was settled next to him, I let him process for a bit. We could see Ember at the table with her friends from where we were parked. She was animated and laughing.

Finally he spoke, "She looks just like her. *Just* like her."

"That's what Nix says, too." I folded my hands on the steering wheel. I'd stay with him until he was ready to move.

We sat in silence for a while as Merck indulged in watching her. The tinted windows gave him that freedom.

"All this time, I mean, you must have seen her?"

Vivacious. Ember lit the whole shop up. People turned their bodies toward her, like flowers to the sun.

T sat at a table a few down from the crew, watchful. It gave me peace to know she was on it. I could focus on Merck.

"I had to stop. When she was a kid, it hurt so much. And I was having a real problem not fighting for her. Getting involved." He rubbed his chin.

It wasn't for me to judge. He had to get by in whatever way made sense to him.

"I mean, what if I got involved and she wasn't mine? I just... shit, I've made mistakes. Maybe." He couldn't take his eyes off her.

"That girl would love a father."

I saw the future. This headstrong young lady getting to know the man next to me, who was harder on himself than he needed to be. He was a good man and put his neck on the line for me many times.

He looked at me like I'd said something shocking. "It's too late. She's grown."

I shrugged. I wasn't interested in telling him how to live his life. But this girl, Nix's sister, she was getting under my skin. Despite her big personality and confidence, I knew that she felt a touch lost. It made sense. She lived with an aunt. One that didn't seem to mother her up too much. She wasn't allowed to know her brother. Had no idea who her father was. Or if it was Nix's nightmare, deceased dad.

"It's never too late to love someone." I fiddled with my sunglasses.

We were quiet for another fifteen minutes before he spoke again, "How's her brother?"

"Nix is good. In love. Happy. It's nice."

I saw a smile inch up on his face. "That's nice. Kid deserves happy things. His mother wanted him to have good things."

"You know, you have an in with me. Whenever you want. I know you've always wanted a kid."

Merck's eyebrows drew together. "I have you."

I felt my heart kick-start. "Yeah, of course. But you could have her, too. She'd be lucky to know you. She's dropped out of school. I'm trying to force her back into it. Just a little guidance, you know?"

"I've been scared for so long—to screw up, maybe I can't imagine making it right." Merck rubbed his hands on his dad jeans.

"Come on now. You're a hero. You've protected this city for years and years. She'd be proud to know you. You want me to steal some hair from

her brush? She's living with Nix and me." I kind of regretted offering that because that felt like a betrayal of Ember.

He shook his head. "I always believed she was mine. I wouldn't need proof. I mean, if she wanted it, of course."

He was starting to think about it. And that was good.

"You want to come to dinner? Tell her in a safe space?" I snuck a peek at him and watched his familiar face go through a kaleidoscope of emotions.

I knew he thought about Kinsey, who was still with us despite all of the health issues she faced.

"I could come to dinner?" He was testing the thought out. I didn't want to seem too anxious.

I wanted Merck to have a win. And Ember was headstrong, but an open soul. I had suspicions that a reveal of information and identity would go well.

"Where's her aunt?" Merck was picturing all the different outcomes now, like a cop would.

"She's still at her house, pissed. She wants Ember to get married. She's mad that Ember's living with us." I put my sunglasses in the cup holder.

I watched as he weighed Aunt Dorothy's concerns while tilting his head back and forth.

I spared him from having to pass judgment. "We recognize it's not ideal. I've got T on her as security."

Merck snapped his head around. "T? The T? *Your* T?"

Then I was full-on grinning. "Yeah. She's back. We're cool.

She's... talented." I tried to remember that Merck was the other side of the law.

I pointed her out to Merck.

"Well, I'll be damned. That's wonderful news. I always liked T. Glad she's back." Merck grabbed my shoulder and squeezed.

"Yeah, it's great." I didn't bring up that I smashed her heart to smithereens on the regular like a fucking asshole. "How about Sunday? For dinner?"

"I think I can manage that. I'll have Kinsey's sister come sit with her." He looked terrified.

"Send me a text how you want it to go down. Do you want Nix and me to tell her, and then you show up—you want to be the one to tell her? Think on it. Don't decide now."

Merck inhaled and exhaled slowly.

"You really think this is a good move?" The old man put his hand on the door latch.

"I think it's going to be hard on you, because this is always hard on you, but I really believe it's best for Ember." And that was the truth. It was clear that Elise was the love of his life. The poorly timed love of his life.

"Okay, I'm there. For dinner, this Sunday."

I could virtually hear his nerves revving up, but it was good. This was good.

"It's a plan." I nodded as Merck exited the Hummer.

I'd put this in motion before checking with Nix, but it was a gut instinct.

Hopefully, it was the right one.

I met T's gaze. Even through the tinted windows she found me. I watched as she banged out a text and then looked at me again.

You cool?

I nodded and waved. I had to manage three more meetings before I got home. One loan shark was coming in early, wanting his payments too soon. Another pawnshop had been selling off stolen stuff from a recent rash of burglaries in a retirement community, and the last was a pimp who was beating one of the girls.

By the time I got home, T and Ember were there already. The loan shark now had a brand new broken femur and a newly rejuvenated sense of loyalty to me. The pawnshop owner sent me selfies in front of all the different addresses that Nix had hacked from the police report, returning the property that he still had in the store or cash taped to the inside of the mailboxes of the stuff he didn't have. And the pimp was currently trying his hand at being a mermaid. It wasn't going well when I left.

My reputation was carefully maintained. I wanted people to trust me and fear me in equal measure. So far, I was doing pretty goddamn well.

39

Merck had been texting me in the two days he had to stew about meeting Ember again. He hadn't changed his mind, but he wondered what to bring, what to wear, if he should provide a side dish.

It was sweet to see him so excited. When I approached Nix later in the evening after I got home to the girls, he was thoughtful for a while.

He asked my opinion, and I offered that I thought it was a good choice. Merck was a good dad. At least, from my standpoint. Nix brought up that having a cop in our house was a tricky situation. We wanted him not to be watched or tagged as our friend, and we didn't want our people to think we had switched sides at all.

We settled on letting T smuggle Merck in. And Merck had left it up to Nix and me to decide what to do about Ember. We debated the merits of telling her and then letting Merck reveal it.

In the end, we decided it wasn't fair to spring the news and the man on Ember in the same night.

It was late on Saturday when we all convened. Both Becca and T made themselves scarce. Nix and I had tipped them off to what was going down. They would be on standby if Ember needed some female interaction after the news we had for her.

Finally, when Nix and I had settled into the living room, Nix texted for Ember to drop downstairs.

She gave us both suspicious looks when she got to the living room and folded her legs crisscross on the sofa. "You've all been too nice to me lately. And now you're staring at me weird. What's going on? Are you kicking me out?"

Her phone was clutched in her hand. I had a thought. "You alone in that phone?"

"What do you mean?" She hugged it close to her.

"You don't have any of your friends on FaceTime or anything, right?" I waited to see what her body language told me. Sure enough, I was right. She pressed the buttons to show me that she was no longer broadcasting the discussion to God knows how many people.

"I'm in trouble, huh?" She was starting to shut down.

"Baby girl, no, we have news, though. And we're going to deliver it to you like people who care about you." I sat forward and put my elbows on my knees.

Nix nodded. "It's nothing scary."

Ember nodded and looked from Nix to me and back again. "Okay, I don't know what to expect, but okay."

I waited for Nix. I felt like the news should come from him. If she had questions about Merck, I would share.

"You and I, we might not have the same dad—which you've known." Ember's eyes grew wide.

"Well, it turns out, we know who Mom was involved with around the time you were conceived." Nix cleared his throat. "His name is Merck. Well, that's his last name. Animal said you met him the other day? His first name is Patrick."

I watched Ember carefully. She was holding her breath and seemed reluctant to blink. Ember pursed her lips and took all her blinks at once.

"He's a retired cop. Just retired this year—actually." Nix reached out and held Ember's hand.

She looked like she was trying to figure out a very hard math problem. Nix shrugged at me. "If you have any questions, we're here."

Ember pulled her hand away from Nix's and stood. "Wait. You know my father? How long have you known this?"

Nix stood as well. "A few years now."

I didn't like the turn this was taking and made sure I had some of the blame. "I've known since you were a kid."

"Oh. Sure." Her eyes filled with tears. She was mad. Really mad.

She seemed to start and stop a few questions before running her hands through her hair. "This is... something."

Her face was getting red and Nix gave me an alarmed look.

"So, today is the day I get to know what you both have known all this time?" Her voice was thick with the tears she wasn't shedding.

"Baby girl, it's just the way fate laid it out the other day. Merck's a great guy." I held out a hand to her. I was used to her sneaking hugs with me. That she would turn down the contact made me realize that this wasn't going to end well.

"Yeah, I've got to go." She turned and walked out of the living room.

"Shit," Nix and I said at the same moment.

We trotted after her. She went straight to her room and started to pack.

This was not what I'd pictured at all.

Nix stood in the doorway. Becca came into the hallway and stood off to the side, waiting to see if she could help. I didn't see T.

Ember was throwing things into the suitcase that she'd dragged into the house when she'd first arrived.

Nix tried to figure out how to approach her. "Listen, this is a shock—we get that—but what are you doing?"

She stopped with her back to us, clothes in each hand. We watched as her chest expanded with deep breaths.

When she turned to face us, she was composed. The tear tracks made a few pinstripes on her cheeks. "You knew this and didn't tell me. All this time, I've been thinking I'm part of this family." She walked slowly up to her brother, toe-to-toe. Nix looked broken. "And you knew who my dad was? And kept that from me?"

Nix slowly nodded. It was the truth.

"So, am I just a houseguest? A pet? I don't deserve to have that knowledge?" Ember made two fists and held them straight down.

I tried to help. "It's not like that at all. Nix loves you. We love you. And Merck—he hasn't wanted to interfere with your life..."

She turned to face me now. The betrayal was deep. I instantly felt how wrong it all was from her point of view.

"I never had my mother. Not a day that I can remember. I was six months old when she died. Sometimes, I try to pretend I can remember. Aunt Dorothy would tell me that I looked like her, so I'd look in the mirror and pretend to be her—tell me she loved me. That's how fucked up I was." She wiped at her tears that flowed freely now.

Nix held out his arms to her for a hug. Now that I was thinking about it, she was hugging him all the time she was here, too. And I knew my boy. Opening up for a hug was a huge deal for him.

She pointed at his chest. "I would have given anything —*anything*—to know you. To not be so, so alone." She took a second to sob before forcing herself to stop.

Ember backed up, turning to her suitcase and closing it. She didn't take time to zip it, just held it in her arms. "And he was out there? In this town? Has he always been in this town?"

She looked from Nix to me and back again. Nix nodded, arms still open.

He looked like he was going to cry, too.

Ember looked down at her suitcase. "I could've had a family. All this time."

Nix and I were blocking her doorway. She stepped closer to the exit. "Please let me leave. I'm done here."

Nix rolled his head to the side and dropped his arms, stepping to the side.

He was crushed.

I held out my arm. She wouldn't look at me. "Ember, you can't go. It's the middle of the night."

Her chin started to quiver, and then she quietly added, "You've been trying to get me to leave since I got here. Some wishes get granted, Animal."

I looked to Nix who nodded once, letting me know he wanted her to be allowed to make this decision.

She didn't even have shoes on as she slipped by me. She was on the phone on her way down the stairs. "Jet? Can you come get me? I'll be walking out on Route 8."

Becca stood in the hallway. Nix's jaw was twitching. He didn't want to break down, but Ember leaving was killing him.

I felt my phone buzz. A text from T.

I'm on her. I'll keep her in sight.

I showed my screen to Nix, who read it and handed it to Becca. Becca seemed to already know this was the plan.

"We figured." Becca handed me back my phone. I pounded out a quick reply to T. I saw Ember's canvas sneakers and grabbed them. Girls didn't leave my house like it was on fire. I took the stairs three at a time and snagged one of Nix's hoodies as well. I had to sprint to catch up to her, her suitcase dropping clothes on the driveway like she was leaving a trail on purpose.

I caught up to her and stopped in front of her. She was sobbing. I wanted to pick her up and bring her inside. I could overpower her, but that wouldn't be fair. I tossed Nix's hoodie over my shoulder.

I dropped to my knee and held out her left sneaker. She stared at it for a beat and then jammed her foot into it. I held out the right sneaker, and she did the same. I took the suitcase from her and stuffed the clothes that were falling out into it and zipped it up. Then I offered her the hoodie, and she slipped her arms in. I pulled the handle out of her suitcase. That way she could at least have shoes and some warmth, and her damn drawers would stop falling out as she walked.

"Ember, you don't have to go. Be mad here. Come in and throw stuff at us. Please."

After taking the handle, she maneuvered past me. I wanted to say more. Tell her that her brother was devoted to her. Crazy about her. He loved having her know him.

She looked over her shoulder and barely got the words out, "I thought we were friends."

I put my hand to my chest. I hadn't thought about this from her point of view. It had been a mistake to treat her like a privileged kid. She had a past that haunted her, too.

I let her walk away. Just before she was out of sight, T rolled her motorcycle past me, quietly following Ember.

I noticed T was packing heat and had a few knives with her. No one would hurt Ember. I turned and went back inside. Nix was in the foyer waiting. When I came back in alone, he stood rigid for a second and then put his fist through the wall.

40

Animal

I called Merck to tell him the bad news. He slayed me with his understanding. He told me he would just save the presents he had for Ember in case she ever did want to meet him.

Nix was a goddamn basketcase. I knew he was getting updates from T, who was tailing Ember better than a pile of CIA agents.

But it was sad in the house. Sad without her. The first night she'd spent at Jet's house. She'd snuck in through his bedroom window. I thought Nix's head would pop off. Ember was with a girlfriend the second night. The third night, she was at another friend's.

"She's fucking homeless. My sister is homeless." Nix had punched at least five more holes in the walls. He wasn't dealing with things well.

Becca did her best. She offered to go speak to Ember, but she had a hunch that Ember might not take the news that everyone had stayed away all this time very well.

I kept up our business. I met with the Feybis who were complaining about a Kaleotos encroaching on their territory. I beat some heads. I met with the Kaleotos. Compromising between the two families sometimes felt like handing a bunch of middle schoolers' weapons. Sometimes they just had to be forced to face each other and hash it out.

On my way home, I passed the bad part of town that Debra, Helena, and T hung around back in the day.

I saw Ember's brown hair with streaks in the center of a group of guys. She was laughing and smoking a cigarette under a streetlight.

I parked a block away and got out of the Hummer.

If Ember saw me, she played like she hadn't. I knew T was somewhere close, but I couldn't see her.

I was just about to text you.

I looked at T's message and leaned against a car. The group couldn't see me, but I could make out some of the words they were saying and Ember's giggles.

I sent T a question mark.

Her friend dropped her off down here. I don't like this crew.

I was ready to go in and bang some heads.

She's taking some risks.

I sighed. Ember was hurting and wanted to numb that.

Stay hidden. I don't want her to know she's being followed.

I slid my phone into my pocket. As the group came into view, the tone changed. Ember's laughter went from flirty to a little shrill.

I saw the hand motions of the punks in a circle around her. They were up to something. Ember was in over her head.

The one with a slouchy hat went low behind her and picked her up. The one across from them grabbed her ankles. The cigarette tumbled from her hands. Her laughter went to a quick screech.

Another put his hand over her mouth. He yelped as she obviously bit him.

I saw T headed at me. She hadn't listened, but as the situation escalated, I wasn't sad to have her with me.

I hit the mouth cover expert with one quick punch to the back of his neck. He went down like an empty sack.

These guys were used to trouble, because they were ready to fight immediately. They didn't know that T was there, and she was double fisted with Tasers. Between the current she launched at two of the men, and with the knee-swipe-punch combo, she had three men on the ground before they knew they should be scared of her.

I had dropped one, but we still had two left. And they were holding Ember.

To her credit, she was struggling like a beast. I came low and lifted Ember away from them. I set her on her feet as the one who held her ankles took a swing at my head.

I ducked, so it was just a brush of knuckles, but what sounded like a wildcat ripped through the night.

T. I turned and put myself between Ember and the guys in time to see T decimate them. She was like a choreographer of pain. There were cracking bones and demoralizing punches. I didn't even have to help her.

"Shit, girl."

I turned to see a shocked Ember staring at the groaning bodies.

T detached the Taser wires and took the weapons with her. I grabbed Ember's hand and made sure I had T.

We double-timed it to the Hummer, and then we were rolling out. I glanced at Ember as we passed under some lights. She looked embarrassed. I wasn't taking her back to her girlfriend's. I wasn't taking her to Jet's. I had one option if she wasn't willing to come home with me.

"You want to come home? Or otherwise I'm taking you back to your aunt's."

She gave me a dirty look as I announced my intentions then she nodded once. T was in the back seat. I knew she was forcing the situation, making sure Ember and I sat next to each other. I had about ten minutes to make a difference.

"Ember, Nix misses you. We all miss you," I started with honesty.

I was wrong in assuming she was just a kid, because she had true insight. It wasn't fair to assume she was unaffected by her situation just because she'd had a person to stay with.

Ember tapped on the glass with her pinkie. "You know, I think a lot of people make choices for me. Decide what I can handle. Decide what I need. More than I know."

"We care," I interrupted.

She looked at me without the flirty teasing. Just betrayal. "You knew who my dad could be, and you sat with me how many times and that information wasn't on your tongue? Do you know how that makes me feel?" Ember twirled her long hair into a loose ponytail and then pulled it over her shoulder. "Expendable."

"It's not like that. You're right. We should have told you. Your brother and I both think of you as the little girl that was better off being separated from Nix's life." I turned toward her aunt's house. "Nix's father was not a good man. He was dangerous. That's what we were perseverating on. Not trying to make you feel like less."

Ember lifted her shoulders and her eyebrows at the same time. "That settles it then. Good job. You were right. Now take me back to my aunt's, the place I left on purpose."

"Will you come back?" That was my preference, if that was an option for her. Maybe I hadn't been clear.

"Nah. I'm nobody's burden. I can take care of myself. And I *will* take care of myself. You can tell T to stop following me, too." Ember grabbed the door handle.

I glanced in the rearview mirror. T's face registered the rejection, and we met our gaze in the reflection.

It was hard to be in the wrong. Ember had a lot of great points, but her life was influenced by Nix's decisions and mine.

"Baby girl, we can't leave you unprotected. I'm sorry. You can be as independent as you want, but we're watching you. We can't have one of our associates pick you up and do you harm to get to us." I parked in front of Dorothy's house.

She turned to me. "So, you and Nix, you get to decide to be whatever you are that makes money. That needs guns, that needs scary meetings, and I just get to reap the benefits of that?" She used air quotes around the word "reap".

"Life isn't fair." I had no good response, really. It had to be this way, even if she was pissed about it.

Ember popped the door open and shook her head. "Leave

me alone. I want out. I don't need anyone." She stomped up her aunt's driveway. I watched as she knocked on the door. It took a while, but her aunt appeared and waved Ember inside.

She at least had a place to stay that Nix had wired with cameras.

T opened her door. She put her hand on my shoulder before appointing herself the job as Ember's guardian. "That crew will be watching for her. Tonight wasn't good."

"Thanks, T. I'll see if I can get out ahead of it and see if the assholes are talking about her. Stay safe." I patted her hand once, and then she was gone.

T's years as a homeless person gave her the heartbreaking knowledge of how to stay outside for extended periods of time. It couldn't stay like this indefinitely. I needed T on bigger jobs and as my confidant.

41

I was an insomniac. A hidden talent. When I was a teen, I was able to stay awake for days at a time. If I didn't take anything to sleep, my eyes just wouldn't close on their own. So watching Ember was as simple as skipping my dose of Benadryl and Melatonin.

As a kid, I'd lie awake watching my mother make horrible decisions. I knew now that it was her illness making her swing from one task to another without being able to focus. She'd start to bake a cake, then walk away from the oven to paint a mural on a wall.

I remembered burning myself on a black, smoking cake as I

pulled it out of the oven with a bath towel. I forgot how old I was, but I ran my hand under cold water after dragging a chair over to the sink, and I knew then I was the adult in the situation. Not in those exact words, of course. But I realized that I was in charge. Not tall enough to reach the sink, but I knew not to walk away from a hot oven.

People who knew us would always exclaim that I was old for my age. There was a parade of neighbors and friends who helped. Their names would blend together. I should be thankful for the adults who stepped up when they saw my mother and I struggling, but I was just trying to survive and find good things to look forward to the next day. At night in my bed after Mom crashed, I would whisper out loud, "Tomorrow will be a better day."

I shuffled my feet as I settled into the trees alongside of Ember and her aunt's house. I wanted to make sure that none of the men who had been part of messing with Ember would follow her here.

I'd stay until morning or later if I had to.

Animal and Nix were men. In their eyes Ember had it all. A roof. No one hitting her. I was sure they pictured love.

But I had empathy for a girl who felt alone in a world full of adults making choices for her.

I watched as a light came on in Ember's room. Her curtains were pulled back, and I felt a pang of empathy when she fell onto her bed crying.

42

For days I watched her. Absorbing from a distance as she fought with her aunt. Judging from the body language, Aunt Dorothy didn't have a lot of gumption in her gut. Ember was rebelling, maybe a late start on her teens. Maybe her brother's alternative lifestyle had started a fire in her.

She had visitors. Jet had come by more than once. Her girlfriends came, and there were promises at the front door to stay in contact while they were away at college.

It's where Ember should be now. At a college miles and

miles away from this. From Nix, from Dorothy. From my prying eyes.

Nix would send me updates on Ember's cyber searches. It was invasive and creepy, but it was how he maintained his illusion of control.

Nix had baggage—that much was obvious—but we all did. Hell, I was making do in the woods by Ember's house because I loved a man who wouldn't love me back in my lifetime. That was its very own season of a reality TV show.

Animal showed up with an earpiece and a listening device. A duffle bag of more clothes and food, too. He looked haunted and stayed to chat for a while. He missed me, I could tell. It messed with my head and my heart.

When night descended at Dorothy's, I snuck in and installed the device in Ember's room. Everyone had slept soundly through the break-in.

After I relayed that to Nix, Dorothy conveniently won an alarm system that he could control from his basement. We had both eyes and ears on her now, adding to the previous coverage.

Ember was getting restless, though. Her aunt was mentioning her getting a job at least once a day.

When Ember got the message that changed her world and ours, I had just finished texting Animal to check on Nix. He hadn't responded to my messages, and usually texting with him was lightning fast. His brain was plugged into his computer and phone.

Ember started screaming, and I blew my cover and took off running.

43

I knew what we did every day was dangerous. Shit, we'd been in enough fights that coming home alive wasn't a guarantee. But this was too much. I never pictured this.

Overconfident, I guess I was. I figured we'd either kill or be killed. Seeing Nix being tortured rocked my core. Shook my brain. And it made me feel more helpless than I'd ever felt in my life.

The videotext that had come on Ember's phone depicted Nix strapped to a chair. Electrodes were taped to his head and chest.

He was hit with voltage, and a scream ripped from his mouth that seemingly was sheer reflex.

Then the video cut out.

T's jaw was tense, and her eyes had a wild gleam to them. She was worried. I was worried.

"How's Ember?"

I was trying to think of Nix's girls because he'd want me to think of them.

"Wardon is with Ember. I have two on Christina and three on Becca." "Okay. That's out of the way. Do we know where this is? Who is doing this?"

I tried to make a clear thought happen. My mind screamed.

T pulled on my forearm and led me to the basement. She went to Nix's computer and brought up an application. She had the password. While she worked, she informed.

"Nix and I have been following Albany and Breston Pharmaceuticals. Recently, he found a split between the father and brother and Albany. Nix tapped into a warehouse that he thought belonged to her. We talked about it the other day. The place is outside of town, by the river. It has an inordinate amount of cameras."

She pulled up the feeds that she had, but most of them were dark.

"We need to get Van over here to see if he can get these going. See if we can get a location, at least."

Van was one of our tech guys. He'd apprenticed under Nix a time or two. Not nearly enough for me to trust him with Nix's life, but this was what we had to deal with.

I fired off a text demanding that he show up.

"I've got to go. I need to leave now." I didn't have a plan and was too worried to make one.

"We have to make sure there's a way to get him out. You

both dead helps no one." T had her hands on my shoulders, the fingers biting into the muscles there.

T forced me to sit in front of the other computer. She pulled up a still shot of Nix taken from Ember's phone. "Tell me how you would get out of this. Clear your mind. How would you find him? Look at the picture. Look past Nix, see what the room has, what they are doing to him."

I did look. And my mind crumpled. T was on the phone and typing on two other computers on the opposite side of the room. She was able to put one foot in front of the other.

But to lose Nix. I couldn't. I just couldn't. I knew he was counting on me. Even if he didn't admit it to himself, his heart was hoping I would know what to do. I was big. I was strong. I fixed all his stuff.

T was onto a new conversation, using Google Translate to talk to a foreign person on the phone. It all seemed like a nightmare.

She pointed at my computer, and new video was air dropped in.

Okay. I had to contribute. Panicking like a little old lady wasn't helping. I looked from the blueprints to the room and back. They had access to water. They were using some sort of mask to drown him almost to death.

I felt the pain in my lungs—sympathy pain. It would hurt so much. Focus. They had electrodes hooked to his head, his chest. They needed to have a feeder for that. It would be specially wired. Being shocked was inhumane. Horrible.

"Tell us about Havoc?" I played the audio. There was no accent from the inquisitor.

Nix answered with a smirk, "Fuck You in the Asshole with a Cactus." They strapped the mask on him again. I raged at the image of the fear in his eyes. He was scared.

I made my hands into fists and slammed them on either

side of the computer. I felt her hand on my shoulder, comforting me.

"We'll get him out. You know we will."

Sure. She was so sure. She believed in me. Refused to do anything but, actually.

She concluded the two conversations and pulled a chair up next to mine. "I think we can do it this way. We have to get in. We don't have time to educate an army. We'll have them on standby. We have to sneak inside. Do we have some fuses for some timed bombs or explosives? Can you make me some that have a stretch of time on the fuse?"

I faced the blueprints and the picture again. Nix needed me to get him out. That much was for sure.

And I could do it. Implement some of the things that T was suggesting. I could maybe—maybe defeat the men in the room and get him out. I could get Nix out of the compound. The plan clicked in my mind like it had been in there the whole time.

Maybe that's why I had to come to terms with putting it together. I could get Nix out, but when I saved him, I would be taking his place.

And that's exactly what I had to do. I turned to this beautiful, badass woman, and I laid out my plan. She listened without judgment. She knew me that well. That I would die to save this man was a given.

I respected her more for not fighting me on it. My T. I started making a few calls of my own. I knew a guy who could get me the fuses T suggested in no time.

All I needed was a Trojan horse to get me in the front door and T in a boat out in the river behind the compound.

I'd come by water, and Nix and T would leave by it. Breston would be thrilled to have me—after I'd killed as many of those pharma heads as I could—that they would drop their interest in Nix long enough for T to get Becca, Ember, her mother, and

Merck out of town. Between all of us, we had enough money to live two very lovely lifetimes. I mean, they had enough.

I would not live through the night. T nodded somberly when I told her how it was all going to go down.

The preparations took four hours. Every minute made me angsty. I had to explain to Becca that she needed to be ready to get Nix to the hospital. I had my guy drive her in my fastest car. T double-checked they both had each other's burner numbers.

If everything went as planned, it would take me about forty-five minutes to walk through the room they were torturing Nix in. He had to make it. I had to believe in his inherent toughness. He'd taken more shit than anyone. His father had prepped him his whole childhood to handle pain.

T and I set up everything we needed. I made sure she knew where my Will was. Where my hidden funds were. The closer we got to go time, I was ready. I wanted to save my boy. I texted the attackers on Ember's phone, after they would not pick up a phone call.

I need proof of life.

I wasn't sure they would comply. They weren't asking for a ransom. Yet. Which was good. They'd need him alive to ask for that. Unless the entire reason they took him was to break me. They were already succeeding there.

As T and I made our final choices in the weapons room in the basement, I saw my man. The video had a man in a hazmat suit holding up an iPad with the time prominently displayed.

It was current. Nix was bruised and battered. Alive, but hanging from rubber chains. The video bounced around on purpose. I was still taking notes mentally of what I would face when I got there.

My first thought was that we were being attacked when I

felt the needle slide into my neck. I swatted at it and turned. The only thing that stopped me from throwing a punch was T's determined face. She was just finishing up pressing the plunger and pulled out the syringe.

She helped me to the floor as best she could, but I was a lot of man at the whims of gravity.

She was taking me out of the picture. As she handcuffed me, I tried to talk, but I knew the fast-acting bullshit we kept in those needles had already started their process.

I was a hostage in my body and in Nix's house.

I wanted to holler at her. That she was going to get killed. That she was going to get Nix killed.

But she already knew that. She didn't need my words. I watched her through a hazy focus as she pressed a kiss to my lips.

No speech. No hype up. My T was low-key going out on my suicide mission.

She threw a sniper rifle over her shoulder and walked out the door.

Then I fell into the deepest sleep of my life, filled with concern.

44

These bastards were better than the average assholes I'd dealt with in the past. They were intelligent. They had thought about the ways I could get out of their grasp. I was still working on an exit plan, but the small cement room that I was being held in was windowless. I was hanging from the ceiling. They had thick rubber worked into a chain. These chains were around my wrists in such an elaborate way, my double-jointed fingers were no use.

They were using electricity and water alternately as the method of torture. They knew what they were doing on a molecular level. These fuckers were industrial.

I was coming to terms that I wasn't going to make it out of here. They wanted me to flip on Animal. Turn on Animal.

Not in a million years.

Not even for Becca.

I'd been in a ton of shitty situations in my life, and I'd gotten out of all of them pretty much on my own.

I was under my bed watching when my father killed my mother when I was a child. I'd been captured on purpose as an adult and had to get out of that, too. It made me think—obviously erroneously. They were going for the water again.

The system for drowning me looked very similar to an oxygen mask, but did the exact opposite.

My shoulders were stretched way past the point of use. The muscles were like warm taffy. I realized that they were having trouble getting the water mask on me because I was heaving out groans. The pain was incredible. Tears were sliding down my face and insultingly going up my nose when I sucked in precious oxygen. I was being gluttonous with the air because soon it would be gone. Getting any extra moisture up my nose pissed me off.

I wondered where Animal was. I knew Ember was safe with him. I had to believe that. And that he would get her far away.

The men were in white zip-up jumpsuits, like I was hazardous waste. They were the kind of professionals who knew exactly how to kill a man because they read it in a textbook and performed it on cadavers before ever implementing the torture on a living person.

There was a knock on the door.

I watched as the tallest of the four pulled off his safety glasses. "What's this?"

He met the gaze of all the others in the room. Everyone shrugged.

The tall one hit the intercom on the wall, but there was no response.

The soft knock sounded again. The shorter man walked over and looked through the peephole. "It's a chick."

I kept my eyes on the tallest one. He had the contraption it took to get my arms out of the elaborate rubber chains that were hanging me from the ceiling. Just the tips of my toes were touching the cement floor.

The shorter one swung open the latch and pushed open the lock.

The door swung out, and the girl was admitted. I tried to get my eyes to focus on her. I fully expected it to be Albany, Animal's nemesis.

The black heels were ankle cracking-ly tall. The legs were nice. The black dress was painted on. Her face was classically stunning, the makeup obviously professionally applied. Her hair was swept up off the back of her neck. I looked at the face for a few beats before I placed her. I made sure not to show my surprise.

T.

T looked like a mix of a model and royalty. She had a thick silver band as a necklace and a matching one on her wrist.

"I'm sorry? I think I came into the wrong room? I was with Mr. Feybi and just wanted to pop into the powder room."

She put one hand out, fingers in the air like she was offended by the obvious stench and sweat in the small room.

"You went the wrong way, gorgeous. Or maybe the right way. Feybi treating you right?"

My captors were smart, but they were still thugs and assholes.

T put her other hand on her chest, emphasizing her cleavage with her deep breaths.

I was slapped across the face and admonished. "Don't look at the lady, you freak."

"Is everything okay? Is he all right?" T playing dumb.

"He's one of the bad guys. He's done evil things. To children. And pregnant women. The worst of the worst. Deserves everything he's gotten and more."

"I feel so safe knowing you guys are here taking care of this kind of thing. Thank you."

I glanced up. I wasn't sure what the hell she was planning on. She wasn't armed, and I didn't see Animal.

I trusted her. I didn't doubt she was completely on my side. She needed me to be at the top of my game, and I was as close to dead as I'd ever been. I didn't even know if I could use my arms.

I swallowed the gag of sadness that hit me. Thinking of Becca, that we'd had so little time together. Thinking of Animal. He would take the loss deeply. Of me. Ember as well. What T was doing, I wasn't sure.

Water was trickling onto the floor. I closed one eye and tried to focus with my right one. The hose that supplied the water mask had a hole torn into it.

As I noticed the leak, so did the other men in the room.

"I'm sorry. That's my heel. I'm so klutzy." I think it was then that things were going to go down, and fast.

Despite the threat of another slap, I lifted my head and opened both eyes.

The men in the room felt the shift. She was not as she appeared.

The alarm started in the men in the room, but T knew it. She snatched the necklace off her neck and twisted it until it formed a blade. Her high heels were also weapons.

This was a girl who knew how to kill people. I was in pain,

half-dying, but I knew she'd win this battle. At least, the first wave of these four men.

She sank her heel into one man's abdomen, and the blood instantly expanded on his white jumpsuit.

Her necklace/blade took another man down, right across his throat. His blood spurt was more spectacular.

The man who grabbed her up from behind just helped her attack the tallest with a slash of her heels again. The last man's body language became more frantic. He grasped at T's throat. I tried to kick my leg out, but it was useless, just a meaningless effort. I had no way to get any leverage.

T was an obstetrician of death. She was incredibly capable at delivering it.

The last man didn't stand a chance. She hit him with the blade she hadn't dropped right into the center of his chest.

The electrodes that had been used to shock the fuck out of me lay on the nearby counter. They were attached to a powerful voltage.

Both T and I heard the pounding of Breston and/or Feybi soldiers coming our way. The door was closed and a pool of water was at our feet.

T finally addressed me, "Can you lift your feet?" I wasn't entirely sure.

She wasn't really asking, though. T ran to me and leaped up, grabbing the rubber chains above my wrists. I crunched my abs and lifted my feet out of the water.

Together we hang as she used one hand to toss her knife in the direction of the wire on the electrodes. As the door opened, the water spilled into the hallway. In the same instant, the wire touched the water.

We could feel the electricity zap through the water and hear the instantaneous screams of the men with their feet in the electrified water.

My legs started to fall despite my best efforts. I had been through too much.

We were chest to chest, and she used her legs to hook under my knees.

She was sheer strength, keeping me from touching the water.

The fuse in the room popped and the lights went out. T let my legs drop. It was wet, but we weren't dead. "You got to get out of here. I can't move."

I heard her splashing around in the dark, the hallway light giving just a hint at what the torture room contained.

She ignored me.

In a second I had a flashlight in my face, then it was aimed above me. T had the small light in her teeth while she worked out the release system.

I heard more voices. "T, go."

My voice was gruff and grumbly.

She got both locks undone, but let my hands stay up as she kicked a body out of the way to wheel over a table.

After she positioned it behind me, she totally ignored my directions.

Male voices were shouting and orders were being issued.

At least the water's electricity had subsided. If the power came back on, maybe T could live through that.

By the time she was done with me, she had me on the wheeled table and dragged it behind her. She kicked bodies out of the way, only pausing to grab guns. She put a machine gun on my stomach. I tried to flop my stretched arms in the right direction.

She tossed another gun from a dead man across her chest. She swung the table around her so she was pushing it.

I forced one hand to hold the trigger. "Lean left."

I sure as shit didn't want to shoot her dead by mistake.

T shifted her shoulders and I started shooting up the hallway behind us.

She kept running me down the hall and seemed to know the layout.

The place was a fortress, though. This was an exercise in futility.

She skidded us to a stop and made a quick right. The door wasn't locked, and behind it lay a line of about ten four-wheelers. Breston probably used them for grounds maintenance or security.

T acted like she and I had practiced this whole thing ten times before.

Her movements contained so much precision.

Instead of going straight out the door we had come in once she had the four-wheeler, she threw it in reverse.

"We're not going to make it." I was trying to get her to understand. Instead, she pulled my head to her chest and covered me as we flew backwards through the glass window.

"Shit!" We bounced clear of the building and halfway down the sprawling hill.

She pulled it to a stop despite the fact that we were starting to take fire. "Listen to me."

T grabbed my jaw. "I have to light a few fuses. I have a different way out, okay? You're going to go on this, and when you stop, you'll be near a boat. Take it through to the river. There's a cell phone taped under the steering wheel. Call Becca and tell her to track the phone."

She stopped her instructions to fire off some return volleys. "You hear me? I know you're messed up, but do this for her. And for him."

"Light the fuse. We'll go together."

She shook her head and threw the four-wheeler into

reverse. "Tell him I only love once." T jammed something down on the gas pedal and I was off.

The vehicle started the descent backwards. When it flew through the fence unhindered, I realized that the hole had been prepped for this very thing.

I grabbed the steering wheel and tried to keep it even, straight.

Sure enough, the four-wheeler drove into the river as far as it could go. I heard bombs going off back at the Breston building, one after another. The man in me wanted to go back and help T. The realist in me knew I was too injured to help. My eyesight was blurry, and I was the most tired I'd ever been in my life.

I had to believe that the woman who had the foresight to get me out of a cement room surrounded by an army had a solid plan and that she would get out. I had to listen to her. I had to force myself to float toward the boat, right where she said it would be.

I used my last bit of energy to fall into the boat close to the motor.

I pressed *start*, and thank God, it cranked easily. It was a fast boat, but I wasn't fit for driving. All I could think to do was reach for the phone. For Becca. The steering wheel was tied in place, and I was moving.

I flipped open the burner phone and Becca was the only contact. I hit her number.

"Nix? Nix?"

She was in a panic.

"It's me, love."

"Nix!" My name was a sob. I heard an alert tone on the phone, like Becca was getting a notification.

"Okay. Okay. I just got an email from T. It says to tell you to motor straight across the river. I can be at the dock. I have the directions. And it says that Animal is in the weapons cellar. Are you okay?"

I really loved the idea of seeing Becca again, but the phone and then my consciousness fell out of my grasp. There was only blackness.

45

I woke up and had to look around the room before I knew what was going on. Before I remembered what she had done to me. She'd sabotaged me in my own place and handcuffed me to the safe handle.

I sat and raged for what had to be forty minutes.

The weapons door flung open and a frazzled looking Wardon was there. The keys to the handcuffs were neatly hanging on the light switch and I waited while Wardon unlocked me.

I rubbed my wrists and shook my arms to get feeling back into them. "I need an update."

He handed me a phone. “Becca’s on this. She has Nix.”

I had no idea how that magic had happened. I stared hard at Wardon to try to gauge if he was lying. Nix had been so incredibly fucked that I had been on a suicide mission to Breston’s headquarters.

I put the phone to my ear. “Becs?”

“I’ve got him. We’re in the hospital. He’s been so hurt.” She had to stop talking for a moment. “But he’s here. He’s alive.”

“Nix escaped?”

I rubbed my head. It hurt so much.

“No. T. It was T. She set it up. Do you know where she is?”

Becca’s question echoed in my head. I handed the phone to Wardon and went to my room upstairs. My phone was still plugged into the charger. I had a text message from her.

> I’m sorry. I know you need him. And I need you to be happy. Just stay home. If you have him, just stay home.

I tried to call her, but the phone went to voice mail. I tried to text, but just emptiness responded.

My heart started to implode because I had the answers I sought. There was footage rolling in the basement.

I ran down the stairs. There were no working cameras on any screen. I couldn’t sit, but I dragged the red dot backwards. Seeing the past, the reason the cameras were off, was a gigantic set of explosions. I went slowly, looking for some sign of her, but my hand slipped.

The footage of Nix’s escape started with T walking into the room dressed to the nines. I sat hard as I watched her movements. An expert. A ballerina made of violence. She was exquisite. Faster, smarter than any of her enemies.

I flipped through the cameras to watch how they escaped. My man was so boneless, it was horrifying. T moved him around like she was born to do it. Eventually, I saw her speak to him, close to his face. Then he was in a vehicle going in reverse. She turned from his fleeing ATV and took on the gunman. The dark flashing with the gunfire. Bombs started. I saw one camera after another lose its feed.

She collapsed under the barrage of bullets.

My T.

I felt myself start to shake. She just lay there, motionless. She didn't move when the men came up to her. One kicked her beautiful body, and there was no reaction. The last camera to the outside, the one that was keeping a silent watchful vigil over T's body, cut out just as a man tried to pick her up.

I was putting it together, the horror of it. She'd saved Nix, and to do so, she'd sacrificed herself.

In the black screen I saw the TV on behind me.

Part of Nix's surveillance, knowing what was on the news, hearing the police scanner.

Explosions at BRESTON Pharmaceuticals.
Police Respond to Multiple Deadly Explosions!

I'd just watched my T die. It was a horrible time to realize that the sheering, gasping pain in my heart was my love for her finally being recognized.

My T.

She'd died saving Nix. She'd trapped me here so I wouldn't complete my suicide mission that I'd laid out with her.

My screaming started in a young place. The girl who would steal me a muffin just so she could watch me eat. She'd killed for me. She'd killed for Nix. Her beautiful brown eyes. I was so sure she would always protect herself, but I forgot that I was the ultimate weapon to her. For her. She'd do anything to make me happy. Or what she thought was happy. My soul was sliced in half. I felt the pain deeply. Without her I wasn't able to cope.

She was my family. My girl. My wife. My T. My greatest love. My only future.

46

I was going to live. I knew that much. The damage that had been done to my body would heal, but it would hurt the whole damn time. My doctor actually consulted with military paramedics to get tips on how best to deal with the recovery from the torture.

My beautiful Becca didn't leave my side. She was very, very angry with me. I took her fuming gratefully. Just to see her. Be with her. Love on her again. Have her hand touch mine. That this love wasn't over yet—I was so grateful.

But she was pissed. She was pissed that I had been captured. She was angry that I was incredibly fucked up. There was a haunted part of her that looked like she'd lost me, and I was sorry for that.

Animal looked a goddamn wreck when he made it in. I told the nurses to lay off the morphine when I heard he was popping in for a visit.

When he entered, Becca went up to him and slapped his giant arm, then gave him a hug. "Goddamn the two of you."

She pointed at us both, then she excused herself to go to the hospital cafeteria.

I'd never seen Animal with the light in his eyes so dim. He was muted. "How's T?"

I'd asked Becca a few times, and she'd tried to text T, but no answer. She reminded me that T had emailed her when I was in the boat, so she must have escaped as well.

Animal sat down like I had hit him with a bullet instead of a question. "Brother?"

I tried to sit up and was met with a wall of pain.

Animal rubbed his eyes over and over, then switched to rubbing his huge man paws on his thighs.

He tried to start a few sentences and stopped.

He was a mess.

This was bad.

This was very bad.

Animal was cool in crises.

"Where's T?" My throat was still raw from the waterboard style interrogation methods. It had only been less than twelve hours.

"She's dead. They shot her."

The room was engulfed in a backdraft of silence. Animal's shoulders started shaking.

"Come here. I can't get there. Come here." I patted the part of the bed near my hand.

Animal struggled to the floor, on his knees. He made his way to the side of my bed like he was praying.

I used the hand I could move as best I could to hook his head and pull him closer.

Animal put his forehead on the edge of my bed and sobbed.

Seeing the big man on his knees made my nose burn and my eyes water. All I could do was awkwardly pat his head.

"She told me to tell you something." It came back to me in a haze. Holy shit. She had been saying goodbye. She knew the second she hit the room I was in that she wasn't coming out alive that night. "Tell him I only love once."

Animal couldn't look at me, but he shook his head, as if hearing her message made it all worse.

He turned and sat on the floor, head in his hands. "I failed her. It was supposed to be me. She took my place."

T had saved my life and apparently Animal's as well.

We were two mobsters. Murderers. Assassins. But we cried in that hospital room together for a quiet girl who refused to let us pay for our sins.

47

Animal

Where she was supposed to be, she wasn't. I'd taken her for granted. I relived the night she told me she loved me a million times since I watched the footage of her getting killed.

How could I have possibly doubted how I felt about her?

If I could only have shown the me in the past a glimpse at the pain I was going through without her. The guilt that resounded in every step, every breath all day, every day without her, maybe I would've known.

A psychologist would have a field day with how easy I was to diagnose. I insisted on more than one woman at a time because I didn't want to feel vulnerable. I was an obvious fucker.

I was wasted. I'd been buoyant for so long, that when I deflated, I did it thoroughly.

Wardon was doing his best. But without T and Nix, my empire was sinking as well. There was a lot of upkeep that I normally had endless energy for. I wanted the hustle. I was hungry for the balance and the control.

But I was haunted now by the girl I loved.

God, I loved her so much. How could I have ever let her walk through this life not knowing that?

I stayed in my room and watched her last moments over and over. I watched her final gift to me. Saving Nix, saving me.

She only loved once. One mom. One man.

She could have been anything in this life. She survived the streets. She survived homelessness. Running a company would've been a piece of cake for her. She had a motherhood about her. God, she would've been an incredible mother. No one would fight harder for her kids.

The past tense thoughts made me ashamed that I was accepting that she was dead. Becca had broached the idea of a memorial service for T. I dismissed it. For a million selfish reasons. I didn't want to say good-bye. I didn't want to make it so real. Even Merck had stopped by to ask me what he could do. Nothing. Nothing was the only solution I had for everyone.

I thought of her mother and hung my head. I would watch over her. I'd make sure I outlived her mother so that she would always be taken care of.

There was a knock on my door. Ember entered despite the fact that I didn't answer.

"Oh, Animal. Look at you."

She was a teenager, but the empathy in her face was far deeper than her age should allow.

"Go home, punk." I had no bite in my words. No joking. Just flat. Ember went to the window and opened it. "Nix's coming home today. Do you want to shower? Get dressed?"

I closed my eyes to the bright light she let into my room.

"He can't wait to get out of the hospital. Says people keep dropping by to see his tats. He's like a mannequin in a store." Ember threw the bottles of alcohol into the trash can without talking about the fact that I don't drink. Didn't drink.

I'd started when I got home from visiting Nix.

The depression matched the way the booze made me feel, though time seemed longer on it.

Ember kicked the clothes on the floor into a pile. She walked into my bathroom and started the shower.

"I told you to leave." Maybe I was a mean drunk. Maybe I was just mean now.

Ember looked a little scared. I regarded her from the bed. I needed her out. She was here despite her deep anger at me for keeping the knowledge about Merck from her. That fight seemed like light years in the past now. I did my best to scare her away.

"Didn't you say you wanted to fuck me? Come on in. I don't have rules anymore. Let's go. You a virgin? I can take care of that for you."

She went from scared to angry in a hot minute. "Don't you talk like that! Not to me."

She stormed to the edge of my bed. If I'd been serious about scaring her, I would've pulled her onto me.

"My brother is on his way home. To this. To you. You're his best friend. Don't you dare think you'll make him feel guilty for being alive."

Ember flipped her hair and her eyes were fire. She was getting a rhythm.

"T didn't want you to make him feel like a trash bag for

living." The mention of her name was a tsunami of pain again. "Get out." I tried to make her go away.

Her anger flooded out of her. "You don't get to change. I count on you being you."

Her youth was shining again. The fear in her face.

"Life changes. People change. Get out. Go to your aunt's. You're not welcome here."

I watched as she came to the conclusion that she wasn't going to be able to fix this. Fix me. Make me better so that Nix could have a happy homecoming.

"Okay, that's how it is for you now. I see." She walked slowly to the doorway. Just before she could have been considered truly out of my room, she looked over her shoulder. "I needed you today. I have a thing that I'm not sure about..."

I shook my head. "Handle it yourself. It's what T would have done." My words were toxic, meant to harm.

They struck their mark. Ember left and closed the door behind her.

The only thing left was the steam escaping from my bathroom from the shower she'd started.

I closed my eyes and had regret. T would have been pissed if she'd seen me treat Ember that way. I forced myself to sit up. The room was spinning. The alcohol was still in my system. I'd shower. Give Ember that much. Give T that much. At least Ember was talking to me.

Maybe I'd make all my choices this way from now on. T's memory would be my jury.

48

Nix was home. I was showered. Ember had helped with her arrival and fighting, even though I was a tremendous dick to her.

I wish I had the will to fix it. I should've had the will to fix it. When I heard Becca pull the minivan into the garage, I opened the door and went to the passenger side.

I had to help him. Even with the dragging depression, I had to see my man walk into our home.

"Sweetness." I opened the passenger door. Nix grunted and tried to smile. "Hey. Glad to see you up." His voice was still hoarse. I bent low and wrapped an arm around his back. Becca walked around and made sure that the doors were open. It was a slow walk, but we made it to the couch.

I helped him sit and Becca brought an ottoman over for his feet. He made all kinds of horrible noises.

He should've been dead. I'd seen the video many times. Bones was a tough fuck. I knew that. I knew he was capable of turning off his nervous system and accepting injury.

Breston had done a job on him. A very scary job on him. We had a ton to discuss. I needed to participate in this life, take control again.

"I'm sorry." He was reading my internal dialogue. I put my elbows on my knees and covered my mouth with my index finger.

"Don't. You didn't do anything." I looked out the oversized window that displayed the beautiful forest. I pictured T taking walks out there to clear her head.

"If I hadn't been caught..."

Becca cleared her throat. "This has to stop with both of you. Blaming yourselves. You knew T. I knew her. She was going to fix it. That's what she did. She made things better for all of us, but especially you two." Becca stopped and her eyes filled up while I looked at her.

T was quiet, but she had a way of getting underneath everything.

Ember walked into the room. "She would've wanted you all to move on. Move past this. Do something else than what you're doing. Get out of this business."

I stood when I saw her enter the room. I held my arms out to her. "Baby girl, come here."

I knew I had to make her feel okay. Nix would kick me in my balls for hurting her. Shit, I was going to kick myself in the balls for it—as soon as I could feel anything other than numbness. She had come to visit both Nix and me. I doubt we were forgiven, but at least she still cared. I should be fostering that feeling.

She nodded the whole way into my arms.

I kissed her head. "I'm so sorry. You were right. It just hurts so much." Nix started to struggle, plainly wanting to man up and get in on the hugs.

Ember pushed away from me and sat cross-legged next to Nix in a smooth movement.

"Stay put. Traveling is exhausting. How are you doing?"

I watched as Bones reached for Ember's hand. "I'm sad. I feel weak. And I wish T wasn't gone."

Becca came close to me and put her arm around my waist. I put mine around her shoulders.

We were a puzzle missing a piece.

"Hey, Mrs. Bones. Can I ask you for a favor?" Becca patted my stomach. "Any tat you want."

"Thank you. It'll need to be big and painful." I wanted it to hurt the whole damn time.

"My specialty." Becca hugged me once more, then she went to sit next to Nix.

I needed time. I needed T. I had to look at the floor. I had not been grateful enough when it mattered.

49

Seeing Animal broken was horrible. His shoulders were slumped. The light in his eyes was diminished.

Having T gone was too much of a shock. She'd been a part of our every day. I liked cracking jokes with her, knowing I hit a good one when she finally smiled. While Becca rubbed my back gently and Ember held my hand—despite her anger with me—I thought about how T had pulled off the rescue of a lifetime.

She had been able to get into an impenetrable fortress and defeat an army all while wearing a pair of heels. The way she thought out the whole scenario—she was a goddamn genius.

She gave me my life. I felt like she wasn't gone. And I couldn't place why. I might have to pursue collecting her body to make it real. I had faced a great deal of death over the years, but this was the first time I had this nagging feeling.

I'd look at my footage from the surveillance. Animal was standing in the living room, but his mind was far away.

I wondered if he'd been watching the video. And then I knew he had. The way he had deep lines on his face. The way he'd cried in my hospital room.

Merck had come to visit me after Animal had left. I wondered about his timing, but it was clear he wanted to talk to me without my brother around. We'd tried to come up with ways to help this man we loved. We were both woefully inadequate at cheering Animal up. Giving him something to smile at again. The loss of T had changed everything that gave him genuine joy.

50

When I opened my eyes, I had to shut them immediately. The white of the room was blinding. I tried to concentrate on whatever I'd seen in the brief glance. I felt too...present to be dead. But as far as I knew, that's what I was.

I had aches and pains. In the distance I could hear machines. Monitoring noises. I opened my eyes very slowly, giving my pupils time to adjust.

The ceiling was white, but had those drop down tiles. The walls were white, but needed a touch-up in parts. The floor had white tiles with a light gray marbling through them. The blanket covering me was white as well. I moved my hands and felt restraints.

I didn't call out, because I didn't know where I was. I wanted the upper hand if I could get it in any way.

I'd gotten Nix onto the four-wheeler. He was in reverse when the first bomb detonated. The bomb that Animal had planned to plant, but I'd set instead.

I wanted to know how he was. Animal. Nix. Becca. Ember. My mom. All these people whom I cared about.

It was not lost on me that I was a loner that had a pack now. Well, had a pack then. Chances weren't good for me here. I went down in a hail of bullets. I couldn't move my torso, but this was different.

It felt like I was cemented into place. I had consciousness, though, so there was that.

A man in a lab coat walked in. He noted my open eyes and pulled out an iPad.

"And you're awake?" He didn't seem friendly.

The man was plain. He could have been a stock photo for "average guy".

"Yes." My voice worked at least.

"That's good. Can you move your feet?" He pointed with his pen at the bottom of the hospital bed I was in.

I couldn't move them. I tried again and again. "No." "That's good."

This made me reassess him. Something was wrong. He should have been disappointed. Maybe my gunshot wounds had paralyzed me.

My heart rate picked up and he noted it.

"Is not being able to move making you nervous?" He tilted his head.

I decided right then answering this man's questions were not in my best interest. I pushed my lips together.

"You'll note that it is very hard to conceal information right now. Do you find me handsome?"

My heart rate went even faster. The words felt like a cough in my throat. It was getting harder to hold on to them. Maybe this was a version of hypnotism?

"You're either pretty good at self-control or we need to up your dose." He walked to the IV hanging near the bed. The tubing snaked under the blanket that covered me. He made an adjustment.

He casually took more notes, checked my pupils, and made various observations under his breath.

After about ten minutes, he asked me the same questions. "Is not being able to move making you nervous?"

I wasn't answering. No way.

"No, it makes me angry." It was surreal to answer when I had no intention of doing so.

The man holding the iPad smirked and gave a thumbs-up to the wall-mounted mirror. A two-way mirror I realized. This man and I were not alone.

"Do you find me handsome?" He waited expectantly.

I knew my eyebrows were furrowed as I gave him what he wanted, "No, you're not my type."

"What is your type?" He opened his mouth as if my words were a treat he could eat.

"Animal. I only love once. So you're the wrong color, height, and most likely, dick size." I was brutally honest. Despite the sassy answer, I felt my rage sliding into fear.

The man's face registered the insult and he closed his mouth.

I was doing what he wanted. I couldn't move anything but my face. Where the hell was I?

"What is this place?" It was clearly not a hospital. He didn't care if I was well; he wanted me to be his guinea pig.

The door to the room opened again. When I saw Albany in a lab coat, certain things made sense.

"T, funny meeting you here." She took the iPad from the man. "She's responding well to the higher dose? Probably did a lot of drugs recreationally. Tolerance can be a bitch to break through." Her tall heels clacked as she walked around the bed. "Your vitals are great. You've been with us for a month now. We really get to know so much about you with this new treatment."

For a month? I'd been here a month. This might actually be a nightmare.

Maybe it was the afterlife—but hell instead of heaven.

"Feel free to say thank you whenever you want now. I was on the team that saved your life."

Again, my usually silent mouth betrayed me. "Fuck you."

Albany laughed. "Sweetheart, don't tempt me. As I was saying, I insisted they save you. You see, the board at Breston was very angry that you'd inflicted so much damage on their property. They weren't ready to be as forgiving as I was. But I noticed you, T. And I'm betting that I'm right. You know everything there is to know about Animal and Nix. And Ember. And Becca."

"I know everything there is to know." The words were like breathing, a reflex.

"You're disappointed in yourself. I can see it in your eyes." Albany put her bright red nail under my chin. I tried to bite it and she pulled her hand away, laughing. "Look at that! Did you see that?"

She faced the mirror on the wall. "Ready to fight even though she's paralyzed. She's exceptional. I do believe we found my protégé."

She turned back to me. "Don't be upset, darling. You're at almost double the dose that it would take to make a man

Animal's size talk. You're a soldier. Never mind that—a general. Is it inappropriate to say I have a huge girl boner for you?" She leaned over me and whispered, "Probably."

"What do you want this for?" I waited, because it was the only thing I could do.

She got a faraway look in her eyes. "It's lonely at the top, you know? All these assholes dragging their nutsacks around like they contain extra brains. I just want to see what we could do. You and my father and brother think they're the only ones that can make our company worthwhile. By the time I have this place up and running, I will be the one that they have to come to and not the other way around." She acted delighted with me like she was my kindergarten teacher. "And I think you and I would make a great power couple."

"You're insane." I tried to wiggle my feet again to no avail.

Albany looked hurt. "You'll come around. See it my way. I mean, there aren't any other choices, really."

I wanted to scream. I wanted to react to this nightmare. But she had a hunger in her eyes that I didn't want to feed. I swallowed my first response. I tried not to show that I had had a very small victory. If for some reason I could control my mouth on this drug, I could manipulate Albany and the situation and then get back to my pack.

51

Albany had other test patients, but she was fascinated with me. I wasn't sure if I was a new plaything or a science experiment. I was in a locked room that reminded me of the psych ward when I was a teenager. It was killing me, though my actual body was healing. I had the care of the best doctors in the world, or at least that was what Albany said.

I believed it when I saw how quickly my gunshot wounds healed. The physical therapist offered a combination of exercises, acupuncture, and electric therapy to get my range of motion back. There was even an herbalist that set up a vitamin, mineral, and protein mixture to speed up the healing.

A plastic surgeon used cutting edge lasers to neaten my scars. They would always be there, but far less obvious in a few years.

I had access to movies, books, some puzzles, and crafts.

I was alive, and I was fighting by not fighting. I remembered how Nix infiltrated the Feybis so he could get information and kill his enemy at the same time.

That was my modus operandi for now. It seemed better to have a plan. And Albany, for all her suaveness, seemed truly alone. I really didn't give a flying fuck about her, but I had to pretend to. It seemed clear that her brother and father had no designs on keeping me alive. But if I accepted her too quickly, she'd see through that as well. So I had to keep my head down and do what was asked. I had to bitch. I had to make a few half-hearted attempts at escape so they would believe me when I stopped trying to run for the open door. Even though it was actually painful to watch it close.

I was being watched at all times. Like prison. Like my worst nightmares. I recognized that I was in a very specific state of peril. And if everything had gone as I'd planned, no one would be looking for me.

They let me have a dull pencil and a pad of paper to draw about two months in. I couldn't stop myself. I drew Animal's face.

I just needed to see it, even if I had to pull his handsome face from my memory. I missed him. He was probably-knee deep in his slut kabob, with Ember giving him the business. When I heard someone coming down the hallway, I reluctantly scribbled over his image and flipped the page. Albany had to believe I was pissed at Animal and Nix. And not that I trusted them to miss me. That I knew that Animal and I would always be headed for each other no matter what had happened to us.

Albany was buzzed in. I talked myself out of poking her in the eye with the pencil. Momentary satisfaction would not get me free. I pushed the pencil into the tunnel the spiral on the notebook made.

She was dressed down in jeans and a white T-shirt today, black flats, and a ponytail. I wondered what was up. She was usually in full siren gear with false lashes and a push-up bra.

She was holding a piece of paper. I hid my irritation when she showed me a copy of the Animal image that she had copied.

"Screenshot of the surveillance, in case you're wondering." Albany smiled and sat next to me on the bed.

I wondered if she knew how many different ways I could kill her. So very many. I closed my eyes as the thought of her warm blood on my hands thrilled me.

"Sleepy?" Albany rubbed my back, running her nails over my spine. "What do you want?" I opened my eyes and pinned her with a frustrated gaze.

She took her hand off of me and smoothed her hair in her ponytail. "Just a friendship, that's all. I mean, I'm keeping you alive, healthy. If not for me and my family's talents, we'd have lost you."

She was narcissistic. I recognized it in the way she phrased her sentences. When I was a small kid, my mom was involved with a person just like Albany. A man named Brit. Mom was pretty and needy, and when she was on a high, there was no one more fascinating in the room. He could make everything about him and expected to be thanked for simple human actions.

"You're right about that. The care here has been pretty interesting," I said it begrudgingly. She was right, though. The crap they were using on me was stuff that only had numbers. Nothing looked like it would in a normal hospital.

"I've got some footage of the man of your dreams today." Albany tapped the paper between us with her red nail.

My throat dried up. I worked at not holding my breath.

"Don't get excited. He doesn't know you're alive." She stood and walked to the window, her back to me.

I was dizzy with the need to snap her neck.

"He's a mess." She looked over her shoulder at me. "If you were wondering."

I tried to borrow Nix's patience. I imagined him in the Feybis' place listening to this type of shit. Possible lies.

Albany was probably lying. I couldn't imagine why they would let her live.

I heard his voice next, and my soul stopped. Albany held up her phone. "No video, but this is audio my guy was able to catch."

The screen was black. Animal was in mid-conversation, and I tried to hear all the things I could between the words.

"Looking good." Animal's deep voice was like a syrup.

"I wish I could say the same to you, sailor. You look like shit." A woman's voice broke the beauty of the recording by just being there.

"I can handle myself." Animal again.

It was a weird clip. This audio had been edited. Still, it was his voice. I tried not to let the way it had been manipulated affect my psyche.

"You miss T?"

The background was slightly different, not as much ambient noise for her phrase.

"She was a legend. I knew I'd never have her forever."

And although it was altered—she was trying to change it—I heard him. I heard his pain, and I knew it was for me.

I kept my face even. Albany had to believe that I was buying the shit she was selling.

If that was recent, like she said, Animal was still okay. I had questions and I swallowed them whole.

"Anyway, I was just wondering if you had some pointers as far as Animal goes. I'm having trouble getting past the night we had together." Albany rocked back on her heels.

I lifted an eyebrow. This bitch had to be kidding. I averted my gaze so I could think of a response. I needed to keep her thinking that I was a pretty docile patient and that I was interested in the bullshit she was strewing around.

"Animal likes loyalty. Have someone offer him an olive branch by sharing information."

It was the best I could do. If I could sway Albany into bringing more intel to the guys, then that would be a good outcome.

"Wow, I think that was a genuine answer. We're growing a bit here, T." Albany left, her flats making hardly any sound on the tile floor of my room.

Little steps. One at a time until I could get out. Get back. Be where I needed to be. Hopefully, any contact from Breston would be a red flag after Nix's kidnapping.

52

A daily stroll with Albany was part of my routine now. I counted snipers as she shared her hopes and dreams. As magnetic as she was in person— especially the first time you met her—there was a shallow vapidness that eventually reared its head. She wanted her father to recognize her. She bitched about her brother trying to run the company. She complained about her situation.

She was the type of person who unloaded and never asked you how your day was. I pretended to be interested, asking questions about the worries from the previous day. Like all narcissists, she required reams of praise. And although I thought it was pretty obvious that I was playing her, Albany could never see it that way. She thought she was the center of my universe. And she thought she *should* be the center of everyone's universe.

Albany got chatty, because eventually she ran out of topics about herself and had to offer options on what was happening around her. She started telling me things, like new innovations Breston was working on besides the drug that had been tested on me. It was used to aid in my recovery, not just torture me. It had kept me still so I could heal quicker.

Every once in a while Albany would threaten me with the truth-telling portion of the drug, but the more I listened, the more she got to talk about herself. I didn't bolt when I started to get opportunities. That was a very tough part. But I remembered how successful Nix was. He was full of information from the time he was in with the Feybis.

Albany would tell me when she saw footage of Animal, claiming she was still sleeping with him from time to time. I doubted it. There was a falseness in her claims.

When my time came to leave, I wanted to make sure that it was worth it. I wanted to hand Animal information that would help him stay out from under the thumb of Breston. And, of course, out from between Albany's legs.

Her plans to use the Feybi side of the organization Animal was running to distribute her new drug illegally was her holy grail plan. A new drug on the streets would be the way she could finally be seen as a major player in Breston.

The thought of this drug she had getting into the hands of the public was terrifying. The truth telling—the paralysis. It would be like a hyper roofie. It was a drug that was a dangerous weapon.

I had enough on her now. It was time. If I was correct about my time in captivity, I had been here about five months. Our daily stroll was upon us in the sun.

I was possibly in a different country. Most of the guards seemed to have a similar accent. Dealing with where in the hell I was was a problem for another hour.

Now it was escape. I asked Albany more questions about her. She was glamorous today, even in jeans. She had pearls on and a dark blazer, nude pumps, and the perfect amount of makeup.

I was in my uniform for my time here. Scrubs and sneakers, my hair in a rubber band. The lavishness of Albany's lifestyle did not spread to her favorite toy of the moment. While she rattled on about her latest car, I counted the snipers again. Jones, the one on the East side, liked to smoke. And from the whiffs I'd gotten, it wasn't regular cigarettes. He was my best bet. I needed his gun and his keys. As Albany gestured with her hands, I was deciding about her fate. To kill or not to kill. She told me how the car drove on her way here to me today. She pointed toward the parking lot as she answered.

I wanted to kill her—for keeping me, but more for sleeping with Animal —but I was making a decision for everyone when I started that war. And I would add urgency to my own capture, assuming I made it out.

For today I would knock her out really, really hard. I knew where to hit her, and I knew her guard wasn't up at all.

As we entered the part of the path that had a clump of trees, I pointed out a pretty bird in the sky. Turning her head was the last thing she would remember doing.

I hit her behind the neck and squeezed a pressure point so she would slide to the ground. Her eyes rolled back into her head.

If I'd timed it right, she and I had between nine and eleven minutes to come out the other side of the path and back into view. I was counting on five minutes of leeway time before any guards realized something was amiss.

I stripped her of her jeans and blazer and made a quick swap. Scrubs wouldn't be great at camouflaging me in public. I patted the jacket pocket and it had her wallet and her keys. The other pocket had her newest cell phone.

She was still breathing, so I hadn't killed her. I felt a pang of remorse and stared at her for an extra beat. I hoped I wouldn't regret leaving her here with her heart beating.

Jones was mid-toke, and clearly not expecting a woman to climb the ladder to his post. He was unconscious before he hit the ground. His M24 and pistol became my property. I took a pull on his joint, trying to settle my hammering heart before I free-climbed out the window.

I had miles and miles to go—and possibly an ocean or two, but I would get back to my people, so help me God.

53

I was continuing without her. That was the extent of what my day entailed. The things we'd set in motion before everything went to shit was what I needed to do.

My sparkle was gone. I linked everything going wrong to the night I'd spent with Albany.

Albany was a waste of a human. It made me feel like gagging when I thought that I'd spent time naked with her. Her whole heritage was garbage. Evil bastards. There would never be enough money for them. They wanted to run third-world countries. They were the kind of people who profited off cancer not getting cured. But I didn't know where she was. Or if she was even on this planet anymore. I'd find her and end her. To feed my newly acquired venom. Someday.

Nix was holding back on hitting Breston harder. We'd demolished the facility Albany was running. T had made sure that the bombs had crippled the whole facility. Thorough.

My girl was good at that.

The pain felt like it was peeling the muscles off of my heart.

My girl.

I had to do this—face the families as a leader. Pretend I was fine. Pretend that I hadn't failed my girl. Failed to protect her. I needed to keep up the façade in hopes of keeping Nix, Becca, and Ember safe. T had arranged it before...well before.

I let Wardon drive me to the meeting. I told Nix not to come. President and Vice President from now on. We lived together, but our security was insane. We tried not to make appearances at the same place anymore.

He'd be watching; he always was. I walked into the warehouse and made my way to the pallets stacked up like a stage. I easily climbed to the top. Fluid. Feline. Like the tigers on my body.

I left my sunglasses on because my eyes might have given me away. My big body and intimating muscles were the only bravado I had right now.

They were talking amongst themselves. This room was danger personified. The rivalry between the two families went deep.

I put my fist in the air and drew their attention. "Kaleotos. Feybis." There was a roar from either side. There had to be two hundred people in the warehouse. My people had the upper level, a single walkway lifted above the crowd.

I was sure that it made the criminals below nervous, as was its intention. "You've seen us at work. In the community. You know you're safer. Your kids don't have to follow you into this life. There's an out for you. Our hookers are happy. Our drug dealers are compensated. The cops are staying off your back. Family on family violence is almost non-existent in case you were wondering. In case you hadn't noticed."

I let the words hang in the air. Applause rose up to meet them. I wasn't even sure it mattered what I said. They needed to see me whole. Competent. Uninterrupted.

It was all a farce, but I could act.

I told them what they wanted to hear and what they needed to hear. Control was mine. After we were caught up on the business, I added a cherry on top.

"On your way out today, just to drive home how incredibly amazing we're all managing, please get your grand bonus from my men."

Another thunderous roar greeted me. My sunglasses stayed in place. Giving this speech without having T's beautiful eyes to look at for a gauge was a sinkhole.

My life would be this way now. This grueling pain. Walking through hot tar. I was living the life she was supposed to have. Taking the breaths I owed her.

The soldiers liked the money. On their way out, the good ones—the ones who were the most loyal to me—made sure to mention T. It was like a backwards funeral in a way. She was involved in so many different scenarios and touched so many different operations. I really wasn't sure how long Nix and I could do this without her.

She was lightning and gone. All that was left was the empty thunder.

54

When I was in the parking lot of our burned out mall, I took my guard down. I let my heart bleed all over itself. Missing T became a symptom of the disease I was slowly dying from.

To have had love and lost it, all at once. I would never love another. I took her vow. I only love once, and she was it.

Lately, I started drinking. I would sleep here in the purple Hummer. Nix and Becca would kill me if they knew that I was out in the open like this and that I did it regularly. It was a predictable pattern.

It was a fairly nice night, so I stumbled out of the Hummer. All the wrong moves, for all the worst reasons.

I found the cement divider that she and I had used as a platform to look at the stars on. It was crumbling, but it was still here. Like me.

I sat on it and stretched out as best I could. I had been a skinny tall thing back then. I dropped the bottle of Jack and was surprised when it rolled instead of breaking.

Usually, I spoke to her in the Hummer. My special angel. I wasn't sure where she was actually. If there was a hereafter. Maybe hell. She'd killed a lot of people. Which was okay, because we'd be there together someday.

I reached my hand backwards to where she was so long ago. I hadn't come to appreciate her sacrifice. I was still angry. It was supposed to be me. I was the savior. I was the protector. I was Animal.

I fell asleep like that.

Hours later, I woke up alive. Another half-assed attempt at being with her had failed. At least I was sober enough to drive now. It was dark when I let myself back into my bedroom.

I looked into the mirror on my door when I closed it.

She was there.

T.

She was wearing jeans and a white hoodie, no makeup and a huge smile. Such a weird combination for me to put in my head. Like, maybe I would picture her in a wedding gown or something more special. I'd dreamed of her, but I felt as awake as shit.

I had to try talking to her. I was desperate.

"T?"

I couldn't believe my eyes. Her laughter hit me next. It was soul-cleansing.

"T?"

I spun to see if the reflection could possibly be true. I grabbed her hand.

It was obviously a hard hallucination, or I had drunk myself to death in the Hummer.

T patted my hand again. "It's me. I'm here."

"What the fuck?" I touched her hand with both of mine and fell to my knees. I reached out and pulled her to me. This dream was so real I had to be dead. There were no other options.

I hugged her middle, resting my head between her breasts.

Her stomach gurgled. I tipped my head back so I could look at her. Her brown eyes were sparkling.

"I'm here. I was captive. All this time. I got out a few days ago. I didn't want them to track me here."

She was saying reasonable things.

"I saw you die. On the video, I saw you die." Her laughter turned to sadness.

"Oh, Animal. I almost died. They kept me alive because they're evil, but very good at what they do. I'm here. With you. I came back." T opened her arms.

My T, who didn't like touches too much, helped me as I staggered as I stood. "Whoa, there we go, big guy. How are you doing there?"

I hugged her for real. Encircling her in my arms as my heart rejoiced. I felt the unrealness seeping away. She was here. This was life, and this was T. I made sure to look her in the eyes.

"I love you." My throat dried up as I watched her hear it.

The familiar pain was just behind her eyes. "I know. We're family." "No. I love you. I want to make a family with you. We're not related. You're my wife."

She rubbed my arms. "Let's hug it out, okay? Have you been drinking? And you're never drinking."

"You're not getting it."

She hushed me with a pat on my chest.

Finally, I was able to get enough of my equilibrium underneath me to spin her and press her against the door.

"I love you. I have been dying for you since I watched you die. I can't take a breath without missing you. Not as a friend. Not as family. As my partner. As my woman."

I brushed her hair out of her face. What had she been through? Was she really here? I pushed her white hoodie off of her. She allowed it.

I took the hem of the shirt she had on underneath and lifted it up. I saw a gunshot wound on her stomach. I pulled it all the way off of her and held her shirt in my hand. With the other, I used my fingertips to scan her body. At least five gunshots.

Healed and well-treated, obviously.

"T?"

She shivered and I put her shirt back on her. I was clumsy about it, but she helped. Then I helped her put her hoodie back on.

"I don't understand. Tell me how to understand this."

T hesitated a few times, and then she put her hands on my face. "I came back. To you. For you. I love once. I love you."

I wanted to show her my tattoo on my back. I wanted to hug her so tight to my chest that I could feel her heartbeat. I needed to call Nix and Becca and Ember.

But there was only one thing I *had* to do.

I leaned down slowly, because our first kiss had been one of the worst nights of my life so many years ago when she left as a kid. And if this was all real, if my T was back, then this was the best night.

I came in very slowly. I kissed her forehead, then the tip of her nose. I'd never felt anything like putting my lips on hers.

Galaxies collided, souls rejoiced, and in the smallest part of me and the smallest part of her, two teenage kids clung to each other, wondering what the hell had taken us so long.

"My wife," I told her with sureness.

I watched as her eyes filled with tears. There was almost a fight in her.

She pointed to my chest. "I knew that. I was just waiting for you to figure it out. I guess all I had to do was die."

She was making light of it, but I wouldn't allow it. "Wait. Don't leave." I went to step away from her and then thought better of it. I grabbed her

hand and tugged her to the center of my room.

"What are you doing?"

She was admonishing me, but I heard the happiness in her voice. I took my silver tiger ring off my hand. It was too big and manly, but I wasn't wasting time. Not a second.

"T." I was very sober all of a sudden, though I knew I'd have to convince her of it again and again. I took to my knee. "I call you my wife all the time. Please, can I be your husband?"

I held out my ring for her hand.

She shook her head over and over. "What? This is... You're out of your mind right now. What about all the ladies?"

I had been wrong before about thinking I needed other women. When T told me that she loved me, I slept with others. I slept with her enemy. It was her all this time.

"There's been no one. I was never going to touch anyone else for the rest of my life." T looked at me like I had spoken a different language. "I get it. You're going to have to process this, and I'm going to have to earn you. You can say no. Actually, you deserve to say no. And if you do, that's fine. I'll live in your house, and you can take others if you want. And I will wait, forever if I have to."

She took the ring out of my hand and twirled it in hers.

She amazed me. The beauty in her thick hair, her deep brown eyes.

Seeing her moving was my dearest wish. She was here, a miracle.

She grabbed my hand and slid my ring back on. I wasn't even disappointed. I would be hers. The king to her queen. I owed her Nix's life and mine.

"I don't want this ring."

I nodded. "That's okay."

"I don't need a ring." She made sure it fit back on my ring finger.

"Whatever you say." T twisted it so the tiger was facing the right way.

And then the hair in front of her face again, the closed door.

"I already told you. I love once. But I'll take you as a husband, too." My eyes were wide. "What? Is that a yes?"

She nodded and smiled. God, she was gorgeous. She was everything.

I stood up and bundled her in a hug.

"You're my T."

T let me kiss her and even returned it. I was immediately revved up. "I love you."

"And I love you."

"Okay, let's go. We have some really, really good news to share with our people." I opened the door to my room. I kissed her four more times in the hallway before I let her come downstairs with me.

"We have so much to talk about." She reached over and patted my hand. I pulled out my phone and texted Nix to meet me in the living room. The reply came immediately. It was time for some more reunions.

55

I smiled at him when he looked over his shoulder to make sure I was still there. Maybe it was a dream, like he kept saying. Animal was touching my hand, my cheek, treating me like I was a goddess in his presence. I'd never seen him drinking before, so this might be how he was when alcohol was involved. But the love he'd professed felt real. And I knew him.

I was really excited to see Nix, Becca, and Ember, hopefully I could see the teenager soon.

It wasn't a thing I thought I'd be able to do again in this

lifetime. He turned to me at the bottom of the stairs with his arms wide.

I took the hug, smiling into his chest. I put my hand on his heart, feeling it beat.

"You're stubborn, you know." His deep voice echoed in his chest.

"How so?" I wound my arms around his middle.

"You refused to do it my way. Maybe I would've had the same outcome as you? And you would've been able to be here, safe."

He'd have anger down the line. I was expecting that. It wouldn't change the fact that I was right. To me, it was the only way to do it. The choice to trap him in the weapons room was so clear it was crystal.

"I had an opportunity, and I took it. I'm a go-getter." I was in his arms after all these years.

"Let's go show you off to these guys. I want to make sure you don't disappear into thin air." He put his massive arm around my shoulder.

God, I hoped he meant this. My heart would be a pile of mush if he took this attention away tomorrow. And I didn't think I could watch him with another woman now and allow her to live. He'd proposed to me basically.

Animal slipped his arm from my shoulders to my hand and pulled me behind him.

We walked into the living room, and Nix and Becca were curled up together, talking and holding hands like teenagers.

I waited as Nix looked at Animal first. The respect and brotherhood in his man nod made my heart happy. Then I watched as his gaze slid to me.

He was not expecting me. That much was clear.

"Shit! Holy shit." Nix stood and had to catch Becca as she

about hit the floor. He snagged her before she could hurt herself. "Shit."

Becca gave him a very displeased look before tracking his line of vision to me.

She just stared at me for a few seconds. I tried for a smile and wiggled my fingers.

"T?" Becca was able to speak.

I shrugged. "It's me. I'm alive."

Nix and Becca swarmed me. I was in the center of a group hug. They both had a million questions and asked them at a rapid pace.

"I was captured, and I escaped. Now I'm back." That was the worst summary ever, but it was the quickest I could offer. "They let me know you guys were okay, so that helped." I didn't want to get into what I knew, or what we had to do still. Tonight I wanted to be home. I met Animal's dark brown eyes. He was starting to believe this was real. That I was real. Nix looked like a beaming new parent.

The family we'd created was almost completely whole again. As soon as Ember knew, I'd feel more comfortable. I knew I had made the right choice, and the concern washed away.

56

Animal

She was slight. In the big scheme of things, there wasn't very much of her. But in presence, in power, she was a legend. I held out my hand to her. I wanted to touch her. My ghost. My angel. My warrior. My T.

My attention was making her softer. She was batting her eyelashes just a little more, like a magic spell, and for some impossible reason, I was the ingredient she wanted.

"Listen, I love you, but I'm taking my wife upstairs." Becca whistled, and Nix slapped me on the ass like a jerk.

T took my open hand and I led her behind me while our friends catcalled us. When we were almost to my bedroom, I felt resistance on my arm. She'd stopped walking. I turned and took a few small steps until I was toe-to-toe with her.

"What?" My voice was deep and husky. She could tell me anything. I would be at her feet forever no matter what.

Her devotion deserved to be multiplied and returned.

"Not here." She pointed at my bedroom door.

And then I understood. There was a history in that room with other women. With Albany.

"I'll burn it to the ground for you." I held her other hand.

She bit her lips as they struggled to form a smile. "Not tonight. I need you for other things."

I would let her set the tone and the mood.

"How about the gun range?" She licked her lips.

"You want me to go with you to the weapons room where you attacked me with a syringe last time?" I gave her a stern look.

"Yup, that's the place. I like guns. They turn me on."

"Say no more." I took a second to go into my bedroom and get the immense bottle of lube. I could only be so spontaneous with what I packed in my pants. I made sure her hand was still tucked in mine when we took the stairs down. T giggled a few times, and I knew it was the prep lube that was bringing it out in her.

Nix and Becca were still in the living room. I gave them a salute and marched past. Then we took the next set of stairs to the basement a level further.

I didn't bring toys. Nothing. It was different—what I wanted to do with her.

After grabbing the keys and unlocking the room, I opened the door. Before I let her in, I snagged some pillows and blankets from Nix's stalker hideaway that he no longer used for his surveillance of Becca.

After I had enough soft things to make the indoor gun

range more comfortable, T and I went into the room and shut the door. I set the lube down on the floor like a pretty lewd promise.

This place functioned as a panic room, though we'd never had to use it for that. The previous owner was prepping for a zombie apocalypse. I flipped the lock and set the lights to dim.

T and I stretched the blankets onto the floor, and then she kneeled down on them like we were having a picnic in a meadow instead of in a cement bunker with egg carton foam and firepower on the walls.

I did the same. I reached for her hand again and rubbed her knuckles with my thumb. She made a subtle hum.

"Do you forgive me? For taking your place?" T's eyebrows furrowed and she looked at our clasped hands.

I nodded for a while as I tried to find the words. "I was mad. No lie. I was so mad that it was you and not me. *I* could protect you. I can protect you."

"And *I* can protect you." Her face held a wisdom that was righteous. "You did." I leaned in and kissed her lips gently. Reverently. "You did it,

T. You saved Nix that night. And you saved me about two hours ago."

She gave me gentle kisses back. T reached her hand up and touched my cheek, running her thumb across my bottom lip. "I've wanted this—it feels like—my whole life."

I felt her yearning in my chest. My mind flashed through the different times she made herself scarce while I took women up to my room. I felt shame.

"Don't. Don't beat yourself up. I didn't want you to force it. Remember what I told you? When I first told you I loved you?" She let her thumb rest on my chin.

The kindness in her brown eyes was endless.

"I remember."

I got how she felt now. It was undeniable. A force to be dealt with. A pure fact. You could write my feelings for T on a monument now. They were permanent.

"And now it makes sense." I bent my neck so I could kiss the tip of her thumb. I wanted this to be special for her considering it was what she was waiting for since we were teens.

The setting was the worst all of a sudden. There were no candles. She wasn't draped in diamonds. There was no champagne. I told her as much.

She laughed at me. "Do you think that's the kind of girl I am, Animal? I mean, really, how do you think it'll be with me?"

I laughed with her for a moment, just joining in the sound that I was addicted to. She was stumping me. I wanted to be everything she'd hoped for.

"I don't need props. I just need you."

For the last five months, this was my wildest dream. My heaven. My answer. I eased down onto the blanket and patted my chest for her head.

T's hair tickled my arm.

"I always wanted to be the best. The most a girl has ever dealt with. Maybe I'm competitive." I had so much to explain to her. Excuses and reasoning. We were going to spend a boatload of time working up to getting naked. I revered her.

She flipped over on her stomach and looked at my face. "Stop. Talking. To. Me." She emphasized each word with a light touch on my face. My nose, my lips, my cheek.

I was getting in my own head, psyching myself out. I put my hands on her face and gently pulled her toward me. I nipped and kissed her. God, how long had it been since I kissed a woman? Maybe the last time I did it was my early twenties. It felt too intimate to explore someone's mouth.

But her lips—free of lipstick—had this taste, this flavor.

Sharing oxygen seemed natural because she was bringing me back from the dead by doing that very thing.

I was buoyant. I felt my personality coming back to me. My joy and confidence had been buried.

She was my foundation.

T eased her body on top of mine. I took my hands from her face and put them on her hips. T's weight on me felt like it was keeping me grounded. She put her hand on my head and ran it down my hair while we kissed, pausing on my ear.

Her touch was burning a trail on my skin. I watched as her eyes grew wide as I swelled between us.

She pushed herself to sitting until she was straddled on top of me. Her hips rocked back and forth, rubbing herself along my length.

Her jeans would have to disappear soon. My heartbeat was picking up. Her hair tumbled over one shoulder and she gave me a smile that told me she was happy to be where she was. I took her hoodie off.

I let my hands feel her body. We knew each other so well, but never like this. Her abs surprised me when I felt the slight indent of the muscles there. I let my thumbs brush the underside of her breasts through her shirt.

T was quiet and reserved. That was how I had her categorized in my mind, so when she pulled her undershirt over her head and easily took her bra off, I was amazed.

It was incredibly hot and sweet at the same time. No pretense of getting to know each other this new way. She was my T, and nothing ever was so right as her looking at me with her beautiful breasts bared.

I took my time exploring this treasure she'd offered me. The size, the weight, how playing with her nipples made her face pink a bit. I sat, and she pulled my shirt off as well.

I hugged her to me, our chests touching. This was a good position for us.

I was just a bit taller than her now.

The kissing started again, the forbidden kissing. I was kind of glad I'd abstained, because it gave me a whole new level of intimacy.

T put her hands on my chest, over my heart, and I did the same.

I had to talk. I was a talker. She needed to hear all the time how grateful I was.

"We're alive. Together."

She nodded. "This is good."

More kissing. I enclosed my hand around her hair and used it to gently aid me in kissing her deeply. I touched her neck, her shoulder. I took a break from the kissing to see her gunshot wounds again.

"You're a terminator. How you moved. How you saved." She winked at me. "I got certain skills."

Sassy T was a rare one. I loved it. I loved her.

My hands went around her waist, with my thumbs resting above her hips.

I wanted to be inside of her and do this again.

Her jeans were more of a task than I wanted, and I cursed them as she and I worked together to get them off. It stopped being even foreplay, and we decided to just get rid of all the clothing between us. I stripped as she did the same.

When we were naked, she stood there expectedly. Not ashamed, not trying to lead me on, just mine. She halted me, turning my shoulders. "What's this?"

My new tattoo. How could I have forgotten? I ducked my head, grinning at her and turned.

Becca had inked an expansive capital letter T on my back. It took up all the space on my shoulders, and my spine was highlighted as well.

Her hands ran softly over the whole thing. “You weren’t kidding. You missed the hell out of me.”

I turned and faced her again. “Did you ever doubt I would? Wait, don’t answer that. It’s for you, of course.”

I drew her into a hug. It was much more than what I was used to. I normally equated this feeling with a goal to get to an end.

With T, it was just how our story continued. I started kissing her again, but stopped to turn her around so her back was against my chest.

I ran my hand from her navel to her hip to her thigh.

She turned her shoulders and offered me her mouth again. How had I ever resisted her pink, full lips?

I touched her between her legs with both hands at the same time. My fingers were knowledgeable, but I tried to go slow with her. Let her acclimate.

When she seemed to be going limp with her moans and pants coming closer together, I twisted her by the hips and got to my knees.

She opened her mouth and I got to watch as she licked her lips. T put her hands on my shoulders as I inserted one finger and my tongue found her clit. I used a wide flat technique as I felt the inside of her. Mine. This woman had my name in her blood.

I added another finger and used my mouth to make sure she was ready. Faster, I pumped inside of her. Her knees went weak, her hands tangling in my hair. I took her weight on my hand, holding her up with one arm. T started to rock on my fingers.

She switched her hold to my bicep. It was at its largest and hardest as I held her up.

Girl loved the muscles, and I felt pride swell up. I was a good package, and I was all hers.

She was close to coming. I could feel the pulse inside her start to become a heartbeat. I stood and pulled my hand out from between her legs.

I lay back on the blankets.

"Ride my face. I want to taste the first of the many, many orgasms I'll bring you to."

Her lust was at its peak. On her way to straddle my mouth, she took a second to gently rock her hands up and down on my length. Then she inched up my body and planted her knees on either side of my head. I embedded my tongue as deeply as I could and inhaled.

Her scent was perfection. How had I missed out on this all this time? I'd never get over all the times I could have been wearing her as a facemask. I used the fingers on my right hand on her clit, massaging and rolling it while she convulsed with my touch.

My tongue went at a fast, strong pace.

T did in fact come on my face. Her first orgasm for me tasted like forever.

For the first time in my life, my heart and my dick felt the same way. Big, ready, and in love.

57

I literally did not know my body could do what Animal was doing to it. I was seeing white, having trouble breathing, and I was in so much pleasure it actually was edging on pain.

And I hadn't even gotten his big ol' dick inside of me yet. I was filled with the dirtiest of thoughts. And they were all allowed, because tonight, right now, Animal loved me.

Intimate didn't even come close to what we were doing to each other.

What he was doing to me.

He reached up and grabbed my breasts as I tried to keep

myself steady. I didn't want to put my full weight on his face, but he was making it really hard to have any kind of awareness.

Finally, I couldn't take it anymore. I was screaming, and my throat hurt. I tumbled off of him.

He caught me with one arm before I hit the floor.

He was so easy with me, with my body. Honestly, I knew he was a professional, basically, and that made me super jealous, but also wildly turned on.

I was ready to move on, to catch my breath and my heartbeat a little when I was on my back. Animal took one of my legs and pushed it out of the way. My orgasm that I thought had completely spent me was just a prologue.

He was at me again. His mouth sucking on me while his fingers did things inside of me that thrummed whole new sensations.

"Oh God. Oh *GOD*."

I tried to wiggle away from him, because it was too much. He put his hand flat on my stomach, holding me in place and somehow pushing down lightly and rubbing me from the inside. Instead of a G-spot, he found my whole goddamn alphabet inside. When all of his attention and touch ended suddenly, I almost felt like crying. I mean, it had to stop, but it felt so good I never really wanted it to.

I heard the noise of a wrapper and then the wet sound of the lube he'd brought with him like a threat.

And then his mouth was on my breast. I arched my back and pulled on his broad shoulders. There was so much of him, but he moved elegantly like the dancer he was. He paid wild attention to my clit again, both thumbs rubbing and tugging until I was cursing. I didn't understand why I was getting this onslaught until he slipped the tip of his dick inside me.

"Can you take it, T? Is it okay?"

He'd prepared me. I lifted my hips with purpose and locked my eyes on him. I took a few more inches for myself until I couldn't get any more from the angle I was in.

"Make it count," I dared him.

Animal's eyes rolled back in his head briefly before he repositioned me, mumbling about opening my hips. He added more lube, and the coolness of it added another layer of sensation. And then he was entering me.

He widened me, stretching the entire way. He had to go slow at first. There was no other way. He pulled out slowly, and I became a straight whore in my head. I just wanted more. Harder. All of him was tremendous. It was taking me out of my mind.

He added more lube. Now I knew why the bottle was so big. He was so big. I could even tell where the head of his dick was, could feel every inch. He started to go faster, and as much as I wanted to add to his motion, I had to hold still and take the hammering. He focused on the back and forth while pinching my nipples hard.

He was good at this—knowing how to keep me stimulated that I would want this monster he had between his legs.

Animal swirled his hips, stretching me even further. He let go of my nipples, but kissed each one after he did. Then he was back with his thumb on my clit, pressing it and thumbing it as he increased his tempo. I lifted my ass and tried to hold still for him.

His pleasure was something I daydreamed about. I had no idea it'd be this vivid. That I would only feel, not think.

The flashes of him that I begged my mind to remember were of glistening muscles. God, he was so strong. Handsome. His dark skin and beautiful eyes reminded me of a work of art in a museum.

But more than that was the look in his eye. He was cherishing me. He looked at me with lust. He looked at me with love.

Animal loved me the way I loved him.

And when he came, he said my name over and over.

"T, T, T!"

I wrapped my legs around him and pulled him close to me, as deep as he would go.

His weight on top of me was everything I'd ever hoped for. This was it.

This was love. This was making love.

I wasn't wrong. I only love once.

58

Animal

I remember thinking of all the guys I knew falling for a woman and becoming lovesick assholes. Like the whole world revolved around the one girl. And if she sent them a text, they would stop mid-sentence to answer her back—forgetting anything we were talking about when they were done.

And I judged them. I thought I had a better handle on manhood. On my brain. On my dick. I even felt that way about Nix. Don't get me wrong. I love my boy to have happiness. And his skeleton lady friend could not be more perfect for him. But I thought it. I thought he'd softened. Became whipped. Less than flattering things passed through my head. I'd never tell him, of course. Or anyone for that matter.

But now. Sweet Lord now.

T was here, naked in my arms. Spent in my arms. I wanted to kill something and eat the heart in front of her. I wanted to start eight fights and win them all, just so she could be impressed. If she sent me a text, I would drop a nuclear bomb if I were holding it just to see what the text said.

Love was crazy, evidently. I pushed her hair away from her beautiful face. She was bewitching. Did she know? She'd know by the time I married her. I'd have my mouth on every part of her body. I wanted to make her come in so many places she'd have to learn how to say my name in ten languages.

I put my hands on her because she let me. One on her breast, the other on her stomach. I eyed her whole body. I wanted to put my baby inside her. Not right now, but she was tapping into my need to further the species. This was some deep stuff.

I was such a pussy for her, and proud to be that way.

She was home. She was alive. And she was willing to be mine.

Maybe I'd earn the favor of someone up above. I tried not to be a dick about my blessings. Bones. Merck. Pretty Becca and even annoying Ember. I was grateful.

But I messed up. I'd ignored this love right in front of my face, and I didn't have to spend the rest of my life hating it. She was here. I wonder how many months it would take for me to take her for granted again. I hoped I never did. I hoped I was amazed every day from this moment forward that she was my lady.

T pulled my head close, pushing my cheek between her breasts. "That was so..."

I started to laugh, adding, "The best sex in the entire history of the world? Yeah. It was that."

I could hear her heartbeat and see her nipple. I buried my hand into her pussy gently, too. Perfection.

She wiggled and then crossed her legs around my hand. "Just keep that there as a souvenir. Because that was a hell of a ride."

Her hand came around my mostly limp dick. I jolted, but then let her. "This beautiful thing is a weapon. I feel like you just made a replica of it inside my body."

"That's my hope. I wanted to ruin you for anyone else. You're mine. My wife."

She exhaled. "You really mean that? Or is it the whole Lazarus thing that's got you going?"

I lifted my head so I could look her in the face. "Oh, I mean it. And as soon as possible. I'll take you to Vegas naked, right now."

She let go of my dick, and it slapped my thigh and then hers.

"That thing is like an elephant's trunk, my gosh." After she complimented it a few more times, I had to joke with her.

"You want to marry me or my cock?"

"Do I have to pick? I was hoping it was a packaged deal."

"You can have them both. Seriously, though. Vegas, in a few hours, okay?" I kissed her lips deeply.

"When we sleep and eat and face the harsh sunlight, if you still want to do it, we'll talk."

I wasn't scared of her. "It's a date."

59

"What's Ember been up to?" It was morning, and we were in my room.

Animal had left it like a shrine. I even had a phone charger.

"She's taking classes at the community college in town. She's still pretty pissed about the Merck thing, but she's been talking to us. She was worried about me. Missing you, too." Animal was stretched out on my bed. He was a lot, covered the whole damn surface. He was naked. I sat down and enjoyed the view of him in the sunlight from my window. Even lying down his muscles were defined. Any time he moved, a new one flexed.

"I need to go see her." I stood. I was way beyond sore. He and I had been at each other all night. Like we were battling to prove who loved who more. It had been delicious. I'd been saving my heart for him, and damn, I was a whore about him now.

"I'll get her brought here. You're not going anywhere. You and I need to have a heart-to-heart about what happened, what you learned. Bunches of stuff." Animal sat up and pulled himself against my headboard.

I enjoyed his abs the whole time he moved.

"Has she been coming around?" I brushed my hair out. It hurt when I lifted my left arm now. The gunshot wound had torn a muscle there.

"Not really. Nix wants to give her space. And I'm betting the less she's seen with us, the safer he feels she is."

He was silent as I dressed for the day.

"Please don't put that beautiful body away," he pouted.

I had a flare of insecurity. So many women had been under his gaze. Would I be enough? Forever?

"Don't. Don't get in your head. I know that you're going to worry. I promise, you are mine and I'm yours. Gladly. So fucking gladly." He swung his legs off of my bed and enfolded me in his arms.

"Okay," I added as he kissed the top of my head. "I'll believe that."

We went back and forth, but eventually I convinced him to let me go to Ember. She was still at her Aunt Dorothy's. He didn't want me to actually leave. He kept saying he felt like he was dreaming, but I was feeling that way, too. Getting this—to be with him—was making me nervous. Maybe for no good reason. Maybe I'd always be waiting for the other shoe to drop. It was a lot, so soon.

He wasn't my mom. She couldn't escape her behavior if she was off her meds, but he could be different. He could allow himself to be true to me. Love me.

It took kisses and assurances, but he finally agreed that me meeting Ember on her territory was a good idea.

"Can you have Nix text her that I'm coming? I don't want to shock the crap out of her."

Nix was on my request, and I was out the door in the minivan. It was bulletproof and not flashy, which was fine.

I'd stolen Albany's Corvette and driven it to the closest city. It turned out we were in Canada, so although it was a different country, there were ways of getting across the border that weren't too intimidating. I had dumped Albany's car in Albany, which felt pretty ironic and lovely. I switched to a sitting duck utility truck that had the keys left in it to make the drive the rest of the way to Midville. It had taken two days to get home.

Having a shower and my own clothes was incredibly soothing. To top that off, with a naked Animal in my bed? It was wonderful.

But now I had to face Ember. I knew Animal would miss me, and Nix and Becca as well. But Ember had just started opening up to me when I was taken. I worried about her. I wanted to show her I respected the blossom of friendship we'd had. I didn't let people in—obviously. Ember needed someone who had no claims on her. At least, that's how it seemed.

Nix texted me that Ember was home and alone. I went to the back door and made sure my head was covered. My hoodie and jeans could mark me as a teenager or hopefully one of her young friends if anyone untoward was watching.

She let me in, and when I removed my hood, I saw the wariness in her face.

"And we're supposed to trust you? Just like that?" Ember's nostrils flared and she folded her arms in front of her. "I needed you."

She pushed at her long brown hair. I wasn't wrong about the friendship I'd perceived.

I recognized the pain in Ember. I'd left her, and I had a feeling she was like me. I'd handle a situation like this the same way. I'd make people work for the right to be with me again. She was so, so angry.

"I needed you, too." I didn't reach out to her or force the situation. She had to be her own person, and her feelings were relevant. "This is literally the soonest I could escape. And if you don't feel right about this, I'll leave. I want you to trust your gut. If you have doubts, I'll leave until you're comfortable." I held my palms out to her. I had to let her know I valued her opinion. "Even if that's forever."

Ember moved her lips from one side to the other, looking me up and down.

Finally, I watched as her eyes filled up. "I don't want you to leave again." She had a small sob at the last word, and it was a knife in my chest. But it was also resurrection. I wiped at a sympathy tear on my cheek.

"I never want to leave again. I didn't want to leave last time, but I wasn't letting Animal trade his life for Nix's. I wasn't letting them take Animal and Nix from you and Becca. You mean too much to me to allow that hurt to happen." It was a lot for me to say. I hoped she knew how genuine I was being. Speeches were out of character for me.

Her acceptance was quiet, but it was the best. "Okay."

I held out my arms for her, and she trotted into them. I rubbed her back. "It must have been hell for you. Five months." Ember pulled back so she could look in my face.

"I managed. It was something else though." I told her as

much as I could without giving her information that could hurt her later.

We eventually got around to Animal and me. And how we were—as far as I could tell—a real couple. I told her about Vegas and that I wanted her there for the wedding. If it actually happened.

I warned her of Merck's inevitable invite. She thought about it for a few minutes before agreeing that she would attend. I was ecstatic because it felt like she was going to be my guest, and I was proud to have one.

I snuck out the back door and slipped into the woods where I used to watch her. I stayed there for a few hours to make sure she was okay. Wardon was still on duty, so I felt like I could leave. We had a wedding to plan.

But first, Albany would pay. I wouldn't head into my future with her not having to be held responsible for what she had done to my pack.

60

Animal

I wanted to bring Albany Breston to her knees. T had filled all of us in on the things she'd run across while she was captive in Canada, and the scariest part, bar none, was the fact that she and her team were working on a new way to medically torture someone. And that they were interested in selling it legally and under the table.

They were the worst of society. Only money mattered. She never thought about the end result of something that powerful. And she had plenty. Breston had money on money on money.

It was bullshit. You can't take money with you to the grave, so turning it into your god seemed like a waste of time to me.

We were about to have an informational meeting in the basement. Nix liked to go deep where there were no windows and he could be sure that he wasn't going to be overheard. People could call him paranoid, but he basically thought of every possible way he could tap into a conversation and headed it off.

So when we sat around in the basement, the plans to Breston's medical facility in Canada were proudly displayed on the monitor.

T gave us her review of her time there. Where they held the treatments, patients, and labs. She got the sense that most resources were buried in this new drug they were close to perfecting. She explained how it worked, and we talked about the implications and uses. T was fantastic at remembering the tactical stuff, though she was pretty shit at names and descriptions. She did her best. I found it all a turn-on and adorable.

Nix was curious about their cameras and attempted a few rudimentary hacks to see how prepared they were for potential cyber attacks.

It was clear it'd take him a longer time to hack into their systems. We couldn't even fathom how much money we were up against. Her father and brother's company's legitimate product sales were in the billions. But if

Albany got into illegal drugs for them, it could almost be limitless amounts of money.

It all seemed to be a bit much. I didn't know where we would start. Becca, who had been mostly listening, offered her opinion. "You know, sometimes taking little bites out of something is the best way to get it done. I mean, look at Nix's tats. They couldn't be done in a whole day."

Nix turned to her. "How do you mean?"

"Well, how can we take them down in small bites? I mean, things can happen all at once, but on low level stuff." She stood and pointed at the graph we had on the wall of the Breston products we knew of.

"Like, you know an Internet fake rumor can change destinies now. What if we started a fake one about Breston? Something that affected their sales." I watched as an almost angry look crossed T's face. Then it lit up. "That's genius. We can start reports on some of their drugs and some of their products—saying they're harmful or what have you."

We were a flood of ideas, and Nix typed furiously to keep up. We could use the Kaleotos family and my army to start the rumors that Breston was a shit place to do business with. Then we could let the father and the son in on our threats. That we'd tell people that they were poisoning groundwater. That their pills were contaminated. Safety seals could be popped in mass quantities. Nix didn't even bring up how much damage he could do to them on the dark net. Unless they brought Albany to a reckoning. We wanted her in prison, and nothing else would satisfy us.

It could work. At least we could make a dent. Things could happen to them. It had seemed insurmountable when we'd come downstairs, but now on our way back up, we had a solid plan. It would start the next day, and it would take all of us to pull this off, save Ember. We weren't trying to bring her into this business. She didn't need her face tangled into this next level bullshit we were getting involved in.

T was opposed to using me as Albany bait. It took convincing to get her to agree. I had to assure her that I wouldn't do the confrontation alone. T wanted to be there.

After a ton of conversation, we agreed as a group that the best punishment for Albany would be prison. T was adamant that it would have the most effect on the woman. She was very spoiled and yet unhappy. Having to wear shoes in the shower and take a piss out in the open would be the best therapy.

I had doubts, though. I knew my girl. She was methodical and devoted, and she was loyal to Nix.

We started small, with me going alone to Meme's, dancing with some of the ladies I played with before T and I were engaged.

Then Nix used the information from Albany's two cell phones that we had to listen in on a few of her contacts.

Albany was more desperate for T than she was me. The time T had spent listening to Albany had shaken her. Gave her a taste of someone giving an actual shit about her.

Nix placed some bait in Albany's Facebook profile. Tips on where T might be. He used the algorithm they had to put pictures of girls that looked like T in the advertisements. Then he started suggesting T as a friend under a fake profile we'd made for her.

It showed how little Albany actually knew about T, that my girl liked to keep things close to her vest. She'd never post how her lunch tasted on a social network.

Nix tracked it as Albany stalked T's fake page for a few days. Eventually, she requested T as a friend.

We all traded fist bumps. Of course, we could've gone up to Canada and popped her, but we wanted vengeance, not just revenge.

T started flirting with Albany in private messages, asking for forgiveness for leaving. She let her know that I was being a huge dick and Nix was moving against her. Just enough to get Albany on a plane.

When the day arrived to meet Albany, we all went to the airport to wait for her private jet.

When Albany touched down and descended in a thick white coat and glasses, Merck and his men were waiting.

We had handed them so much evidence of Albany working to establish a new illegal drug in America, he was able to arrest her on the spot.

I think Nix, T, and I all had twitchy trigger fingers when we saw her face. I made sure to make eye contact with Albany. When I had her attention, I dipped T into a kiss and we both shot her middle fingers while we made out.

The resulting media hellfire for Breston affected their stock deeply. Just as Albany's arrest was hitting the news waves, reports about the things we'd planted against Breston started to trickle out. Within two weeks, Breston was the top headline in the news. And the bonus? No one was hurt while we destroyed their reputation. Now, they had enough money to fix it. They had billions upon billions to pour into congressional and media pockets.

We had choices to make. The Feybi side of the business was far too risky to keep in the loop. As much as I hated to have them be official opposition to the Kaleotos and my crew, we sliced our relations. The danger was maybe not more pronounced, because if we couldn't trust them, they were of no use to us. But it was more distinct.

They had been working with Albany against us. Had they cornered the market on a new drug, they would have demolished us.

There was a resolution for now. And that was enough for me to smile at my girl.

T and I could get married. We had enough stability.

61

I looked at the ring on my finger. He'd somehow figured out how to make his hospital bracelet from when we were kids part of the setting on my engagement ring. I shook my head and wrinkled my nose at him. We were flying to Vegas to get married. The whole crew was here. Nix, Becca, Ember, Wardon, and even Merck. We'd been through so much. To be able to have a trip where our whole focus was fun and vacation felt like a dream.

I reached out and held Animal's big hand. He lifted my knuckles to his mouth and kissed my ring. I was lost in his deep brown eyes.

It was funny. As a girl and a teen, having dreams come true wasn't something I counted on. It was survival. It was loyalty. But the way I felt about him was a secret wish. I'd pictured my wedding day with him over and over when I was outside overnight.

He smiled at me, then looked over his shoulder, checking on his family. I snuggled against his chest after I was belted in. We had first-class seats and plenty of room. I was finding it odd how easy I could sleep with Animal next to me. He was protection. I felt him kiss the top of my head before I let my eyes stay closed for our ride.

Just before we were wheels down in Vegas, Animal woke me by touching my cheek and then my shoulder. "T, didn't want you to be shocked awake when we landed. Get some good rest?"

I patted his hard chest. "Yeah, thanks. Did you sleep a little?"

He beamed. "No, princess. I'm too excited. I get to make you my legal wife tonight."

I felt myself blush. He was so all about me, and I had to keep reminding myself that it was forever.

That he could be with just one—as long as that one was me.

We all stretched and then grabbed our bags after we got the all-clear from the attendants. Seeing Nix shocked me a bit. It took my mind a while to remember that Becca had smeared his skin with makeup for the trip. Being

completely covered with tattoos was just asking for extreme pat-downs from TSA.

Nix was handsome but somehow too plain. Too someone else. I noticed that Becca kept having to soothe Nix. He didn't like being without his ink.

As soon as we were by the baggage carousel, she passed

him makeup wipes. We all applauded when we had the real Nix back with us. I watched as Merck kept positioning himself near Ember and Wardon. Wardon had a gigantic crush on the girl. It was obvious. Merck was clearly torn between trying to relax and wanting to bounce Wardon like a basketball.

I felt Animal's hair against my neck and his deep voice. "Never miss a trick, huh?"

I turned toward his words and his ticklish mouth. "Try not to."

"So, I have to ask. Are we going to find out what your full name is?" Nix was visibly relaxed now. I wondered if we shouldn't just budget in some extra time for security on the return flight so he wouldn't have to go through the process he certainly didn't like again.

I shook my head. "No, why would that matter?"

Animal put his arm around my waist. "'Cause I'm marrying you so legal and so hard that all the church bells in Nevada will be ringing their asses off."

Becca grabbed Nix's hand. "You know, what happens here, stays here, so they say."

"Including my government name?" I pointed out the few checked baggage pieces we'd brought as they popped out onto the carousel.

Ember stepped away from Wardon, who leaned in, trying to flirt some more. Animal and Nix went to grab the bags.

I watched as Merck seemed out of place. He'd left his wife at home, but wasn't sure really where he belonged. I came up next to him and tapped his shoulder. He turned to face me.

"I know what your name is, and it's real pretty. But it can be our secret." Merck nodded at me with the promise.

Animal knew my name as well, but he was a big believer in self-labeling. I touched his forearm, "Can I ask you a favor?"

"Of course." Merck bent his head like a person who was used to being the one to solve problems.

"My mom couldn't make it." That was a massive understatement, but Merck knew how it was for me, from my past. "So, I don't know who

would, you know, if the chapel we go to even has one? The aisle, you know?"

I was bungling this big ask.

"You want me to give you away?" He squinted one eye, as if he wasn't sure he got my request correct.

I nodded. Maybe it was a stupid idea.

"Absolutely. I'd be honored." He gave me a subdued bow.

"Thank you." I maybe should've said more, but I was hoping he'd understand he had an important role in the ceremony. It wasn't just so he could be here for Animal.

Merck was standing in for the parents in our lives.

Nix teased Animal, whose thunderous laughter was catching. We didn't even need to know their joke. Everyone in our group was smiling, and a few fellow passengers were grinning as well.

We were headed to town with a big job. Time to get all official.

62

She was with Merck and he looked pleased as hell. That was T. Silently making things better before people even knew stuff was amiss. Her watchfulness was superior. That I could love her more today than I did yesterday seemed impossible but true.

Nix was thrilled for me. Apparently, he and Becca had been rooting for T and me since he'd came back from the Feybis.

I was still dealing with some guilt for the lifestyle she'd watched me participate in. I knew she understood more than anyone. But still, I'd make it all up to her. For the rest of our lives. She'd know that she was never second best or always enough. With her, I was unafraid.

I'd set the wedding venue up in advance. It wasn't an Elvis or craziness theme. It was a pretty chapel, and it'd be covered in lavender, T's favorite flower.

It'd been amazing to watch her excitement. Beyond that, she was bashful about being the center of attention. I loved that part, too. Seeing her glow with the sudden awareness that we were all here for her. It was my wedding day, too, but it wasn't really. This was T's moment to shine.

We'd need to get our papers in order first, then the whole group would separate by gender until we met up later. We were getting dressed up. I had my suit and so did my boys. After T and I had our certificate, I kissed her deeply. Becca, Ember, and Wardon were going to a hotel to prepare. Wardon was the hired gun, so he was an honorary girl, and we razzed him about it. I had a few extra security measures in place, just so T could see them and take the damn day off in her head.

I wanted her drinking and laughing and dancing with me without the burden of trying to make sure we were safe. Just joy. That's what today needed.

When we parted, I got Nix and Merck to huddle up with me. I'd done something I wasn't sure about and wanted their opinion.

We all sat at a table. Getting food became a priority. Traveling had stirred the beast in all of us. I noticed how little attention was paid to Nix and his unusual tattoos. Vegas was ready for different, so it seemed. I liked it and wondered if Nix felt it.

When we'd ordered, I laid it on them. "I did something, and I'm not sure if it's a great idea."

Nix twirled a napkin in his fingers. "Shoot, brother."

"So, you both know that T's mom isn't, well... She has issues that are unique." I was second-guessing my impulses. I thought back to how I'd kept Merck's identity from Ember and how poorly that had gone. "I set up a way to live feed the wedding to her mom."

Merck's face showed genuine surprise. "Oh."

Nix nodded. "I see why you're stressing. T hasn't spent time with her mom in how long?"

"It's been years. I've been working with a psychologist and a doctor. This isn't a split-second decision. I mean, I wanted to work her mom into T's life. There have been advances made. We have the means to keep her in comfort. I just hope. I mean, I don't think I know better than T. And I can flip this. Only the doctors know. T's mom has no idea. No one would be the wiser." I tossed up my hands.

Merck offered his opinion, "It's a beautiful impulse, and I see why you're torn up about it. That might be a hell of a surprise. Maybe give her the choice."

I waited while our food was delivered. I really wasn't sure if I'd made the right decision. I mean, getting T's mom more help and qualified, dedicated mental health specialists could be done without contact between T and Anastasia.

But I wanted T to have her mom. I wanted her to have all the people she loved able to see her when I made her my wife. Merck had a point. It was bad luck to see the bride before the wedding, but I didn't want to have the concern to hang over this day.

A wedding gift of increased help for her mom could be enough. It didn't have to be a video broadcast.

I lightened the mood once we were fed, and I texted T that I wanted to tell her about a few of my husband plans before we said our vows.

She agreed to meet me in the hallway in her hotel. I high-tailed it over there while Nix and Merck made sure our suits looked decent.

I knocked gently on her hotel room door with my knuckle. T answered the door with rollers in her hair and a satin robe tied tightly around her.

"Wife." I pulled her into the hallway and closed the door between us and her giggling friends. I ran a hand across her flat stomach. She swayed closer to me with a moan.

"Someday I'm filling this spot right here with little baby Animals and Ts," I growled and nuzzled her cheek. She smelled like conditioner and a touch of perfume. I was hard thinking that her preparation was for me. Her eyes sparkled.

"Why are you breaking the rules? You should be getting into your fancy best." T put her arms around me.

"I realized that I had to tell you something I'd planned for you. I hope it wasn't a mistake, like it was when we sheltered Ember. I didn't want to surprise you at the ceremony." I tilted her chin up so I could look into her dark, coffee-colored eyes.

"You're starting to scare me. What's up? I've already had a glass of champagne, so don't make me think too much."

I could tell—now that she'd said it. She had a relaxed posture. Shit. My dream was her enjoying this.

"Tell me." She made her eyes wide.

"I've been working with your mom's doctors. Just making sure that she has the best and stuff." I looked at her to gauge her response.

She smiled, albeit sadly. "That's nice of you."

"It's not that you didn't already have it set up, beautiful. I just wanted it to be over the top. She loves the house and the friends she has there, but..." I took a deep breath. "I wanted there to be a way for her to participate today, if you wanted it. So I have her therapist and her doctor in on a possible live feed, if you want your mom to see what's going on." I rushed in with the rest of the words, wanting her to know everything before I heard my fate.

T patted my cheek as she sighed. "You're thoughtful. And sweet. And I know that you've been in touch with the doctors, because they told me. So your big secret is less so."

"Okay." I had to give her props for that.

"I didn't know about the live feed, though." Instead of pulling away, she hugged me closer. "I want her here so bad. Every day. She'd love it so much. To see me in a gown."

And then I knew it wasn't going to happen, but I listened anyway.

"When I was a kid, I would pretend to be a bride with a toilet paper veil and bouquet of fake flowers. And my mom? When she was happy? She would sing the wedding march and set up any stuffed animals I had as an audience." I watched as T's eyes filled with moisture. "She's really loving, you know? If she could, she'd be the best mom ever."

I kissed T's nose and her chin and then her mouth. I gave her the start of the next sentence. "But..."

"But I can't do it to her. She's been even for years now. On her meds. She thinks I'm still in another country, so the temptation to reach out to me is far less. They distract her. She's been painting and gardening. She's happy." So much pain in T's voice.

"I'm so sorry. I didn't want to make you sad. I just..." She covered my mouth with her hand.

"No. That you've been working on this? That you remembered her? That you hope for her and me? It means the world. And I know when I miss her, I can do it with you."

She was so strong. Did she know? That she could forgo herself the comfort of a parent for her entire life so that her mom would be okay? Have a good day?

"Your selflessness astounds me. My God, I love you so much." I hugged her hard.

She snuggled herself under my chin. "From the man that's spent his life taking care of others."

Becca opened the door after knocking on it from the inside. "Hey! Put a little space between you! You all can get biblical in a few hours. T has an appointment in here, and it doesn't include you." She wagged her finger at me.

T and I kissed one more time. On my way out of the hotel, I ran my hand over my mouth slowly.

She was one hell of a woman, and I was proud of myself for locking her down.

63

I grinned at Merck as he waited for me in the foyer. Becca and Ember were already inside, and the wedding march was about to begin.

"You are beautiful." He wasn't that kind of guy. He didn't go around telling girls that, so it was sweet how he seemed shy about it.

"Thank you again for doing this." I hooked my arm around his elbow. "Animal was really excited when I told him why I was headed back here." He angled us toward the two big doors that opened into the ceremony.

I nodded. The doors swung open and the music filled the alcove we were in.

Not many people were waiting on the other side, and I was thrilled. A crowd was never my favorite. Being the center of attention was my least favorite thing in the world. But for him, I'd do anything.

I thought about my mom as I looked down at my simple, long, white dress. I had a veil, which I touched quickly. It was far from the getup we'd used to role-play when I was a girl. I whispered a short prayer about her happiness, and then I lifted my eyes to his.

My Animal. So many years he was my first concern when I woke up in the morning. Was he hungry? Was he safe? Being connected to him kept me going when things were hopeless.

I watched as he lost a sliver of his composure. He touched his index finger to his mouth. Nix grabbed his shoulder from behind.

Animal was a beautiful man on any day, but in a tuxedo, he was like a model on a magazine cover.

I only love once. Don't forget.

And it turned out I was right.

64

T in her white gown with her long brown hair softly curling down her back would be the most stunning image for the rest of the days I got to breathe on this planet. Her gorgeous lips painted in a gentle rose and enough makeup to highlight her beauty made the center of my chest hurt.

This woman, who was mine long before I recognized it, made me believe that the universe wasn't just a giant game of chance.

When Merck offered her to me with a backslapping hug, I knew that happiness could be overwhelming.

We said our traditional vows. My voice loud, hers soft. The kiss was a bit too long, but goddamn, T was my wife, so I took my time.

Life started. I carried her down the aisle with my friends acting like fools with the hooting and hollering. We took a million pictures outside of the chapel. Ember seemed like a professional photographer as she made us pose. The night was upon us, and I had set aside a room in a fancy restaurant on the strip. T and I had plenty of champagne on the way, and she was even into it when the tourists made a fuss over us.

The evening was full. We joked and laughed and drank. Merck looked every inch the father of the groom, and Nix was treated like a celebrity because of his tats.

It was a beautiful night. I danced with my bride, slowly and infatuated.

We traded kisses and laughs. What a frigging night. One for the books. When we were all exhausted, it was time to take her back to our honeymoon suite. I hugged everyone. They all shared rooms, though Ember and Wardon had separate rooms. I knew Nix would enforce that. Ember was chilly to us, but thrilled for T, so I hoped that there was a softening there now. We needed Ember back in the fold.

When we got to the honeymoon suite, I had to press her against the door and kiss her while I slipped the key into the door. I carried her over the threshold, then set her down. She laughed when I finally turned her around to see our accommodations.

"Is this the fanciest room in Vegas, Havoc?" It had a 360-degree view of the lights. There was a pool in the center, a spa, and staircases twirling up either side of the giant space.

"Could be." I had requested something ridiculous. Over the top. She deserved every single thing. I was just getting started with my wife.

Her white high heels made her a bit taller than usual, and I watched as she clacked across the expanse of the room. She reached up and pulled her veil out of her hair. It hadn't been so long that it was in our way when we danced. Now it was on the marble. I watched as she took in the sights from our windows. I set the keys and my wallet on the table. I went to the bar and found the audio system. I hooked up my phone, and soon we had her favorite song cued up and in surround sound.

I watched as she looked at the pool.

Just a homeless girl and a hungry orphan living life. I was proud of us all of a sudden for making it.

T winked at me and then strolled over to the pool. She walked into it fully dressed.

"Damn!"

Once she was up to her hips, she dove in. I watched as she kicked off her heels and swam underwater to the other side, her dress flowing around her.

She popped up on the other side, laughing. After splashing in my direction, she dared me, "Come on in! The water's great."

Her wedding dress was pressed against her, and I could see her pink nipples through the fabric now that it was wet.

I pulled off my jacket and tie and hopped in from the side. I was able to pull her to me, still standing. Even in the deepest part, I could still touch the bottom.

She wrapped her legs around me. "Hey."

"Hey, I've been thinking about this for hours with you." I pushed the wet hair away from her face.

"Let's see what that kind of mental prep gets me." She bit her bottom lip. I kissed her while I ran my hands up her sides. Then I found her zipper and pulled it down gently.

"You ruined your wedding dress," I whispered into her ear. She unbuttoned my tux shirt. "I was hoping we'd defile it."

I had to look away while I beamed. Dirty T had to be my favorite.

Because she was full of that for me. Surprises, dares, and temptation.

She put her hands on my face and pulled me back so she could kiss me some more. T eased my shirt from my shoulders and out of my pants. She explored my chest like it was the first time she'd seen it.

"All of this is mine."

Victory in her eyes. We were winning this together. I helped her out of her dress so she was just swimming in a gorgeous bra and panty set and thigh high stockings.

"Oh, yes. This is...everything."

I swung her around and walked her to the shallow end. There were two chairs covered in tile there. I silently thanked the designers, because I had a place to set her down while I undid my belt.

She arched her back and pulled in her legs, giving me a classic pose. I always looked at her wounds, remembering how much it hurt before I was given the chance to have her back.

I got out of my pants and boxer briefs as fast as I could. I was able to kneel next to her and kiss her while my hands felt all the uncovered skin. It was early in the morning, but we had all day, and I wasn't about to rush it. My wife would have so many orgasms that we'd have to rehydrate even though we were sexing in a pool.

Eventually, I had to pay attention to her beautiful breasts. I pulled her toward me so I could unclasp her bra. She reached for me while I was working and grabbed two handfuls of my dick. I had to stop touching her for a minute and brace myself. She was so gorgeous. Having her like this was bringing me close just from her one touch.

"What the hell? You do things to me." I let myself indulge

in her devotion for a few heartbeats. I had to make her stop because I wasn't coming for the first time with my wife in her hands.

I would be deep inside her with her screaming my name even if it killed me. I pulled away from her and lifted her from the seat, straddling it and setting her back down. Now my dick was between us, like it belonged. Her lips were captivating. How did they taste so perfect? I held her naughty damn arms by the wrists so I could take control again.

I put both wrists into one of my hands and inched her panties to the side with the other. I felt a little better when she almost exploded when I barely touched her clit. Her nipples peaked and her shoulders were covered with goose bumps. I knew it was a good time to slide in my index finger. I kissed her again, adding nips and then my tongue.

She was magnificent, her hair soaked and plastered on her neck and chest. Seeing her lusting for me would make me marry her eight more times today if I could. I added another finger and made sure my thumb pressed hard against her clit. My T let herself feel. Orgasm number one was a treasure. Her lips were redder, and her voice was hoarse from screaming my name. I let her have her hands so I could grab a handful of her beautiful breast.

Then she was on a mission. I was concerned for a moment that I didn't have my lube in hand, but she shook her head.

"It's good. I think I've acclimated to my husband's cock."

She swam off of me and motioned for me to join her in the shallow end on the underwater benches. The water was amazing. We were even more agile there.

T shimmied the rest of the way out of her panties. The underwater lights slowly changed color from blue to pink. I wasn't sure how she would make it work, but she put my dick between her legs and eased down on it.

Once I was fully inside her, she sat back and put her hands in the air. "It's all legal now, baby!"

Seeing this badass woman fist pump about having me fill her up was the goddamn best. When we tried to rock, we couldn't get the friction we needed.

I knew I had to look crazy while I was frustrated by the lack of friction. I had enough of playing with her. I slid off the bench. Now, I could stand behind her and fully enter her. It was time. As a male, this was my job. I had to put it to her like she'd paid for it with her life. I thrust in and out of my bride and heard the results and felt the convulsions deep inside of her.

And then I felt the familiar heat. She tossed her head, and her wet hair slapped down on her back. Her ass was wonderful as I bounced off it.

I came inside her, hanging onto the sides of the bench. I went boneless and had to make sure she was okay before I slid back into the water. She rolled off the bench and reached her arms out to me.

"I love you." The feeling overwhelmed me.

She came back to herself, softening her look of passion. She held out her hands to me. I adjusted so we could lie next to each other on the lounge.

Her leg snaked in between mine. The ceiling was painted with stars, and it had mini lights incorporated in it as well.

"I love you," she responded.

The water lounge was lovely. There was room for us both. The stars above us reminded me of the parking lot when were teens. I watched as she used her finger to trace the Big and Little Dippers on the ceiling, so I knew she was thinking the same thing.

"We've come a long way." The sheer opulence around us was overdone. It was designed to make us feel as rich as we possibly could. I loved it for her, even though I knew material things weren't a vast part of her every day.

"It could take as much time as it wanted to, as long as we ended up here." She patted the center of my chest. "Thank you for the lovely wedding." She turned her head to look at me, and I kissed her forehead.

"My pleasure. I'll marry you all you want." I pulled her even closer to me. The lights in the pool softly changed to orange.

"It was sweet how happy Merck was." She outlined some water droplets on my shoulder.

He had been delighted. Seeing him with Ember was a sweet treat as well. It was a great goddamn day. I thought about her mom again, and she leaned in and kissed my neck. "You did good. All of it."

I felt like she was thinking of her mom again, too. I knew how to distract her. The lights changed to purple in the pool. "I'm pruning up in here. You want to take this celebration to another spot?"

I waved my hand and the expanse around us.

She got a deviously naughty look on her face, and I instantly wanted to hear what was going through her mind.

T whispered into my ear even though we were alone. "How about the balcony?"

I looked at her in mock surprise. "You want us to get our freak on outside?"

"Too much?" After she eased off the lounge, she used her wet hair to hide behind.

She looked like a coy Venus, naked in the pool.

"Hell no. I'll make love to you on a jumbotron, whatever you want." I stood and encircled her in my arms.

"Okay. I have a few outfits, though. I need to get ready. And dry up a little. Do you think there are two bathrooms here?"

I laughed. "Um, yes. Let's explore."

Our luggage had been delivered earlier, and it was in the foyer. I grabbed some towels by the stairs of the pool and we both swaddled up.

The exhaustion we should be feeling was not present. Seeing her happy and carefree made me almost as proud as being her husband. She and I should've done this much sooner.

I held her hand as we explored the suite. There were four bedrooms and three gorgeous master bathrooms. When we got back to the foyer, she kissed me and scrambled away from my hands. I didn't want her gone, even for a few minutes.

But I could amuse myself if she insisted on wearing sexy lingerie. I walked into the suite the next floor up. I stayed naked because I knew how magnificent I was without clothes, and I made her happy.

65

I rinsed off the saltwater from the pool in the shower. I couldn't stop smiling. It was a beautiful day. The man I loved felt the same way about me. Maybe I could see the future when I was a kid, and I pictured this exact day.

I looked at my wedding band. It was engraved with a tiger. His had an owl that represented me. Luckily, Animal had connections, and a speedy wedding was easily achieved. I pulled on my tall, black thigh highs. The outfits I'd brought for this honeymoon night were sweet and sexy. This one, though, was like porn in cloth. I wanted to surprise him. Maybe every day of our lives, it would be great for him to find out something new.

Tonight, it would be the faux leather outfit. I turned in the mirror and ruffled my hair so it was damp but with a smidge of curl. I didn't need new makeup. There was a bit of black smudged around my lashes that would do just fine. I gave myself a small spritz of perfume. The thong was crazy and the whole thing was crotchless. I really wanted to wow him.

When I came out, he was buck-naked standing on the balcony. There had been lights on before, but he must have turned them off. It was a great idea. As I walked out, he turned slowly.

I watched as his gaze went from my feet to my face, his smile tugging up as well.

"Damn, girl." He twirled me around while touching all the skin I had available to him. My breasts weren't covered by the corset piece, and he began touching me immediately.

"For you." I ran my hands down his chest and ridges of his abs. I had the pleasure of watching him get hard for me.

"Lucky me."

He started kissing me, grabbing handfuls of my ass while I pressed my chest against his. His dick was long enough that it was touching the underside of my breast.

I sank to my knees and considered it. If most dicks were a meal, he was Thanksgiving dinner. I grabbed his balls in one hand and started on him with my mouth, licking up the shaft and swirling my tongue on the tip. I gently sucked the top, humming and moving my lips in the way that he loved.

I saw him bend his knees and sway.

He put his hands in my hair. "The boobs. The ass. Your tits. Holy fuck." After adding both hands to his shaft, I made it as much of a multimedia production as I could, using my mouth and twisting my hands to give him an overdrive sensation.

I was ready to swallow if he wanted, but soon he pulled away from me. "Nah, baby, I want to be inside you again. It's my favorite way."

Far be it from me to keep him from his favorite. He held out his hand to me and I got off my knees. He motioned to the couch on the balcony. I lay back on it. Animal kneeled next to me and stared at the crotchless part of my outfit.

"This is incredible. It's like a frame around a masterpiece."

I started laughing, but it caught in my throat when he put his mouth on me. He was so incredibly determined to make me come, it was like he had it on fast-forward. His tongue and lips knew exactly what to do. When he added his fingers, I was done. I forgot we were outside and started moaning loudly.

"That's right, T. Let 'em know we got married tonight. You let them know."

Before I could come down from the orgasm, he was carrying me back into the suite. He put me on the bed and crawled on top of me.

"I want some good, old-fashioned lovemaking from you now."

His deep voice was perfect. I watched as his beautiful body towered over mine. I tilted my pelvis up so he could access me better.

"You ready?" He dragged the tip of his dick over my pussy.

I thrust toward him, unafraid.

He pushed inside slowly, letting me acclimate to him yet again. It happened quickly, though, since we had already plowed that road once tonight.

He was so big and long that I was overfull. I loved it. It was so very Animal. Together, we worked on the thrusts so they were more and more intense. He was hitting the spot from the inside that only he knew existed.

I grabbed my breasts and felt a drop of his sweat land in

the center of my chest. I looked up at him. He was intense. This was more than sex. It was the reason people got married in the first place—to be like this with each other.

His orgasm happened first, but as I tortured him with more movement and a swirl of my hips, I hit my own peak again. We were shout-moaning at each other as we collapsed on the bed.

We panted and touched, staying connected as best we could as we fought to catch our breath.

It was a beautiful start to forever. My guy. Just the way I always wanted him.

He held out his arms, and I put my head on his chest as he ran his index finger along the gunshot wound on my shoulder.

"I'm never going to take you for granted, T."

"Hey, you can call me by my real name, if you want. Because we're family. All legal now." I lifted my head and watched his lips.

"I love you, Talon Winters."

66

We were sitting in the backyard of our new place. As much as I loved Nix, he needed his space. Just a few minutes north of his property, I was able to get this house on the top of a small hill.

T came out of the house with two glasses of wine. I'd prepared the fire pit. It was homey. I growled at her a little because her ass in leggings did all the right things.

She glided past me, handing me my glass as she went by. After she'd settled into her spot on the bench near the fire, I told her that we were an all-American couple now. They could shoot a few centerfolds for a home magazine if they wanted. She twisted up her face like I'd said something unreasonable.

"What's up?" I took a gulp of my wine and set it on the stone ledge by the fire. She did the same.

"I need to tell you something."

The air around us seemed to tighten. It was serious, whatever she had to share.

After she took my hands in hers, she offered, "I did something bad, and I don't regret it."

My stomach dropped. I couldn't imagine what she had to say.

"Okay," I responded, bewildered. There was a lot of time from middle school until I met her on the street with hookers. Maybe something had happened then.

T shifted her hips.

I took one of my hands from her lap and rubbed my fingertips on my mouth. I didn't say anything, but I knew she could read the confusion in my expression.

"There's something about me you need to know. When it comes to you? When it comes to people who hurt you? I play the long game. I'm their judge and jury and executioner. That won't change. Ever. It's how I'm made as far as you're concerned." She looked at my feet.

"Just tell me. Come on, T." I grabbed her hand again, making sure she knew that whatever she had to say I was down.

"I set up a wedding present for you, but also it's for me."

I was getting hopeful, but her body language was still guarded. She looked over her shoulder and then leaned forward so her mouth was near my ear. "I worked with the girls we have in the prison. They let me have alone time with Albany." She sat back so we could look into each other's eyes. T continued, "I slit her throat and let her bleed out at my feet. I killed her yesterday. For you."

"Shit." I was shocked. T had me convinced that she was happy with Albany in jail.

T grew more somber. "This is who I am. Who I will always be. If they hurt you, they better stay ready. I will always come for them. No matter who it is."

She took a deep breath.

I licked my lips. This lady. We were tighter than family; we were closer than soul mates. It was bigger than the universe—how it was for us. I leaned forward and lifted her from her seat by her ass. I settled her on my lap. She could tell how much I wanted her.

"I want to marry you again right now. Holy shit. My wife." I kissed her with tongue. She was perfect. Albany's blood was my wedding present. Hot damn.

T seemed concerned at first, but then pleased that I was still onboard with this side of her. She was badass. I loved it. And her.

"Turns out I have a present for you as well."

We kissed for a while before I pulled out the duffle bag from behind the bench.

She seemed genuinely puzzled. "Well, I promised you some time ago that we'd have a house on a hill..." I gestured to our setting. "And, do you remember?"

She thought for a moment, closing one eye. "Something about burning money?"

"Hell, yes." I unzipped the bag. She gasped.

I'd packed it with money of all denominations.

"No. That's too much." She pointed at the contents.

I reached inside and grabbed a handful, passing it to her. "Light it up, wife."

After some hesitation, she leaned backwards to grab our

wine glasses. We drained them, she put the cash back in the bag.

"I have a better use for this now." T zipped it up. "How about we drop it off for Sister Mary at the Benfell Academy, instead?"

I liked it. Showed growth and all that. But I knew my way around some pizazz, and had buried a few sparklers in with the money. I fished out a nice handful and tossed them among the logs. I did use a ten-dollar bill to light the fire though, because I liked to keep promises. Soon, we had a mini fireworks show. I had my wife on my lap and my future ahead of me.

Life was turning out just fine.

NOTE FROM THE AUTHOR

When I was first deciding on my pen name in 2009, I knew I wanted to incorporate Anastasia. It's a family name. My maternal grandmother wasn't in my life physically very much. Manic depression (now known as bipolar disorder) kept her locked away from her family. Connections with us and her daughter (my mom) would send her into a tailspin. Because she loved us so much, she would forget to take her medications. I didn't understand much about it as a child—it was just the way things were. But my mother had an entire childhood filled with the very real struggle of having a mentally ill parent.

You'd never know, though. My mom is a fantastic parent and grandparent. She's fun, loving and incredibly thoughtful. She's also a pit bull for those that she loves so deeply.

The Anastasia on the front of this book is dedicated to my grandmother, but also my mom --who had the courage as a little girl to lie in bed every night and say to herself, "Tomorrow will be a better day."

I can't think of anything braver.

Cheers Anastasia and Valerie.

Love Always,

Deb

NOTE FROM THE AUTHOR

When I was first deciding on my pen name in 2009, I knew I wanted to incorporate Anastasia. It's a family name. My maternal grandmother wasn't in my life physically very much. Manic depression (now known as bipolar disorder) kept her locked away from her family. Connections with us and her daughter (my mom) would send her into a tailspin. Because she loved us so much, she would forget to take her medications. I didn't understand much about it as a child—it was just the way things were. But my mother had an entire childhood filled with the very real struggle of having a mentally ill parent.

You'd never know, though. My mom is a fantastic parent and grandparent. She's fun, loving and incredibly thoughtful. She's also a pit bull for those that she loves so deeply.

The Anastasia on the front of this book is dedicated to my grandmother, but also my mom --who had the courage as a little girl to lie in bed every night and say to herself, "Tomorrow will be a better day."

I can't think of anything braver.

Cheers Anastasia and Valerie.

Love Always,

Deb

ABOUT THE AUTHOR

Debra creates pretend people in her head and paints them on the giant, beautiful canvas of your imagination. She has a Bachelor of Science degree in political science and writes new adult angst and romantic comedies. She lives in Maryland with her husband and two amazing children. She doesn't trust mannequins, but does trust bears. Also, her chunky tuxedo cat talks with communication buttons. So that's fun.

DebraAnastasia.com for more information.

Pretty please review this book if you enjoyed it. It is one of the very best ways to support indy authors. Thank you!

Scan the code below to stay connected to Debra:

facebook.com/debra.anastasia

instagram.com/debra_anastasia

tiktok.com/@debraanastasia

ACKNOWLEDGMENTS

Hubs and Kids: Thank you for letting me flop around as this one took shape. I love you.

Helena: As if Pepper could live without Salt.

Ashley Scales and Stephanie Carter thank you for your eyes and insight.

Tijan: You keep me sane and that's a hard job.

Texas K: I can't wait until we write a horrible book together someday.

Christina Santos, you are the way this train stays on the tracks. I #skull you.

Tina Reber: For watching out for Animal!

FAMILY:

Mom and Dad, thank you so much for keeping a copy of all my weirdness in your house so you have to explain to the neighbors how "unique" your daughter is.

Pam and Jim: Happy marriage!! So proud of you both.

Mom and Dad D: Thank you for treating me like the daughter you never expected to get and also can't get rid of!

Uncle Ted and Aunt Jo: Thank you for being Disney magic, I love you!

BUSINESS BEAUTIES:

Kimberly Brower, you are a rock star. Thank heavens for you, Aimee, and Jess.

Paige Smith for kick ass edits.

Gitte and Jenny from Totally Booked.

Give Me Books Blog.

My Swat Team, Debra's Daredevils and the Beta team! I've got access to the most amazing crew in the world. Thank you!

******FREE BOOK PLATES******

Okay Daredevils. I have literally the cutest offer ever for you. My dad makes my swag down in Florida. He is freaking adorable about it and is very serious about his job. If you want a FREE signed bookplate(s) email my dad and we will send them to you and whatever swag he can fit in the envelope.

To receive an envelope sealed with adorableness and extreme efficiency email: debraanastasiaDad@gmail.com with your full name and mailing address (plus how many bookplates you need!!)

WHAT TO READ NEXT!

Mafia Romance

New Adult Angst

Paranormal